Drea Thew

About the Author

JENNIFER MCMAHON is the author of *Promise Not to Tell*. She grew up in suburban Connecticut and graduated from Goddard College in 1991. Over the years, she has been a house painter, a farm worker, a paste-up artist, a pizza delivery person, and a homeless shelter staff member, and has worked with mentally ill adults and children in a few different capacities. She lives in Vermont with her partner, Drea, and their daughter, Zella.

ISLAND OF
LOST GIRLS

ISLAND OF
LOST GIRLS

a novel

Jennifer McMahon

wm

WILLIAM MORROW

An Imprint of HarperCollins*Publishers*

This book is a work of fiction. The characters, incidents, and dialogue are drawn from the author's imagination and are not to be construed as real. Any resemblance to actual events or persons, living or dead, is entirely coincidental.

HarperCollins books may be purchased for educational, business, or sales promotional use. For information please e-mail the Special Markets Department at SPsales@harpercollins.com.

Library of Congress Cataloging-in-Publication Data is available upon request.

ISBN 978-0-06-144588-0
ISBN 978-0-06-266857-8 (RDS edition)

16 17 18 19 20   OV/RRD   10 9 8 7 6 5 4 3 2 1

For Drea

ISLAND OF
LOST GIRLS

"DIVE, DIVE, DIVE!" shouted Suzy as she clutched the old Chevy's cracked red-and-white steering wheel, jerking it back and forth in her hands, yanking hard on the turn signal lever to bring the ship down.

She knew it was air that made submarines rise and fall, just as she knew what she would see underwater: the octopus, the coral reef, the toothy smiles of sharks as they came in for the attack. She'd been a thousand times, and it was just like in the song her mother sang, about the octopus's garden in the shade. But on her way to the garden, there were sharks to run from, enemy subs trying to torpedo her. She knew what it was like to go down into blackness.

Suzy had these spells, like thunderstorms inside her head—that's how her parents explained it—where she'd black out, thrash around, and wake up confused. Seizures. Storms in her brain. Thunder and lightning. She wore a silver bracelet with her name and a weird red picture of a twisted-up snake on one side, the word EPILEPSY on the other. She took medicine, tiny pills each day.

Suzy was not supposed to play near the old car or the pile of rotten boards out behind her grandma's house. She knew that once people rode around in the Impala with its white stripe along the side; once the bumpers had sparkled and shown reflections of the open road. The radio had worked then too. The engine had hummed. They had pulled the white top up when it rained, some kind of fancy umbrella.

Now, her parents warned her not to play there: *It's dangerous,* her parents told her. *You could get hurt. Don't play there.* But that old car called her, the octopus called her, the mice that lived in the hole in the seat called her. The little mouse babies, pink and blind, that squeaked and lived in a nest of straw between the rusted springs, called out to her, a chorus of high-pitched voices singing through nubs of tiny orange teeth. She'd pulled back the torn red-and-white seat cover and seen them wriggle like the tips of fingers. She brought snacks for the mama mouse: pieces of American cheese, peanut butter crackers, birdseed stolen from Nana Laura Lee's bird feeder.

Suzy knew what mice liked. And this was not just any mouse. This was the secret-underwater-periscope-up-first-officer mama mouse who was friends with the octopus, who told her how to outwit the sharks, who had pushed seven wormy babies out from inside her. The baby mice squeaked louder as they dove deeper into the sea, the water dark as ink around them.

Suzy pushed back her thick blond curls, the heavy ringlets, and squinted through the cracked windshield, out the side portholes. Nana Laura Lee, her mom's mama, called Suzy "Shirley Temple" and spent hours fussing with the girl's hair. She bought her ribbons and bows, sweet little dresses that Suzy promptly got caught on prickers and barbed wire, ripping them until they were only good enough for doll bandages or Indian headbands.

But this afternoon's game was dive down and have tea in the octopus's garden before her daddy came looking for her. So down she dove, running from sharks the whole way.

"HELLO THERE!"

Suzy's shoulders jerked when she heard the voice. It was the voice of a tired man, a man stuck on land, a man who clearly didn't know she was miles underwater now and wouldn't be able to hear him. Suzy wasn't supposed to talk to strangers. She knew what could happen if you did. You could end up like Ernestine Florucci, who had been in the second grade with Suzy and now might be gone forever. Even though they lived in Vermont—where, Suzy now realized, listening to the grown-ups, things like that weren't supposed to happen. Like living in Vermont was a vaccine against bad things.

She pulled the dive lever on the sub and sank further, thought about something she'd seen on the news last week, something about Ernestine, but her daddy had jumped up and turned the TV off before Suzy could hear. The news man in the blue suit was saying something about a confession, which Suzy knew was when you went into a little room with a priest with a white collar. Then the TV snapped off and her parents talked in hushed voices. They had all gone out for creemees—Suzy got a chocolate-maple twist with extra chocolate sprinkles.

"Whatchya doing there?" the man asked Suzy, his voice friendly. He was right beside her now, his hands resting on the chipped red door. He was wearing a green jacket with a badge pinned to the front and carrying a walkie-talkie. This man was a police officer. He had a gun and everything.

She squinted up at him, the light from the midday sun beyond the trees behind him giving him a kind of glow like an angel, like the way the world sometimes looked just before a seizure, like everything had this halo, everything holy.

Suzy heard the sound of dogs barking, coming nearer, men talking, their footsteps cracking twigs, the cold squawk of staticky voices on walkie-talkies. They were coming up the pine needle–covered path that led down to the lake. Was she being arrested? Had her parents sent the police to see if she was playing where she was not supposed to?

"What's your name?" asked the man. He had short dark hair, a little dimple in his chin. "You live near here?"

She was allowed to talk to police officers. She was pretty sure. Suzy blinked.

"My name's Joe," he said, extending his hand. She stuck out hers to shake. His hand was soft and warm, smooth as the skin of a baseball glove. She gave in and told him her name.

"That's a real pretty name for a real pretty girl."

She hated this talk—this pretty-girl pretty-name-pretty-hair-pretty-ribbon, "you look just like a little angel" talk adults gave. She hated the winks, the nods, the little pats on her head, testing the bounce of her curls.

The dogs were there then and men in uniforms, men in wide-brimmed hats kicking at leaves, looking at the ground, letting the dogs pull them around. Big German shepherd dogs, police dogs, dogs that could bite, could crush your hand. Suzy had seen a program on TV about a man who couldn't see and needed a dog to help him. A special dog who helped him cross streets, get on buses, do his shopping. Smart dogs, German shepherds.

These police dogs were over at the pile of rotten wood, the boards with nails that could give you lockjaw, and they were whining, barking, digging at the ground like there was hamburger underneath, some sweet dog treat. Or maybe it was drugs. Dogs could sniff drugs, she knew this from school, from Officer Friendly, who brought his trusty dog Sam, the drug sniffer, with him. Sam wore a leather harness like the blind man's dog, like maybe Officer Friendly was blind, blind to drugs, to danger even, without Sam. Dogs could smell hundreds of times better than humans. Dogs could smell things miles away. Dogs were faithful and friendly and loyal. Dogs drooled. Their feet smelled like Fritos. Their breath could smell rotten like something got caught in their throat and died.

The men in uniforms were pulling at the boards, someone was taking pictures, someone had a video camera. Maybe they were all in a movie, a movie like her Nana Laura Lee had been in. They were all movie stars.

"So where do you live, Suzy?" asked Joe. She told him. She told him her grandma's house was on the other side of the trees there, but that her grandma didn't really live there, she lived far away in a hotel for people who took medicine for their heads. Her daddy was fixing screens on the windows because they were selling the house. She told him that when Daddy was done, they would visit Nana Laura Lee, who lived down by the lake in a faded pink trailer with a hundred bird feeders outside. Nana Laura Lee loved birds. Laura Lee had a white submarine in her yard that was actually a propane gas tank, but ever since Suzy was small, she believed it was a special private submarine for exploring the bottom of the lake. Laura Lee was a little crazy, that's what Suzy's daddy said, but Suzy's mom explained that everyone was really a little crazy once you knew them.

Even Suzy's own mom and dad were crazy, she guessed. They had played in these woods as kids. The pile of rotten boards was once a stage where Mommy had been a crocodile and Daddy was Peter Pan.

The policeman was still talking to her, asking her how often she came out to the woods, how old she was, what grade she was in, if her daddy knew where she was. One of the men in a green-and-tan uniform called to him.

"Sergeant Crowley, we found something!"

And the sergeant named Joe went over, walked through the circle of men and eager barking dogs, got down on his knees, and peered into the hole that had been covered by the wood the men had pulled away.

"Call forensics," he said. "I want the whole team out here. And rope this area off! Now!"

The baby mice squeaked for food, for their mama, and Suzy told them to hush, there were dogs around. She got out of the Impala, hopping over the door that had been stuck closed for years, and snuck up behind the men. She got down on her hands and knees, peered through the legs of one of the men, and saw something down in the hole—some old clothes, dirty, red, and torn; and just when it was coming into focus, just when she saw it had eyes, it had teeth, and scraps of hair, Sergeant Joe was swooping her up, saying this was no place for little girls, asking her to point to where her daddy was, saying not to be scared, that he was going to take her home.

RHONDA FARR HAD two Peters in her life: the Peter she loved but could not have, and now the white rabbit, which she, not unlike Alice in Wonderland, seemed destined to chase down the hole. But Alice's rabbit was not named Peter. The only Peter Rabbit Rhonda had known was the one in the storybook by Beatrix Potter, a common brown rabbit with a white fluffy tail, who just couldn't stay out of poor Mr. McGregor's garden.

On the other hand, Rhonda's Peter Rabbit was Ernestine Florucci's rabbit: all white and, as she would tell the police, about six feet tall.

"A rabbit?" the state troopers would ask, hands poised to scribble notes in black pads. "Six feet tall? Are you sure?"

Though the police were skeptical, Ernestine's mother, Trudy, believed Rhonda's story; she believed her but refused to forgive her.

The lives of Ernestine, Trudy, and Rhonda—maybe the lives of everyone in Pike's Crossing—had changed forever in about three minutes. The time it takes to soft-boil an egg.

IT WAS WELL past Easter when Peter Rabbit appeared to Rhonda, swooping away little Ernestine. It was the fifth of June, and Rhonda had pulled into Pat's Mini Mart to fill her tank so she could make it to a job interview in Burlington that afternoon. She was running late, but she needed to stop, there was nothing in the tank but fumes. She also thought she might see Peter. Rhonda had been nearly out of gas all weekend, waiting until today to stop, because she knew Peter would be at the garage.

Visiting him before the interview, even just a quick *Hey, how's tricks, Ronnie?* would give her a little jump start. She avoided his house because then she'd have to make small talk with Tock, come up with some excuse for stopping by, and, most painful of all, Suzy would come out and circle around her, jumping up and down—a cherubic reminder of the futility of Rhonda's situation.

It was a perfect early-June day, the temperature hovering in the mid-seventies. Rhonda drove with her windows open, inhaling the scent of newly mown grass and just-opened lilacs in people's yards. The campgrounds around Nickel Lake had opened on Memorial Day and Rhonda could smell the smoke from the campfires. Brightly colored blow-up toys hung from hooks on the rafters in front of Pat's: sea monsters, inner tubes, a small yellow raft, and a grinning crocodile with handles and cup holders. Overpriced bundles of camp wood were stacked below. Two ice machines stood to the left of the front door and a sign in the window promised cold beer, camping supplies, and night crawlers inside. Summer was here. And there was Rhonda, overdressed in a pressed white shirt and khaki suit. She eyed the crocodile longingly.

The interview she was probably going to be late to wasn't even for a job she particularly wanted. It was in her field (she'd graduated two weeks before with a BS in biology) and would look good on her résumé: research assistant for a University of Vermont study of zebra mussels—invasive mollusks that were hell bent on taking over Lake Champlain, encrusting water pipes and ship-wrecks on its floors, crowding out the natives.

Pat's Mini Mart was the only place in Pike's Crossing to buy gas. It was also close to Nickel Lake, so they got a lot of business from campers and folks with summer cottages. Pat's was also rumored to be the best place in the area to buy lottery tickets. They'd had a jackpot winner two weeks before—two hundred fifty thousand dollars—and a five thousand dollar winner before that.

Rhonda would later learn that it was the lottery tickets Trudy Florucci stopped for that day. She carried her lucky numbers in the pocket of her acid-wash denim jacket along with enough money for four tickets and a pack of menthol cigarettes, the no-name brand that was cheaper than regular brands like Kool, which was what Trudy smoked when her husband was alive and she could afford such luxuries. Trudy would tell all of this to one of the state troopers, spilling out painful little details of her life to an utter stranger at the most awkward of moments—and it would make Rhonda cringe. As if Trudy had opened her mouth, pulled back her cheek, and shown the cop a raw and seeping canker sore.

PAT'S HUSBAND, JIM, was the one who pumped the gas at the full-service station. Full service was a funny way of putting it, Rhonda thought, because Jim never washed the windshield and when asked to check the oil, he grumbled and banged around under the hood so ferociously you were sure never to ask him to do it again. That day, Jim, who was skeletally thin and alarmingly tall, sauntered out in his blue coveralls, looking especially bored. His dark hair was slicked back and he wore several days of stubble.

"Fill her up today?" he asked, just staring out over the roof of Rhonda's car. He swatted at a bug by his left ear.

Rhonda nodded up at him from the open window of her blue Honda. She smiled, but he did not seem to see. Jim unscrewed the gas cap, selected the grade—regular (he didn't bother asking)—and began to fill her tank.

"Peter around?" Rhonda asked, trying not to sound too hopeful as she peered into the garage.

"Took the day off," Jim said, and Rhonda felt her heart sink. *Stupid, stupid, stupid,* she told herself.

"All by myself here," Jim said, sounding a little bitter. He rubbed at his earlobe. The bug had gotten him after all—probably a blackfly, it had been a terrible year for blackflies.

Pat was out getting her hair done, Rhonda would learn later, which was why, when Trudy Florucci pulled up in the rusted-out Corsica, parking in front of the ice machines, Jim left the pump running to go back into the store to take care of her. Pat usually ran the cash register; she ran the whole place, actually—dealing with the books, the deliveries, carding high school kids for beer (a task she took pleasure in). What she did not take pleasure in was when a new delivery driver or salesman went right for Jim with questions, requests, sales pitches, assuming he must be in charge. Some even called him Pat. She took to wearing a large nametag that said PAT, STATION OWNER AND MANAGER. That day, Pat was gone, getting her three-month perm down at Hair Today.

Trudy left the engine running, thinking she wouldn't be long, that she should leave the radio on for her daughter, little Ernie Florucci, who sat strapped into the backseat with its faded upholstery riddled with stains and cigarette burns. Ernie had just been picked up from school. She was wearing a red corduroy jumper and had her brown hair in pigtails held with matching red elastics. Ernie was in second grade. *Second grade,* Rhonda would think later, trying to go back in her mind to what she had been like at that age, how vulnerable she must have been, how small and insignificant.

Trudy had left the radio playing, the volume up loud enough that Rhonda could hear it from her own car. It was country music, which Rhonda never listened to, even as the radio stations that played it seemed to multiply, so she didn't recognize the song. It was a love song maybe, a song about heartbreak—*aren't they all,* Rhonda would later think.

The music was distracting to Rhonda as she sat nervously going over what she might say in the interview, what questions they might ask. She had spent the past two days reading up on zebra mussels so she would sound smart, informed. She wanted the researchers to know she cared enough to do her homework. She was rolling over these facts in her mind, thinking about the sneaky destructiveness of the invasive species, about the photos she'd seen of larger native mollusks smothered by zebra mussels—when the third car pulled into the lot, right alongside Trudy's Corsica.

It was a gold-colored Volkswagen Beetle, and Rhonda's first thought was *Shit, Laura Lee Clark.* Tock's mother. Rhonda put her head down, pretending to study the dial on her radio. She was not in the mood to make chitchat with Laura Lee, who was sure to bring up Peter and Tock (*such a happy couple,* she was fond of saying), and little Suzy's latest brilliant endeavor (*a genius,* Laura Lee insisted, *my granddaughter's a genius*). Rhonda kept her head down, but glanced up just enough to see the driver open the door and climb out. That's when she saw that the car was not driven by crazy old Laura Lee Clark at all, but by a large white rabbit.

"You mean someone wearing a rabbit suit?" one of the state troopers would ask her later. "Like the Easter Bunny?"

"Yes," she would tell him. "Of course. A white rabbit suit. A costume. It was a man wearing a costume."

"How do you know it was a man, Miss Farr? With the costume?"

"I don't know, I guess. It just . . . it just seemed like it would be a man. And he was tall."

"Six feet tall," the trooper repeated back to her, reading from his own notes.

But the truth was, when the rabbit got out of the car, there in the Pat's Mini Mart parking lot at quarter to three on a Monday afternoon, it didn't occur to Rhonda that there might be a person inside. He hopped like a bunny, moved quickly, nervously, jerking his big white head one way, then the other. He turned toward Rhonda, and for an instant he seemed to stare at her with his blind plastic eyes. She imagined she could almost see his nose twitch as he gave a slight nod in her direction.

Rhonda watched as the rabbit rapped on Ernie's window with his big white fluffy paw. The little girl grinned up at him and pushed open her door. He leaned down and Ernie touched the bunny fondly on the head, right behind its ears, and unbuckled her seat belt.

The rabbit held out its paw and Ernie took it in her own small hand, stepping from her mother's car to the gold Volkswagen, getting in the passenger seat without a struggle, without any hesitation. The little girl smiled the whole time.

THE GOLD VOLKSWAGEN had a dent in the rear bumper.

That was all Rhonda could tell the troopers when describing the car. She told them how, at first, she thought it was Laura Lee, then it turned out not to be. She hadn't thought to get the license plate number.

"But it was a Vermont plate? Not out-of-state, Quebec, like that?" one of the troopers asked.

"Yes, Vermont," Rhonda said, hating herself for not even thinking to notice the plate and commit it to memory. "I think so anyway."

"Okay, was there anything else distinguishing about the car? Some rust? Was there anything in the backseat maybe?"

"I didn't see into the backseat. And no, it was just a gold bug. Nothing unusual except the driver."

"The rabbit," the cop said, a trace of skepticism in his voice. He was the shorter of the two and Rhonda believed he couldn't have been more than nineteen, barely over adolescence. The rash of pimples at his temples looked painful, more like boils, really, under the shadow of his wide-brimmed hat.

"Yes, the *rabbit*." Rhonda's voice shook a little this time, from nerves and frustration, the frustration of having to explain herself again and again, of knowing what Trudy said was true—it was Rhonda's own fault that Ernie was gone. She had taken no action. She watched the small girl in the red jumper be taken as easily as she had watched life unfold beneath the lens of her microscope: as a passive observer slightly in awe of the sight before her.

This was not who she was. She was a doer, someone who made lists. Someone who was methodical and looked at things with a keen, scientific eye. She always knew the next logical step in any situation. But for some reason, that afternoon, she sat staring, paralyzed, dumbfounded. Hypnotized by a white rabbit.

The other trooper was with Trudy on the other side of the store. Jim had pulled the folding chair with the ripped padding from behind the counter and set it up beside the candy rack, next to the Hershey bars and Good & Plentys. Together, he and the policeman had guided the nearly hysterical Trudy to the chair and were doing their best to calm her. Only moments before, when it finally sunk in that Rhonda had seen the abduction and done nothing, Trudy dove at her and tried to put her eyes out with her freshly manicured nails. Trudy's nails were no joke. They were two inches long, filed to points, and showed off a fresh coat of a reddish orange that reminded Rhonda of a bleeding Creamsicle. The taller state trooper, the one who seemed to be taking the lead role in the investigation, pulled Trudy off and led her across the store to the chair Jim was setting up. Rhonda stayed with her back against the beer cooler, her head bowed.

"You did nothing!" Trudy called back. "You sat on your fucking fat ass and watched my little girl get taken away!"

Rhonda did not consider her ass fat but, compared to Trudy's size six figure, Rhonda was a big girl—a chunky, five-foot-five-inch size fourteen who carried most of her weight in her torso. Rhonda's face was round too, and she was forever trying to find a haircut that might help make it seem less so.

Once the taller trooper had settled Trudy into her chair, he resumed his questioning.

"Is there anyone you know who might have taken your daughter? A family member? An ex-boyfriend, maybe?"

"I'm a fucking widow! I don't have any boyfriends. I have Ernie and my sister and that's all." She began to cry, mascara running black streams down her pale face, cutting tracks through her foundation.

"Please, ma'am. I'm sorry. I know this is hard. But has Ernie told you about anyone? The parent of a friend, maybe? A stranger watching her play?"

"It was the rabbit!" Trudy cried. "Fucking Peter Rabbit! Oh, God!" She was sobbing and fumbling in the pocket of her denim jacket for the new pack of cigarettes and her lighter. Lottery tickets fluttered to the floor. The tall state trooper leaned down and picked them up, held them in his hand while she lit her cigarette, studied them like they were evidence.

"She's been telling me for over a month now about Peter Rabbit visiting her. Taking her to Rabbit Island in his submarine. She even drew pictures of it. Christ! I thought it was all made up!"

Jim sauntered over and put a reassuring hand on Trudy's arm, giving it a squeeze with grease-stained fingertips. "I called over to the beauty shop. Pat's on her way. Don't you worry, Trudy. Ernie'll show up. Just like that girl down in Virginia. They found her safe and sound, now didn't they?"

Rhonda thought of eight-year-old Ella Starkee, the little girl kidnapped in rural Virginia last month and found in a hole ten days later. She survived by catching rain in a rusty tin can and eating earthworms. Rhonda shivered. Trudy glared at her, eyes glazed with fury.

"The fat girl knows more than she's saying," Trudy spat. "I mean, why the fuck else did she just sit there? She probably knew the guy. They were working as a team. She was the lookout. Don't kidnappers do that?"

"We'll investigate her thoroughly, ma'am," said the cop.

The shorter trooper with the bad skin led Rhonda outside, where they stood talking on the oil-stained pavement.

Rhonda watched Trudy stare out at her through the glass window with its collage of beer and cigarette signs. WEDNESDAY SPECIAL: 5 CENTS OFF EACH GALLON OF GAS ALL DAY!!! MECHANIC ON DUTY, promised another. But where *was* Peter?

Trudy continued glaring out at Rhonda like she expected to suddenly notice a white fluffy tail peeking from beneath her blazer.

WHEN DETECTIVE SERGEANT Joe Crowley arrived at Pat's Mini Mart, he called in a team to come and search the area. More state police arrived along with a white forensics van. They took pictures. They searched the parking lot for tire tracks and other evidence. They dusted the passenger side of Trudy's car for fingerprints, even though Rhonda had made it clear that the culprit's hands were well covered. After all, the bunny had furry white paws.

Crowley put out an APB for the gold Volkswagen, for Ernie Florucci. He issued an AMBER alert. He sent the taller trooper home with Trudy, instructing him to pick up the girl's rabbit drawings and a recent photo of Ernestine. The trooper helped Trudy up out of the tattered chair and gently handed her the lottery tickets he'd been holding.

"You can't forget these," he told her with a wink. "I've got a feeling they're real lucky." Trudy gave a half smile and stuffed the tickets into the pocket of her denim jacket, then walked to the car, leaning into the cop as he guided her, his arm around her waist.

Sergeant Crowley had an air of authority that made Rhonda relieved and hopeful. If anyone could find the little girl and the rabbit, Crowley could. He was in his mid-forties (her father's age) and wore his salt-and-pepper hair very short. He had on dark trousers, a white shirt, and a dark green tie with a gold clip. He looked, to Rhonda, like a man who had been in great shape once, an ex-athlete who blew out a knee and had let himself fill out a little.

"Miss Farr, is there anything else you can tell me about the rabbit? Anything at all?"

"No," said Rhonda, shaking her head. There was nothing else she could tell him. Not about *this* rabbit, but once, long ago, there had been *another* white rabbit and he too, in time, had somehow slipped away.

APRIL 11, 1993

THERE WAS SNOW in the woods. Her feet were slipping as she ran in her good yellow Easter shoes, ankles numb from cold. Lizzy was beside her. They were holding hands. Laughing each time they fell. Lizzy wore matching yellow shoes with pale satin bows: she had seen Rhonda's and begged her mother to take her to the mall for an identical pair. It was like that with the girls: whatever one had, the other longed for.

Lizzy and Rhonda told everyone at school they were twin sisters living as cousins, when the truth was they were not related at all. But still, the other kids believed the story about them being twins. It was an easy lie to believe, because they looked so much alike: two chunky girls with straight, dark, tousled hair, dirt under their nails, funny overbites from sucking thumbs too long. They were quiet girls with big brown eyes. Koala bear eyes, lemur eyes, eyes that seemed to take up their whole plain faces.

They had been best friends since before they learned to talk—sharing a sandbox, being walked by their mothers in matching pink strollers down to the lake. And when words came to them, they seemed, the way their mothers described it, to develop their own secret language—a coded communication that no one else could understand, full of words such as *daloor*, *ub*, *ta*, and *skoe*. Their parents were worried that the girls would go on speaking this way to one another, would have no need for the rest of the world, for words like *cat* and *swim* and *thank you*.

Sometimes Rhonda thought about this when she looked at Lizzy—how once upon a time, all they needed was each other.

They had been born two days apart, this much was true, though they made up the lie about being from same mother—how Rhonda stayed in after Lizzy came out and their mother didn't know about the other one until she went to the bathroom a couple of days later and out popped Rhonda.

"Into the toilet!" the girls would holler in their singsong voices, identical in pitch and tone. "Rhonda fell into the toilet!" Which didn't seem like a bad beginning, just a funny one.

PETER WAS RUNNING ahead of them, closest to the rabbit. He had his father's red wool hunting cap on over his blond curls but he hadn't worn a jacket. He was thirteen and Rhonda knew that as a general rule, thirteen-year-old boys didn't believe in jackets unless it was way below freezing. He had announced that this was the last year he'd do the egg hunt: Easter baskets were kids' stuff.

Rhonda and Lizzy rounded a bend in the path, and Lizzy hit a tree root and tripped, falling, pulling Rhonda down on top of her, both girls cackling, their good Easter dresses ruined already.

"Eew!" Rhonda complained, pushing herself up. "What have you been eating?"

"Sardines," Lizzy said, smiling.

"Gross! For breakfast?"

"My dad says they're full of calcium. You know, 'cause of the bones and stuff in them. They're the latest part of the Rockette regime."

"Your breath smells like cat food." Rhonda took off down the path, toward Peter and the rabbit, Lizzy right behind her.

Rhonda thought the entire, ever-changing Rockette regime was stupid, even the name. She thought the dumbest part of all was that Lizzy had never even seen the Rockettes except on television. How can you decide from some five-minute routine on a twenty-inch television that that's what you want to do with your life? But Lizzy was determined. And to be a Rockette, she kept reminding Rhonda, you had to be at least five foot six.

"I'm way too short, Rhonda."

"You're ten! You're totally average for ten."

"Neither of my parents are tall. I've got short genes. It's a curse."

So, in addition to practicing eye-high kicks, Lizzy ate weird, allegedly tallness-enhancing food and avoided soda, which she swore rotted your bones and stunted your growth.

"Besides," she said, "soda's full of sugar. And who's ever heard of a fat Rockette?"

PETER AND THE rabbit had reached the stage. The rabbit jumped into the driver's seat of the old abandoned convertible and pretended to drive.

"Over here!" Peter shouted. The girls raced to catch up.

There, in a nest of snow tucked into the backseat, were the three plastic eggs that marked the true beginning of their hunt.

"Oh!" Lizzy exclaimed, clapping her hands together, like the eggs were a strange surprise—not the very thing she'd been looking for.

Rhonda bent down and picked her egg up out of the car. Tucked inside the orange egg, like a fortune in a cookie, was a message: *Go to the top of the hill. Look next to the rock.*

She gazed up at the rabbit, who was standing on the hood now, hands on his hips, impatient and ominous with his huge paws and ears, the plastic cartoon-style eyes scratched from years of Easter rentals, the white fur dingy and smelling of dry cleaning chemicals.

Rhonda took off to the top of the hill, leaving her two friends to their own quests.

It went on like this for almost an hour. Zigzagging through the woods, finding an egg, following the clues inside to get to the next one. She'd run into Lizzy and Peter and they'd compare hiding places and messages, but always with the breathless urgency to hurry back to the hunt.

Rhonda's breath was smoke. She wheezed from exertion. The rabbit darted in and out of trees, taunting. Pointing in one direction, then another. Holding his head and belly as he doubled over in silent laughter when she slipped and fell, when she believed him and went the wrong way looking for her next egg. Trickster rabbit.

When at last she grew tired of the game and was too cold to go on, the rabbit appeared, took her hand in his white fluffy paw, and led her to a small clearing. There, on top of a large, flat rock was her orange basket, shimmering with green plastic grass, stuffed full of chocolate bunnies, eggs, and jelly beans. He nodded down at her, and just for a minute, before she picked up the basket, he led her in a celebratory dance, their own little joyful bunny hop, one furry arm around her waist, the other clutching her cold fingers in his thick paw. There were none of the high, Rockette-style kicks Lizzy was famous for, just a clumsy little slippery-soled shoe shuffle. They stomped a little circle in the snow, then he let her go and, with a wave, turned and hopped back down the hill.

Rhonda took her basket and raced through the woods to her house with its warm, familiar smells: coffee, cinnamon buns, bacon. The table was laid out for Easter brunch. Peter was already there, the contents of his own basket spilled out on the couch. Rhonda saw right away that he'd gotten comics and a pocketknife. She had Silly Putty and lip gloss. Peter was picking black jelly beans out of the mixed bag and throwing them up in the air to catch them in his mouth. He'd seen a guy do this with peanuts in a western and had been working on it ever since.

Rhonda couldn't remember ever not having Easter brunch with Peter and Lizzy. Her dad and Peter and Lizzy's dad, Daniel, had grown up together and been best friends forever. They were practically brothers, Rhonda heard her dad say once. And the Shales lived next door—a quarter mile down Lake Street, a little closer if you cut through the woods.

"Where's Lizzy?" asked Aggie, Lizzy and Peter's mom. She wore a lime green dress that showed her knees, shoes with heels, lipstick, and rouge. Her short, spiky hair was dyed magenta and stuck up like she'd just been struck by lightning. She had a highball glass in her hand even though it was only ten in the morning. Her hand trembled slightly, as if holding the glass took all her strength.

"Still in the woods with the rabbit," Rhonda said.

"They'll both end up with frostbite," said Aggie.

"It's not *that* cold, Ma," Peter said, opening his new knife and running his finger across the blade.

Aggie fixed her eyes on Peter, drained what was left in her drink, and rattled the ice like dice in a cup. Rhonda could smell her perfume, which seemed both sweet and rotten—like a Venus flytrap, Rhonda imagined.

"Coffee's ready," said Rhonda's father as he held out a cup to Aggie. His dark hair was cut short, and he had on a white button-down shirt and tie, which made his face and hands look tan even though it was April; Clem had the kind of complexion that left him bronze year round.

Aggie squinted at him, put down the glass, and took the steaming mug. Rhonda's father sipped at his own coffee, keeping an eye on Aggie the way you'd watch an unpredictable dog who might lunge and bite at the slightest provocation. He set down his coffee, reached into his shirt pocket for the unfiltered Camels, and lit one, using the three remaining fingers of his right hand as expertly as if the other two had been missing all his life.

When Rhonda was a little girl, she used to sit on his lap and ask him to tell the story of how he lost his fingers.

"It only took a second," Clem would explain, Rhonda on his lap running her tiny fingers over the scarred nubs where his two missing digits had been.

"Daniel and I were at the mill, working on a big order of beams with Dave Lancaster."

Rhonda would nod. She knew Dave. He was the boss at the mill. He'd once gotten into a wrestling match with a black bear, and if you weren't careful, he'd offer to show you the scars, which were on his butt.

"I was guiding a piece of hemlock through the saw," Clem would continue. "Daniel was behind me."

"And he had a seizure," Rhonda would say, having the story memorized.

"That's right, sweetie. He fell against me and I wasn't expecting it. My hand went right into the blade."

"Did it hurt bad?" Rhonda asked.

"No," Clem answered. "It happened too fast and then after, I was too surprised. I was in shock."

"In shock," young Rhonda would repeat back to him, thinking about electricity, how she was not supposed to go near outlets or play in thunderstorms because of shocks.

"It was an accident," Clem would tell her.

"But what happened to your fingers?" Rhonda would ask, squirming on her father's lap.

"I guess I don't know," Clem would answer.

Rhonda would imagine the fingers lying there in the sawdust on the floor of the mill, still warm.

"I think your fingers were lonely for your hand," the little girl would say, and this would make her father—who once admitted that on some mornings he thought he could feel himself wriggling those fingers awake—smile a sad and longing smile.

RHONDA'S MOTHER, JUSTINE, shuffled into the dining room from the kitchen, her feet in worn pink slippers. She had on her usual outfit: a matching sweat suit; this time, for Easter, she'd worn one in pale lavender. She carried a fresh tray of cinnamon buns and placed it in the center of the table.

"Justine," Aggie said, her voice thick with an alcohol drawl, "you've outdone yourself! Everything looks *won*-derful!"

Justine nodded and went back into the kitchen to make waffles and, no doubt, hide out in the breakfast nook with a cup of black coffee and a romance novel. Rhonda thought she should go help her mother, keep her company at least, but she found herself planted by the French doors leading from the dining room to the patio, scanning the tree line at the edge of the yard for Lizzy and the rabbit.

"Maybe they got lost," Rhonda said to no one in particular. She turned back to see Aggie lean over and pull the cigarette from between her father's lips and place it in her own, taking a long, deep, lung-killing drag.

Rhonda went back to looking out the window, breathing onto the cold panes of glass to leave a film, then drawing in the condensation. She drew eggs. And a crude-looking rabbit with uneven ears.

"There they are now," Peter said. He'd come up behind her

and rested his chin on her shoulder, his black-jelly-bean-scented breath hitting her cheek, making her feel warm all over.

Through the trees came the rabbit with Lizzy sitting high up on his shoulders, like an Easter queen in her yellow dress and shoes. She was laughing, swinging a pink basket full of candy as the rabbit jogged with her across the lawn, holding her legs against his chest with huge white paws.

Once inside, the rabbit set Lizzy down, then walked over to Aggie, whispering something in her ear and grabbing her rear end. She leaned back into him, wiggling her butt against him and laughing. She turned around to face him and tugged gently at his crooked white ears.

"Take this silly thing off, Daniel," she said, and the rabbit took off his head, tucking it under his arm.

Daniel's shaggy blond hair was sticking up at funny angles. He had a thick walrus mustache, which he'd had the whole time Rhonda knew him. It was the kind of mustache food got caught in. The kind that tickled when he leaned down to kiss your cheek or blow on your belly button.

Peter snuck up and snatched the rabbit head from him, dropped it over his own head. Daniel let out a howl of mock rage and chased Peter around the dining room table. Lizzy squealed with delight and took Rhonda's hand to watch the chase. Justine came out of the kitchen, pink-covered romance novel in hand, to see what all the fuss was about. Aggie reached into Clem's pocket and grabbed his pack of unfiltered Camels, shook one out, and lit it with a match from the book Clem kept tucked in the cellophane. She crossed her arms and watched the chase through a haze of smoke, her eyes focused not on her husband or son but on the French doors beyond them, which had been left open. Aggie looked out onto the patio expectantly, as if she was waiting for some uninvited guest to arrive. Or maybe, thought Rhonda, she was planning to make a break for it.

The oversized rabbit head shifted as Peter ran, turning him into a life-size bobblehead doll. When Daniel caught Peter, he held him upside down, shaking him while Peter bucked and squealed, "Enough, Dad! I give!" until the large rabbit head slipped off and landed softly on the thick beige carpet, mesh eyes fixed on the French doors, like it, too, was dreaming of escape.

The rabbit is a rabbit is a rabbit. His ears are keen. His nose twitches. He scratches an invisible itch with his white fluffy paw. Cocks his head, listening. He does not speak. He never speaks, just gestures, nods, shakes his head. It's amazing what can be communicated without words.

The rabbit cannot believe how easy this is. How the girl has come to trust him, to love him. They try to play crazy eights because she says it's her favorite game, only he can't hold the cards. She laughs. There's something about her laugh. Something that makes the rabbit feel alive in a way he hasn't in a long, long time.

She's a sad girl. Her daddy died not long ago. And her mommy is so caught up in her own grief that she can do little to comfort the child. But the rabbit knows how to make her smile. The rabbit has come hopping in like the hero in a fairy tale, banishing sorrow.

And the little girl has named him Peter. He does not tell her how odd this is. When the rabbit is the rabbit, he has no other, human life. He leaves all traces of personhood behind and becomes something more . . . pure. More perfect.

The rabbit has a name for the little girl, too. A secret name. Birdie, he calls her in his mind.

His darling Birdie, back again.

BACK IN HER car (still parked in front of the gas pumps), Rhonda pressed the cell phone against her ear. She felt keyed up. Cagey. Like she had to do something, but she didn't know what. Tempting as it was to start the engine and crisscross the state searching for the little girl and the rabbit, she knew it would do little good. Every cop in Vermont was on the lookout; every citizen who paid attention to TV or radio as well. Still, Rhonda hated doing nothing.

Peter picked up on the third ring.

"How'd the interview go?" he said.

"Something's happened, Peter." She told him about the kidnapping, that she was at Pat's still and didn't know what to do with herself. When she was through, she heard him cover the phone and mumble.

"Tock's home?" Rhonda asked, her heart sinking a little.

"Yeah, I was just filling her in. We *know* Ernie. She's a friend of Suzy's."

Tock picked up the extension—probably in the kitchen, Rhonda imagined. She pictured Peter in the living room, sitting on the brown couch, his feet up on the coffee table. She wondered if he was wearing sneakers or work boots.

"Jesus, Ronnie," Tock said, "a white rabbit took Ernie?"

"It sounds crazy, I know, but . . ."

"The world is full of crazy shit, Ronnie," Tock cut her off. "Jesus Christ, it's just like the girl in Virginia. There're some real wackos out there! I think you should come over. We'll grill some steaks and have a good soak in the hot tub."

"Yeah, come on over, Ronnie," said Peter. "Have dinner with us." Rhonda heard movement, the squeak of couch springs. Peter was adjusting himself, probably sitting up straight, getting ready to reach over and hang up the phone once she agreed. Peter always seemed anxious to get off as quickly as possible when Tock was around.

"Okay, I'll come. I'll be there in half an hour or so." She felt hesitant about accepting the invitation, but didn't want to spend the evening alone, kicking herself in the ass for letting the little girl be spirited away by the rabbit.

She hung up, placed the phone back in her purse on the seat beside her. Then she gazed out through her windshield at Trudy's car, doors open, surrounded by police.

Beetles, too, Rhonda remembered. The TV news shows reported that little Ella Starkee ate beetles. Rhonda wondered what the rabbit would feed Ernie; what she might have to do to survive.

RHONDA STOPPED OFF at her apartment to change and grab her bathing suit. She lived on the top floor of an old Victorian near the center of town. It had been divided into three apartments: the first floor was occupied by the landlord and his wife, the second by their unmarried daughter and her two kids, and the refurbished attic was Rhonda's. The peaks of the roof gave many of her walls a terrific slant. To get up to the apartment, she had to climb a set of spiral stairs behind the house.

Rhonda unlocked the door at the top of the stairs, went straight for her bedroom, and changed, relieved to be out of her uncomfortable suit at last. From the dormer window beside her bed she had the perfect view of the south end of Nickel Lake. She stood for a moment with the curtain pulled back, watching the swimmers and sunbathers at the town beach, wondering if word of the kidnapping had reached them. She had this ridiculous urge to open her window and yell, like the town crier, warning mothers to keep their children safe; to beware of rabbits.

Rhonda turned away from the cheerfully oblivious swimmers with their bright towels, umbrellas, and coolers, and checked the messages on her blinking machine. Only one from a man on the Lake Champlain research team, wanting to know if there'd been a mix-up about the time of her interview and offering to reschedule if she was still interested in the position. Rhonda erased the message. On the way out, she stopped in the hall to glance in the mirror. Behind her were two of the dissection drawings she was so proud of: the squid and the rabbit. Rhonda loved her biology classes and was particularly fond of the dissections. She enjoyed drawing the accompanying diagrams—labeling the parts and sketching the map of organs, going back later with a colored pencil to turn the heart red, the spleen purple, the liver green. She had dissected a sheep's eye, a pig fetus, a pigeon, a cat, a squid, numerous frogs, and a rabbit. She was so pleased with the drawings she'd had them framed and hung them on the walls of her apartment, where some other woman might put family portraits, maps, or posters of babies in sunflower costumes.

Her eye caught on the backward image of the rabbit in her mirror, skin pulled back, muscles and chest wall cut away to reveal the organs. She blinked, grabbed the keys from the table under the mirror, and headed out the door.

TOCK ALWAYS GOT naked before getting in the hot tub, and Rhonda hated it. She hated that the other woman was so slim and muscular, so totally unashamed of her body. Tock peeled off all her clothes as nonchalantly as someone taking off a pair of sunglasses. Peter wore blue swimming trunks. Rhonda wore a black bathing suit, and even in that, she felt too exposed and put a T-shirt on over it.

The hot tub was homemade, as was nearly everything in their small, off-grid A-frame house, which sat on twelve acres of land fronted by a stream at the dead end of a three-mile-long Class 4 dirt road. The road wasn't maintained by the town, so it was up to Peter and Tock to plow and grade it each spring. Rhonda, who didn't have four-wheel-drive, knew better than to attempt a visit in the winter or during mud season.

Tock and Peter had built the house together three years before, giving careful, woodworker's attention to each detail, making the house more like a work of art than a home. They heated with wood, got electricity from solar panels and a bank of batteries with a gas-powered generator for backup.

Rhonda and her father came to help with the house-building on weekends. Rhonda's contribution (aside from entertaining Suzy and keeping her out of harm's way) was measuring and marking boards. Rhonda was afraid of all tools, of the images they inspired—images of herself reaching down to touch the spinning blade of the table saw, of letting the circular saw slip and hit her thigh, of how easy bleeding to death could be; how easy to be marked forever in the way her father was marked.

"All it takes," her father used to say when telling his story, "is one second."

Rhonda knew the story of her father's accident by heart, and over the years had heard not only his version but Aggie's, Daniel's, and Dave Lancaster's. Dave had been boss at the mill then and was also Aggie's uncle. Clem and Daniel worked part-time at the mill through high school, doing everything from bucking the logs to delivering finished lumber. They both went to full-time after graduation. Aggie Lancaster had come up from Maryland to work for her uncle that same summer, having just graduated herself. It was the end of that summer that Clem lost his fingers.

When Dave told the story, usually after a few beers at a family barbecue, he'd swear it hadn't been an accident.

"Daniel didn't fall into Clem," Dave insisted. "He sure as shit pushed him."

Daniel claimed to remember nothing of the accident: one minute he was beside Clem helping him guide the hemlock into the saw, the next he was waking up on the concrete floor, covered in Clem's blood.

Clem always shook his head after hearing Dave's version. "It was seizure," Clem said. "Daniel fell against me on his way down to the ground."

The rest of the story everyone agreed on. Clem jerked his hand away, spilling blood everywhere, but the first thing he did was drop to his knees to check on Daniel. Dave shut down the saw and screamed for Aggie, who was in the front office across the lot.

When Aggie came over, she saw Daniel thrashing and foaming, Clem crouched over him. She saw that Daniel's shirt was covered in blood, but did not understand where it had come from.

"Watch his head!" Clem shouted, having been through the seizures a hundred times, knowing he should not hold his friend down but should do everything possible to not let him bash himself against anything. Daniel's head was near one of the metal legs of the saw table, and Aggie bent down and gently rested her hands on Daniel's jerking head, keeping him from harm. She had never seen a seizure before, never seen so much blood. And only then, when she had her hands resting on Daniel's head, tangled in his sweaty hair, did her gaze fall on Clem's hand.

"Jesus! Your hand!"

Clem looked down at his hand, at the pumping blood, and furrowed his brow as though not quite understanding what he was seeing. He then fell gently backward, still frowning in mild confusion, the color drained from his face. Dave wrapped Clem's hand in a flannel shirt, helped him to the flatbed truck, and gunned the engine all the way to the medical center.

RHONDA AVERTED HER eyes from Tock's naked form (no stretch marks, even!) and took a deep breath, trying to concentrate on the feel of the water around her, which was almost unbearably hot. Peter had spent a summer during high school working at a vineyard in upstate New York, where he had picked up the huge wooden barrel they were soaking in. The water was heated by coils that ran through a woodstove. The three of them bumped knees as they sat on the narrow ledge Peter had built into the side of the huge cask. Tock had just put Suzy to bed.

Whatever else Rhonda could say about Tock, she could never criticize her parenting skills. Tock seemed to be the perfect mother—creative, fun, patient, firm, and always seeming to know the right thing for Suzy.

Tock had moved in with Peter just after graduating from high school and, soon after, announced she was pregnant. Everyone thought they were foolish—too young to start a family. And there went Tock's chance at college, and her so smart! But Tock hadn't wanted college: she wanted Peter and a baby and to build her own house in the woods. She never seemed to have a moment of regret.

Tock leaned over and grabbed a beer from the table beside the tub. She was between Rhonda and Peter in age, one year older than Rhonda and two younger than Peter, and was in better shape than both of them. She wore her hair cropped short, a tight little chestnut-colored cap—she had, Rhonda thought, the bone structure to pull it off. Peter wore his shoulder-length curly blond hair back in a ponytail. At twenty-six, Peter had the look of a man descending quickly into middle age. His hairline was receding and he'd developed a potbelly. He was looking more and more like Daniel every day. All that was missing was the mustache.

Neither Peter nor Tock liked it when Daniel's name came up, and as a general rule, Rhonda tried to keep him out of conversations. But that night, lulled by the hot water, steak, and beer, by the way her knees bumped against Peter's, she couldn't help herself.

"So seeing the rabbit today reminded me of that Easter . . . remember? When Daniel dressed in the rabbit suit and we were all chasing after him in the woods, looking for eggs."

Tock narrowed her eyes. Peter stared down into the neck of his beer bottle.

"I'm gonna go get some weed," Tock announced, jumping out of the tub, steam rising off her lean flanks. Tock grabbed her robe and went through the sliding glass doors into the house.

Rhonda took in a breath, relieved to be alone with Peter but a little panicked by it, too.

She leaned back, her head resting against the edge of the wine cask, her eyes fixed on the stars.

"So do you remember it? You stole the head of his costume and he chased you all over the dining room."

"No," Peter mumbled solemnly. He reached over to get a cigarette from the pack on the table.

"We followed the rabbit through the woods looking for eggs full of clues." Rhonda glanced over at Peter and searched his face for some sign of recognition. There was none. She leaned back against the wall of the tub, closed her eyes, and let the images of that Easter continue to come.

"Lizzy was last to find her basket," Rhonda said, "and when she finally came back into the yard, she was riding high up on the rabbit's shoulders, swinging her basket, playing with his ears." She opened her eyes and looked over at Peter. "How can you not remember any of that?"

He shook his head and said only, "It was a long time ago."

They were quiet a minute, Peter staring down into his empty bottle, turning it in his hand like a kaleidoscope while he smoked his cigarette. Rhonda studied his face, trying to imagine the way it had looked that Easter so long ago, searching for a trace of the boy she'd run through the woods with, chasing after the elusive rabbit. She thought of Peter's sister, Lizzy, whom, like Daniel, they hardly mentioned anymore. She remembered Lizzy and Daniel straggling into the yard, the last to return from the woods that Easter. Looking back, Rhonda thought perhaps it had been a sign, an omen, showing that one day they would both be gone, as if they'd walked into the woods for the egg hunt and never come back.

"I'm sorry I brought it up," Rhonda said. "It's just that I'd forgotten all about it until this afternoon. It's not every day someone sees a huge white rabbit."

"Or a kidnapping," Peter added, leaning over to stub out his cigarette, seeming relieved at the chance to change the subject. He still didn't look her in the eye. Rhonda slouched, sinking deeper into the tub, her chin resting on top of the steaming water.

"I feel guilty as hell sitting here drinking beer when that little girl is out there somewhere because I let the rabbit take her," Rhonda said.

"What were you supposed to do, Ronnie?" Peter asked.

"I don't know. Beep the horn. Get out and yell. Call 911—that's why I have the frigging cell phone, right? Notice the license plate. Anything. I just sat on my ass. I felt . . . I don't know . . . drugged or something. Hypnotized. Like the bunny put some kind of spell on me. And I was scared, Peter. I mean, it wasn't until they drove off that I even realized I'd been holding my breath the whole time. My heart was racing."

"Of course you were scared," Peter said.

"And now I'm just sitting here soaking in this fucking tub when I should be out there doing something."

"What is it you want to do?" he asked.

"Find Ernie."

Tock returned, a lit joint in her mouth.

"We should check out the eleven o'clock news," Tock said. "I bet they'll have something about it. Hell, maybe they found her by now. Maybe it was just some kind of prank."

"Who would pull a prank like that?" Rhonda asked.

"I dunno," Tock said. "Maybe someone got the idea because of that girl in the hole in Virginia. It's been all over the news for weeks. Maybe it's just some gung-ho kid and he'll just drop her off down the highway once he realizes what a totally fucked-up thing he's done."

The Virginia girl, Ella Starkee, was found by a farmer and his border collie. The farmer and the dog had since made the rounds of every morning news show in the country. They posed with Ella for the cover of last week's *People* magazine. The little girl was all smiles, rosy-cheeked, hair neatly braided.

Rhonda found herself wondering what size beetles the little girl had eaten—tiny ones or something more like a June bug. Something substantial.

"Where were you today, anyway?" Rhonda asked Peter. "Don't you usually work Mondays?"

"I took the day off to go hiking," he said.

"All of you went?" Rhonda asked.

Tock passed the joint to Peter, exhaled, and said, "No. He snuck off without us. Suzy and I packed a lunch and drove out to the trailhead to join him, thinking he'd be up at Gunner's Ridge, but he wasn't there. So we had a little girls'-day-out picnic of our own."

"I hiked a different route," Peter explained. "Over by Sawyer's Pond."

"I bet the blackflies were god-awful," Rhonda said.

"Not too bad," Peter told her, examining his arms. Rhonda didn't see a single bite.

"So you said the Florucci girl is a friend of Suzy's?" Rhonda asked.

"Yeah," Tock said. "They're in the same class. Suzy went to Ernie's birthday party back in March. Lives with her mom in a little trailer out on Meckleson Hill Road. Kind of a dump. But Ernie's a good kid. She's been out here to play a few times, right, hon?"

Peter nodded.

"It could have been Suzy," Rhonda said.

Tock shivered and looked away.

"That little girl could be cut into a hundred pieces right now and I could have done something to stop it," Rhonda said. "I could have at least remembered the fucking license plate."

"You're too hard on yourself, Ronnie," Peter said, reaching through the water to take her hand and squeeze it. "You need to let shit go."

Like I let Ernie go? Rhonda thought to herself. She looked up into Peter's watery blue eyes and let her fingers squeeze back. *Like you let Daniel and Lizzy go?*

LIZZY AND RHONDA danced through the woods, hurrying to the stage. Just a month before, they'd chased the rabbit down the same path, but now the snow was gone and the maple trees that were mixed in with the spruce, hemlock, and white pines were just beginning to leaf out. It had rained the day before but now the sun was out and the woods smelled green and loamy.

Lizzy was singing "Achy Breaky Heart" and getting the words wrong, which cracked Rhonda up.

And if you tell my heart, my achy breaky heart,
I might throw up on this man . . .

Lizzy spun in a circle, then put her hands on her hips and kicked her right leg up high. The move was more karate than Rockette.

They had just come from Lizzy's, where she'd changed from school clothes into a leotard, leggings, and turquoise leg warmers, then showed Rhonda the metal bar her father had installed at the top of the closet doorway.

"What's this for?" Rhonda had asked.

Lizzy'd jumped up, grabbed the bar, and hung.

"It's going to stretch me," she'd explained. "If I hang for fifteen minutes a day, I'll get taller. Guaranteed."

Rhonda figured about the only thing that was going to get stretched out was Lizzy's arms, which would leave her looking more like an ape girl than a Rockette, but Rhonda knew better than to say anything.

"And look," Lizzy had said, pulling first one leg, than the other, over the bar and letting go so that she hung upside down in the doorway. Lizzy closed her eyes and hung, focusing, no doubt, on stretching herself taller as her face grew redder and redder.

"Easy there, Rocket." Rhonda turned and saw Daniel standing in the doorway to Lizzy's bedroom. "You don't want to burst anything."

"It's Rock-*ette*, Daddy," Lizzy said, pulling herself up, then jumping down and straightening her leg warmers. "Come on, Ronnie, Peter's waiting."

THEY FOUND PETER sitting cross-legged in the center of the stage, puffing on his homemade corncob pipe; the air sweet with the smell of the cherry-flavored tobacco he swiped from the general store. In the afternoon sun that came down over the tops of the pines into their clearing, lighting up the stage, Peter seemed to glow. He wore faded brown corduroy pants and a green chamois shirt. And a crown made from woven grapevines stuffed with an assortment of leaves. He looked, to Rhonda, like a fairy prince— something you'd come upon while lost in the woods, then you'd blink and he'd be gone. So Rhonda blinked, just to see, but Peter was still there, radiant as ever.

Lizzy and Rhonda hurried up onto the stage, holding their breath in anticipation: maybe today Peter would tell them about the play.

He'd been keeping to himself for weeks, locked in his room, spending afternoons at the library and coming out to the stage on warm days after school to write in his notebook. No one was allowed to disturb Peter when he was writing a play. And only when he was finished with the script and all his production notes, would he reveal anything.

Peter got to his feet, smiling impishly at the girls. He reached out his hand to Rhonda.

"Come away with me, Wendy," he said.

And Rhonda took his hand without hesitation, without any consideration of who Wendy might be or where he wanted her to go. Together, her hand tucked into his, they jumped off the stage and ran around the clearing like crazy birds, cawing and laughing, Peter yelling, "Isn't it wonderful to fly?" Lizzy sat on the edge of the stage, clapping and laughing with them until finally, exhausted, they came back to the stage and collapsed at Lizzy's feet. They were both on their backs, and Rhonda's head was resting on Peter's chest, going up and down with each breath he took. Lizzy lay down with her head on Rhonda's belly and her legs over Peter's, the three of them forming an imperfect triangle.

"Have you guessed yet?" Peter asked.

Rhonda's mind was spinning with possibilities: a play about birds? Greek gods? Fairies maybe?

"*Peter Pan*!" Peter said at last. "We're going to do *Peter Pan*! It'll be the best play yet. I'll play Peter. You, Ronnie, are Wendy. And Lizzy, you are the infamous Captain Hook!"

THEY HAD DONE other plays, of course—plays Peter had written, and ones they'd made up as they went along. Short, predictable dramas about knights slaying dragons, cowboys killing Indians, cops shooting criminals. Last year, Peter even let the girls talk him into doing a play about a roving band of gypsies. Peter played the gypsy king, Rhonda was the queen, and Lizzy her treacherous sister who was also in love with the king. Lizzy poisoned Rhonda, who got to die a spectacular, three-minute death on stage. Peter, the gypsy king, had Lizzy hung then stabbed himself in the heart with his dagger, cursing the wicked ways of women, damning the gypsy life. This followed the formula of most of their plays: all the important characters died at the end, even the hero. Only in *Peter Pan*, everyone would live.

"Everyone but Captain Hook, that is," Peter explained. "He gets eaten by the crocodile."

Peter, as writer, director, and star (not to mention the oldest kid in the neighborhood), made the rules, and, as they got older, the plays got more complicated, as did the rules. But from the beginning, it was a strict rule that the plays were not to be discussed with outsiders. No one was allowed to hear about the play, or see any part of it performed until the opening night, when it was for paying audiences only. Rehearsing a play was like training to be a ninja, Peter said. You cleared your mind of everything else and developed your art in secrecy. You strived for perfection.

Some children wanted a tree house, a secret fort somewhere, but these kids wanted a stage of their own, and they got their wish. They'd built a stage out in the woods three years ago, in a clearing between Rhonda's house and Peter and Lizzy's, right beside Clem's old, rusted-out Chevy Impala convertible, parked there the year Rhonda was born. Clem and Daniel helped put up the stage, doing all the sawing and heavy lifting, letting the kids pound nails.

The stage went up like a strange life raft marooned in a clearing surrounded by tall white pines. It was built from two-byfours and tongue-and-groove boards taken from an old silo that had been torn down a few miles away. The back of the stage was a framed wall from which they hung sheets with scenery painted on (which Rhonda, as resident artist, was always responsible for). There was no curtain. Sets were changed out in the open, for the audience to see. To the left of the stage sat Clem's old red Impala with its top down, and this was often used as a prop. It had been a cop car, a gypsy wagon, and now, Peter was explaining, it would become a pirate ship complete with mast, sail, and a skull-and-crossbones flag at the top.

Rhonda opened the sketchbook she'd brought and started to work on designs for the boat as Peter talked, throwing ideas at her. Drawing was the thing Rhonda did best. She could draw better than she could act, and she was by far the best artist in her class, if not the best in the whole school. Writing and directing the plays was Peter's job, costumes and choreography were Lizzy's department, but the scenery was up to Rhonda.

They were just in the planning stages now. They'd spend the next weeks painting scenery, making their costumes, designing the sets. When school let out and the summer kids came to the cottages around the lake, Peter would hold auditions and they would begin rehearsing every day.

"And this is where our crocodile will lie in wait," announced Peter, pulling open the trapdoor in the back of the stage floor. It led to a hole the kids had dug underneath. The hole was four feet wide, four feet long, and four feet deep. The trap door above it was designed so that evil wizards could appear and disappear, so that the dead could rise from quiet graves.

"But who will be the crocodile?" Lizzy asked, nervous about who was going to kill her.

Peter shrugged. "Don't know yet. But that crocodile's out there somewhere, I can feel it!"

JUNE 6, 2006

THE HOLE ELLA Starkee was left in was nine feet deep, and the floor, said the article in *People* magazine, was roughly the size of a wooden shipping pallet. The kidnapper, whom Ella came to call The Magic Man, covered the top of the hole with boards and leaves. He came to visit every day. The article didn't say what he did during these visits, only that he used a ladder—fashioned from saplings lashed together—to get down into the hole to see her. Each day, he brought her one butterscotch candy, golden as sunlight, with crinkly cellophane wrappers that she saved and sucked on long after the candy was gone.

PAT'S MINI MART had transformed into the Find Ernie headquarters. Pat and Jim had cleared the shelves in the back aisle of Ho Hos and Smartfood, and moved the shelving units into storage.

They were replaced with a long row of folding tables, piled high with flyers, envelopes, and legal pads. Extension cords and phone wires snaked out from behind the deli's meat case, powering the laptop computer and two cordless phones. Those who stood too close to the work area for long, Pat roped in—"Surely, you have five minutes to stuff envelopes?" or "How about manning one of the phones for ten minutes, while Alison here takes a break?"

Pat's nephew, Warren, who had just finished his freshman year of college down in Philadelphia, had driven all night to get there to help out. His job was to collect all the phoned-in tips, jotted on the legal pads, into a database on the laptop. Karen Boisvert, who worked for IBM, had set up a Find Ernie Web site, complete with all the latest news and a form to submit possible sightings and leads. Peter had been there, working right beside them, until Crowley pulled him into Pat's office for questioning.

Rhonda was sitting next to Warren and his laptop, answering phones. Warren wore a Penn State baseball cap and a hemp necklace with brown and black beads. His eyes were bloodshot from not having slept the night before, and he seemed to have a strange, boyish addiction to hot chocolate with mini marshmallows (he was on his fifth cup since Rhonda had been there).

So far, it was mostly dead ends and crackpots calling: a woman who had a dream that Ernie was in a well, a man over in Chelsea who said he believed there were rabbits living among us, wearing people suits. Rhonda drummed her fingers on the table, got up, and paced. Surely there must be more she could do. She had shown up at Pat's first thing in the morning, as soon as Peter called to tell her about the gathering of volunteers, and she'd been sure then that today they'd find Ernie.

Pat had seemed overjoyed to see Rhonda: she caught Rhonda up in a tight embrace and said, "How awful for you to have seen such a thing. You must be a wreck! But don't worry, we'll find her. You mark my words! I bet she'll show up this very morning!"

Pat led a small group through the streets of Pike's Crossing, then into the woods bordering the state forest. They were gone most of the morning and came back for lunch and went out again, to continue combing the woods with Pat cheering them on, saying she was sure they were going to find Ernie that very day.

Rhonda had believed Pat, had even let herself fantasize that it would be her who took the important call; she who put together the string of clues that would lead the cops to Ernie. But now, here it was, a little after three p.m.—twenty-four hours since Ernie's kidnapping. And the most productive thing Rhonda had done was to keep the coffee pot full.

"Fuck," she mumbled to herself, then started organizing papers and pens—busy work. Useless. Little Ernie Florucci's face stared up at her from the flyers strewn across the table. MISSING, said the bold red letters at the top of the page. Underneath was a snapshot of Ernestine taken just the week before. She was wearing a flowered sundress and sitting in the dull yellow grass of her front yard, a plastic kiddie pool in the background. She had dark brown, straight hair done up in pigtails. Her small nose was dotted with freckles and she had a slight gap between her two front teeth. She was smiling up into the camera, squinting a little, like the sun was in her eyes. Or like she couldn't make out something she was looking at in the distance.

"I'm sorry," Rhonda whispered to the little Ernie as she put the flyers in a neat pile, then sat back down in her chair, willing the phone to ring.

"What'd you say?" Warren asked, looking up from his computer. His eyes were a deep, rich, chocolaty brown. A little sad and totally sincere, like the eyes of a basset hound. Rhonda imagined the string of girls Warren must have back in Pennsylvania.

"Nothing," Rhonda said, looking away. She leaned back in her chair and turned to see if there was any sign of Peter yet. No. Still in the office with Crowley.

Rumor had it, among the other volunteers, that Peter had the distinction of being Crowley's first suspect. Rumor also had it that the police had impounded Laura Lee's Volkswagen and that they'd found one of Ernie's red pigtail holders in the front seat. Rhonda herself had overheard Crowley ask Peter if he had a set of keys to his mother-in-law's VW, when she went back to get more pens from the storeroom.

"I did," she heard Peter admit. "But I lost my key ring about a week ago."

Rhonda could picture the key ring: a half dozen or so keys attached to a bottle opener and, of all things, a small white rabbit's foot for luck.

Afraid of being caught eavesdropping, she grabbed the box of pens and returned to the phone table, where she resumed drumming her fingers, waiting for the phone to ring. It was bullshit that Crowley was wasting his time questioning Peter. Everyone, it seemed, was wasting precious time.

By the cash registers, Pat was holding a small press conference, her arm around the silent and tearful Trudy Florucci.

"It's times like these," Pat was saying, "that pull a community together. The people of Pike's Crossing are not the sort to just stand back and let tragedy overtake them. No, the people of Pike's Crossing are going to go out there and find that little girl. Mark my words: we will find Ernestine Florucci. We will not rest until she is back in her mother's arms, safe and sound."

Rhonda caught Warren's eye. "God, I hope she's right."

"She is," Warren said, chewing his lower lip. "Aunt Pat is hardly ever wrong. And once she makes up her mind about a thing, there's no stopping her—she's like a force of nature."

Rhonda glanced around the room at the whirlwind of activity Pat had put into motion in less than twenty-four hours, and nodded. "That I can believe."

Rhonda and Warren were the only two volunteers for the

moment. Peter was stuck in back with Crowley, the others had left.

"So you believe her, then?" Rhonda asked.

He set down his paper cup of cocoa, leaned in closer, and nearly whispered, "Wanna know what I believe?"

Was he flirting? Had *she* been?

Rhonda suddenly felt horribly guilty. How could she even be thinking about some unattainable guy while Ernie Florucci was still missing, being held under lock and key by the rabbit, or worse?

"No matter what happens, we've gotta think positive," Warren said, as if reading her mind. "Thoughts have power, Rhonda. That's what I believe." He leaned back in his chair, closed his eyes tightly for a minute, then opened them, looking at her.

Rhonda shook her head. "*Actions* have power," she told him. "Ernie's not just going to come walking back on her own. Someone's gotta go find her."

AS THE PRESS conference was breaking up, a woman in hospital scrubs and white clogs came in. Behind her was a girl Rhonda guessed to be about twelve, shouldering a heavy-looking knapsack and looking flushed and out of breath, like she'd run the whole way.

The woman in scrubs embraced Trudy and whispered something to her. The girl headed straight for the folding tables, opened her knapsack, and pulled out two large plastic containers.

"I've got cookies and brownies for you guys," she said, smiling. She addressed both of them but was clearly focused on Warren, who, with his disheveled teddy bear looks, was an adolescent girl's dream. "I baked them myself. I'm Katy," she said, extending her hand to Warren, "Ernie's cousin."

She wore jeans, canvas sneakers, and a black T-shirt with a large-eyed anime character on it.

She extended her hand to Rhonda, though even when Rhonda took it, Katy stayed focused on Warren. Katy had long, straight, blond hair that she wore pulled back in a braid. She had braces, but didn't seem the least bit self-conscious about them. When she smiled, she showed her teeth and the metal flashed like jewelry.

Warren peeled back the lid on the brownies and dug in. "These look amazing. You're our savior."

Katy grabbed an empty chair and pulled it up between Rhonda and Warren, turning it so that she sat backward, legs straddling the seat, arms wrapped firmly around the wooden back.

"Anything new?" she asked. Again, the question was clearly directed at Warren.

"Not much on our end. Crowley's been in there talking to the mechanic who works here, Peter, for about forty-five minutes now," Warren reported.

"My mom said they found the car the guy used but they don't think the owner's involved. Belongs to some nutty lady who didn't notice it was missing. Lives over by the lake."

"You mean Laura Lee Clark," said Rhonda. She felt odd discussing the details of the case with this girl. But still, it was good to have an in with Ernie's family—to hear what the police had been telling them.

"Peter's mother-in-law," Warren added. Clearly, he'd been paying attention to the rumors and gossip of the day.

"Not technically," Rhonda corrected. "I mean, Peter and Tock never got married."

"But they have a kid, right?" Katy asked. "A friend of Ernie's. My mom said Ernie would go over to their house to play. This Peter guy *totally* knew her."

"Just because he knew her doesn't mean he did it. I know Peter, all right? He would never do anything like this. Ever. I'd bet my life on it."

Katy and Warren exchanged a *yeah, right* look.

"You guys know about the drawings, right?" Katy asked. Rhonda nodded. Warren shook his head, said, "What drawings?"

"She made these pictures of her and the rabbit going on all these adventures together. He'd take her to this place called Rabbit Island. I bet that's where she is right now!"

Warren frowned. Chewed his lip. "Rabbit Island," he muttered.

"Time to go, Katy!" called the woman in scrubs, who Rhonda figured must be her mother. Trudy was still holding on to her arm, like she might crumple and fall without the extra support. Trudy glared at Rhonda with such fierce hatred that Rhonda felt her stomach do an icy drop down into her bowels.

"See you guys later," Katy said, taking her leave.

"SO HOW WELL do you know Peter?" Warren asked once they were alone again. Peter and Crowley were still hidden away in Pat's office—it had been nearly an hour.

Rhonda took in a breath while she considered what to say.

"We grew up together. Next door neighbors. He was like my big brother."

"You know, I thought you guys were a couple at first. Until Peter started talking about his wife and little girl," Warren said.

"They're not married," Rhonda said again, as if that made any difference. "And no," she continued, allowing herself for half an instant to imagine that alternate universe where she and Peter *were* a couple and had been living happily ever after all along. "We're just good friends." She gave him her best and-I'm-just-fine-with-that smile.

Warren nodded, plucked at his goatee. "So do you think he could have had anything to do with this, or is Crowley barking up the wrong tree?"

"No question. Wrong tree entirely," Rhonda said. "He's wasting valuable time."

"But if it was his mother-in-law's car . . ."

Didn't I just say they weren't married?

"We don't know that for sure. I was actually thinking I might take a ride over to Laura Lee's after I leave here. See what her story is."

"Mind if I tag along?"

"What? Why would you want to do that?"

"Curiosity. And besides, what else am I gonna do? Uncle Jim and Aunt Pat are all caught up here and it's not like I know anyone else in town. Come on, you can show me the exciting sights of Pike's Crossing." He flashed her a warm smile that Rhonda, in spite of herself, found impossible to resist.

"I don't know if Laura Lee's trailer counts. She's kind of a nut job," Rhonda warned.

"I like nut jobs. Come on, every great sleuth has a sidekick, right?"

"I don't know . . ." Rhonda said. She eyed the hallway leading back to the office, thinking of Peter. Ridiculous. She didn't need his permission or approval.

"Okay," Rhonda agreed. "Why not?"

LAURA LEE CLARK'S trailer rested on a cinder block foundation about one hundred feet back from Nickel Lake. The trailer itself was an old metal one, covered in faded and peeling flamingo-colored paint. The yard was a forest of lawn ornaments, whirligigs, bird feeders, and bird baths. Rhonda led Warren through the gnomes, colored gazing globes, and wooden cutouts of fat women bending over, showing their knickers. Rhonda was trying to seem calm and composed, but inside, she was fuming. She had learned, on the drive over, that Pat, who had been friendly to the point of near nausea today, considered Rhonda a suspect.

"What did your aunt say to you on the way out?" Rhonda had

asked Warren. There was something odd in the way the ever-friendly Pat had pulled Warren aside and whispered in his ear just before they left the Mini Mart together.

Warren's face reddened a little at Rhonda's question.

"Come on," Rhonda said. "I thought you were Mr. Think Positive, Surround Yourself with White Light and Don't Ever Tell a Lie."

Warren laughed, chewed on his lip. "Hardly."

"So really, what'd she say? You both looked all serious and conspiratorial."

"She told me to stick close to you," he admitted.

"Why, does she think that bunny's coming after me next?" It hadn't occurred to her until that moment. The rabbit, she recalled, had gotten a good look at her. She was a witness.

"Not exactly," Warren said.

"Well, what then?"

Warren worked at his lip some more.

"She thinks," he paused, "that maybe you're involved somehow."

"What, like I helped with the kidnapping?" Rhonda's voice raised in pitch.

"Relax," Warren said. "Pat's just a leave-no-stone-unturned person."

"So that's why you wanted to come along? To keep an eye on me?" She was furious, mostly with herself for thinking that Warren had come along for other reasons.

"Nah," Warren smiled. "I came along 'cause I thought you were kind of cute." He winked. "Listen, I can see you're on the level. I'll talk to Pat."

Rhonda kept her eyes on the road, hands gripping the wheel as she drove down toward the lake. They passed the Ducharme farm—a Jersey cow was poking her broad snout through the roadside fence, seeing if the pickings were any better out there.

"So what is it you're doing at school . . . computer science or something?" Rhonda asked after a few minutes of silence.

Warren laughed. "I'm a film student."

"Really? You make movies?"

"I've made one. A documentary about this place I used to work at: Story Town. It's like a theme park with buildings and characters from classic stories. You know . . . like the old woman who lived in a shoe, Jack and the Beanstalk, that kind of thing."

"Just don't tell me there are any big white rabbits," Rhonda said.

"Nope. Not a one. And my movie is more about the stoner culture of the kids working there than the characters themselves. Humpty Dumpty was a dealer. Cinderella was sleeping around."

"Ah. The dark underbelly of children's entertainment," Rhonda said.

"Exactly," Warren said. "And I've gotta admit, when I heard it was a rabbit who took this girl, it sounded right up my alley. I thought that maybe, I dunno, when it's over, when Ernie comes out okay, I could do a little movie about it. You know . . . interview people and stuff. It's a helluva story, don't you think? I mean, this could be way bigger than what happened to that girl in Virginia."

THEY CLIMBED UP onto the tiny Astroturf-covered porch, ducking the bird feeders that hung along the edge of the overhang. Warren tapped at a set of parrot wind chimes while Rhonda knocked on the screen door.

"If you're the goddamn press, I don't have anything to say!" came a voice from the depths of the trailer.

"Laura Lee! It's Rhonda Farr!"

"Ronnie? Goddamn! Come on in."

Laura Lee greeted them in the kitchen, which was done in

white and turquoise and looked as though it hadn't been either remodeled or cleaned since sometime in the sixties.

Laura Lee had giant red curls that must have taken hours to put in and were up so high and stiff above her head that Rhonda wondered how the poor woman kept her balance. Her eyes were painted silver and blue (nearly matching the kitchen décor) and she had two circles of rouge on her cheeks. Her lips were hot pink. She wore bright yellow stirrup pants and a T-shirt with a sequined parrot on the front. In one hand, she held a highball glass of pink wine with an orange slice, in the other, a thin cigarette.

"I thought you were from the papers." Laura Lee swayed toward them as she spoke, then jerked herself back so fast she stumbled. "Reporters came by earlier. They've been calling all day. I finally took the goddamn phone off the hook. Are you going to introduce me to your adorable boyfriend, or not?" Laura Lee touched Warren on the cheek. "God, you're a looker!"

"Laura Lee, this is Warren. He worked with me today at the volunteer center."

"Volunteer center? What are you, out collecting for charity? AIDS? Those bums, whatayacall'em now, homeless? Ha! Orphans, maybe? Oh, whatever it is, I'll throw in a buck. Why not?" She turned and found her purse on the kitchen table and began fumbling to undo the clasp.

"No, it's nothing like that," Rhonda said. "Pat set up a center at the Mini Mart for volunteers to help find Ernestine Florucci. We answered phones. Made posters. That kind of thing."

Laura Lee scowled at her. "Good for you, sweetie. Good. For. You. Is that why you're here? To see if I've got the little dove tucked away under my bed? Well, you don't have to bother. The police already checked."

"No! No, Laura Lee. That's not it at all. I was just hoping you could tell us about your car."

"My car? Everyone wants to know about the goddamn car. The police took it, *impounded* it. They insist it was used in the kidnapping. Said they found some kinda evidence. Ha! I don't know a thing about it. I take it out once, maybe twice a week. I haven't driven my goddamn car since last Thursday! It's been sitting in the driveway the whole time. The police had me down at the station all morning taking down my whole life history. Hell of a way to get your biography written, huh?"

"So you didn't notice if it was missing?" Rhonda asked.

"Sweetie, I was here with my Lifetime movies. All the fans were blasting. I had a few goddamn glasses of sangria—I think I've earned that much, don't you? I wouldn't have noticed if the devil himself came prancing up from Hades and took my car. I can't see the driveway through the living room windows, and the shades were drawn anyway to keep the heat out. I didn't hear a goddamn thing. I got this telephone call around ten after three. Some lady from my credit card company wanting to offer insurance at a reduced rate because I'm *such a good customer* or some such bull crapola. Ha! The police tracked her down and that proved to them that I was home. As if I were really going to dress up like the goddamn Easter Bunny from hell and steal a little girl! Absurd! Don't they know who I am?"

Rhonda gave Laura Lee a weak smile and glanced over at Warren to see how he was taking all this. He seemed to be eating it up. He was smiling away at the crazy woman, and before Rhonda could keep the conversation on track, he went and blew it.

"You're an actress, aren't you, Miss Clark?" he asked.

"Why, yes I am! Have you seen my work?"

"Warren's a film student," Rhonda said. "He makes documentaries."

This news produced a warm glow in Laura Lee.

"You sure do look familiar," Warren told her. "What have you been in?"

"Oh, far too many pictures to name, young man. Hundreds. Why, I bet if we were to turn on the TV right now, one of my pictures would be showing"—and before they could talk her out of it, Laura Lee was headed into the living room and reaching for the remote.

"Sit, sit." She gestured toward a faded love seat covered in a crocheted afghan. "Don't mind the African," she said. Warren gave Rhonda a startled look. "I put it there to hide a hole in the sofa. Goddamn cigarettes!"

"It's lovely," Rhonda said, touching the gaudy afghan and biting her lip to keep from laughing. "Did you make it yourself?"

"Hell no! Yard sale," Laura Lee said, then turned her attention back to the television. "Here we go: *Earthquake*. I do a great scream in this film. God, I hope we haven't missed my part! Chuck Heston was just a *dream* to work with. And I don't care what kind of goddamn right-wing gun-nut wacko he is, either!" She held up a hand to silence any argument from Rhonda or Warren. "Ava Gardner, on the other hand, was a total bitch."

"You must have had quite a career," Warren said. Rhonda reached over and pinched him, her hand well hidden by the bunched up "African."

"There's nothing like a career in the cinema. Rhonda, honey, I have to say I was always a little disappointed that you didn't choose a life in the footlights."

"Me?" Rhonda asked.

"I mean, I know you were only children when you put on those plays in the woods, but you had goddamn *talent*. I know it when I see it. You had *a gift*." She turned to Warren. "You should have seen her. She was magnificent. In her last role, she was Wendy from *Peter Pan*. She had me *in tears*. And what were you, dear, ten, eleven years old?"

Rhonda nodded.

"I never understood why you kids tore down that stage. You

got yourselves all banged up. Probably could have been killed. And what for?"

Rhonda shrugged. "It was a long time ago. I can't remember." She reached up and brushed back her bangs, feeling for the thin scar above her left eyebrow.

"Goddamnedest thing!" Laura Lee told Warren. "She and Peter were both cut in the same place when the back wall came down. They both needed stitches. They have the *exact same scar*. Show him, honey. Show the young man your scar!"

Rhonda pulled her bangs back down protectively, shook her head.

"You ask Peter to show you his," Laura Lee said. "It's the craziest thing. The scars couldn't be more alike."

Warren looked at Rhonda, waiting. Rhonda stared at the television. A huge dam was cracking. She wasn't big on seventies disaster movies, or any movie made in the seventies, for that matter—they were all so meandering, overloaded with characters. It occurred to her that this might be a topic of conversation with Warren.

"Laura Lee," Rhonda said, "can you tell me who else had keys to your car?"

Laura Lee sighed dramatically.

"Back to the goddamn car. That's easy, dear. Only two people: Tock and Peter."

Not the answer she'd been hoping for.

"No one else?" Rhonda asked.

Laura Lee thought a minute. "I've had this car since 1979. Can you believe it? And I bought it used! These things go forever. Of course, I keep it garaged in the winter and I don't do much driving—where's an old lady like me going to go? Ha! No, dear. No one else has keys. Except . . ."

"Except?"

"Nothing. It was a hundred years ago. And it doesn't matter

now." Laura Lee reached for her glass of sangria and stared into it with concern, like there was a tiny drowning man among the ice cubes.

"What?" asked Rhonda.

"Daniel. I used to let Daniel borrow my car. He always had a key."

*S*he calls his car a submarine and this pleases him. He mimes putting up a periscope, looking around. Lets her have a peek.

"No sharks," she tells him.

He nods to show they are safe. She will always be safe when she is with him.

He takes her to their secret place. It's private. Cool and shaded. They won't be found here.

Rabbit Island, she calls it.

He chases her in a friendly game of tag. She's zigzagging through the trees and stones, laughing.

He remembers the first Birdie, how they would play hide-and-seek all day. She was so good at hiding. She could find a tiny place and fold her body up, filling the space like a hermit crab. She'd wait so quietly, so patiently to be found.

The rabbit chases this new girl and he's laughing too. Quietly laughing because at last, his long-lost Birdie is back. And he's not going to let any harm come to her this time.

MAY 23, 1993

"TAKE IT OUT," he urged her.

Rhonda laughed.

"Really. It makes you talk funny. And it makes your lip stick out."

She pushed the retainer forward with her tongue, pulled it out with her fingers, holding it like something extra delicate, exotic: a pink beetle with thin, silver legs.

"That's better," he told her.

They were hidden underground, buried together like secret treasure. The trapdoor on the stage floor was closed over their heads and they sat in the small hole, face-to-face, breathing in the damp smell of earth and roots.

She studied him in the dim light that came from the cracks in the trapdoor above their heads. They were sitting with their legs crossed under them, facing each other. He was wearing his Peter Pan costume. He smelled like leaves. And she was wearing the white Wendy nightgown, her hair tied back with a ribbon.

"So you want to know the truth?" he asked.

"Yes," she told him.

"Are you sure you're ready?"

She laughed.

"Then quit laughing. Just relax. I'll tell you how it is: first, you start with a little kissing. Then the guy feels the girl up. You know, touches her boobs and stuff."

Rhonda wrapped her arms around her chest, concealing her painfully obvious lack of boobs.

"Then he touches her between the legs to see if she's ready," he explained.

"Ready?"

"You know . . . ready for him."

She nodded, but had no idea what he meant.

"For his penis," Peter said.

"Oh," Rhonda said matter-of-factly. Her mouth felt suddenly dry. She swallowed hard.

"He puts it inside her and they move together so that it goes in and out."

"Why?" Rhonda asked.

"Because it feels good, stupid!"

"Oh," she said again.

She couldn't wait to tell Lizzy all of this. But then, as if reading her mind, Peter put a stop to her plan.

"Rhonda," Peter said just before opening the door so they could both head home for supper, "you can't tell Lizzy I told you this stuff."

"Why not?" Rhonda asked. Peter had never asked her to keep a secret from Lizzy before.

"Because she'd be weirded out. It has to be our secret. Okay?"

Rhonda nodded, slipping the retainer back into her mouth, smiling. She and Peter had a secret. A secret that made her feel all tingly and strange, like a walking lightning rod.

JUNE 7, 2006

"SO ARE YOU gonna tell me about this Daniel guy, or what?"
Warren asked. He'd quizzed her about Daniel when they left
Laura Lee's the day before, but she'd put him off, saying she
needed time to think. Now here it was the next morning and they
were working the phones at Pat's. He was sucking down a large
hot chocolate and Rhonda had a cup of French roast. Warren
had shaved around his goatee and his hair was still damp from a
shower.

"Not much to tell. He's Peter's father."

"So is he the kind of guy who would take a little girl?" He
cocked his head to the side, waiting for her answer.

"No. It's impossible."

"Why's that?"

"He disappeared twelve years ago."

"Disappeared?"

"Yeah. One night he was there, with all of us, and the next morning, he was gone. We all thought he'd show up eventually. That he'd gone off on a bender or left town to avoid paying back a gambling debt or something, but no one ever heard from him again."

"Spooky."

"His daughter Lizzy was my best friend. Peter's sister. And, um, she disappeared three years later when we were freshmen in high school. Lizzy left for school one morning with just her book bag and was never seen again."

"Wait a sec," Warren said. "Peter's sister disappeared?"

Rhonda nodded. "Her dad came back for her."

"If it was Daniel, why didn't he take Peter too?" Warren asked.

"No one knows," Rhonda said. She picked up her cup of coffee and drained the last lukewarm sip. "Everyone wondered, but no one knows. The police looked but couldn't find either of them. Lizzy was one of those faces you see on milk cartons and in Wal-Marts; one of those parental abductions. Her mom pretty much lost her mind after that."

Rhonda thought of Aggie's steady decline: the drinking, the increasingly strange behavior. How she started to play with her hair, pulling out one strand at a time, working at it for hours until she looked like a dog with mange. She got paranoid, accused Clem and Justine of knowing where Daniel was and not telling her. She drank to excess, drove her car into Clem and Justine's house, and bit the earlobe off a police officer who was sent to investigate a report of a woman dressed in only her underwear trying to steal avocados at Price Chopper.

Aggie eventually ended up in the state hospital for six months, then went off to her sister's in Maryland. When her sister got burned out, she had Aggie moved into a sort of residential hotel for the mentally ill.

"And you're sure it was Lizzy's dad who took her?" Warren

leaned toward Rhonda. His breath smelled sweet and chocolaty and she let herself wonder, for exactly one second, what it might be like to kiss him.

Rhonda nodded.

"Positive. Two weeks after she left, we got a postcard. There were a few more, all saying she was doing fine and telling about adventures she was having with Daniel. The last one was from San Francisco. I was a junior in high school then. The card just said she was taking singing lessons, which was really weird." Rhonda closed her eyes, tried to remember the sound of Lizzy's voice and couldn't. What she remembered instead was her friend's habit of singing the wrong words on purpose, trying to get a laugh.

"Weird?"

"Lizzy gave up speaking after her dad left. Wouldn't talk to anybody. Three years without a single word. Then she writes that she's taking singing lessons." Rhonda laughed weakly, and began peeling the lip off of the now empty paper cup in her hand.

Warren nodded. "Freaky."

"Yeah," Rhonda agreed. "We were close, then the summer Daniel left, everything just kind of fell apart. Things were never the same."

"That must have been really hard. Your best friend just disappearing like that."

There it was. The thing she'd longed for from Peter over the years. Just a simple acknowledgment of how hard it was on Rhonda, on all of them. How hard and wrong and terrible the whole mess was. Instead, she heard it from Warren, practically a stranger, but with those two sentences, a thousand times more empathetic than Peter had ever been. It didn't seem fair. But life wasn't, was it? She looked down at the photo of Ernie on the MISSING flyer, then went back to working at tearing apart her cup.

"It *was* hard. And the hardest part has always been not knowing what happened to Lizzy. We never heard from her again. She and Daniel just snuck off and made this whole other life some-where and none of us ever knew why."

Warren nodded. "Two lost girls," he said.

"What?" Rhonda's cup was in shreds. She scooped the torn pieces into a pile.

"Lizzy and Ernie," he said.

Rhonda let out a breath of air through her teeth. "The two have nothing to do with each other, Warren."

Warren began picking up the torn pieces of Rhonda's cup, studying them like they were evidence. "I'm just saying that I think things happen for a reason, it's just that we don't always know what the reason is." He gnawed his lower lip, then contin-ued. "I don't think it was a mistake or just shit luck that you were here in the parking lot at the Mini Mart when Ernie was taken. You were meant to see it, meant to get involved."

"I don't buy it," Rhonda said, scooting her chair back, away from him. "Life *is* all about shit luck and random chaos. That's how the universe was created. It's why we're all here."

"YOU SHOULDN'T BE here," Trudy hissed at Rhonda.

It was lunchtime and Katy and her mom showed up with a cooler full of sandwiches for the crew at Pat's, with Trudy Flo-rucci in tow.

"Aunt Trudy, she's here because she wants to help," Katy said.

"Make her leave," Trudy said to Pat, who had stepped in to intervene.

"Trudy, she's . . ." Pat started to say.

"I made the sandwiches. It's the one thing I've been able to do to help since Ernie was taken. It took every ounce of energy I had. And I'll be damned if that little twat is going to sit on her fat ass eating *my* sandwiches thinking she's some kind of fucking hero when it's her fault Ernie is gone!"

Pat nodded at Rhonda, who stood up on shaky legs. Pat put an arm around her, guiding her toward the back of the store. "Go hide out in my office till she's gone," Pat whispered. "We need you here."

Rhonda did as she was told, taking a seat behind Pat's massive desk. In the corner, a small TV was tuned to CNN. On the wall beside her was a clipboard with the employee schedule on it. Pat's desk was cluttered with magazines, newspapers, printouts and MISSING flyers with little Ernie peering up, smiling. In the middle of the chaos was a large granite rectangle, similar to a grave marker, the words PAT HEBERT, STATION OWNER AND MANAGER engraved on one side. Beside it was a framed photo of three little girls, one of whom was most definitely Pat at ten or eleven. It was odd to see that Pat had been young once, but somehow comforting to see that, from appearances anyway, not much had changed. Pat looked serious, the oldest girl of the group, the girl who was obviously in charge. The middle girl had a complacent, buck-toothed smile. The littlest one, the girl on the end, had her hair done up in ribbons and looked a little mischievous, like the minute the photo taker turned away, she'd pull the ribbons out.

In front of the photo in its heavy metal frame was the issue of *People* with Ella Starkee, the farmer, and his border collie on the cover. Rhonda flipped it open, scanned the article, which she'd already read several times.

Ella's kidnapper met up with her on her way home from school. He asked if she wanted to see a magic trick. She shrugged. He pulled a coin from his ear and gave it to her. As she palmed the shiny quarter, he grabbed her wrist and pulled her into his car.

"Coast is clear!"

Rhonda jumped. Warren popped his head through the doorway, his smile sweet and slightly apologetic, like Trudy's behavior was somehow his fault. "Katy's still here, but her mom and aunt are gone. Come on out and grab a sandwich."

Back at the volunteer table, Katy pushed a tuna on wheat toward Rhonda, who refused it, though she was starving.

"My aunt Trudy's not herself," Katy told Rhonda. "She just wants someone to blame, you know? And I'm sure that when she gets her head back on straight, she'll see it wasn't your fault about Ernie. I mean, I can see that clear as day, you know? What were you supposed to do? The guy grabbed her and was gone."

Rhonda nodded. *Gone. Hopping off into the sunset, hand in paw.*

"So this is what I've been able to figure out: the rabbit had been visiting Ernie for at least three weeks. The last time we know he saw her for sure was this past Thursday: Ernie told her mom she missed the bus and the rabbit brought her home. She drew pictures of him hiding in the bushes by the playground at school and talking to her through her bedroom window. But most of the pictures looked like this," Katy said, slipping a page surreptitiously out of a school binder that said GIRLS RULE in sparkly letters on the cover—a bright crayoned drawing labeled RABBIT ISLAND in crude letters.

"Shouldn't the police have this?" Warren whispered.

Katy shrugged. "Ernie made so many drawings of the same scene. Crowley got all of them. I figured I should save one, just in case we never get the others back, you know? They're evidence now. And it didn't seem right to give every last one away. It seemed like, I dunno, bad luck or something. Like I was giving away every last piece of her."

How pleasant it looked, Rhonda thought, like a scene from a brochure showing a tropical island getaway. She studied the palm trees, the multicolored rabbits lounging on neat rows of rocks in the sun, the pale clouds shaped like hopping bunnies. The island was surrounded on all sides by dark, shark-infested water. A small black fence circled the island, and to get in, you walked through a swinging gate guarded on either side by giant bunnies. Pulled up in the water next to the gate was a small brown submarine.

"That's obviously the Volkswagen," Warren said, pointing to the sub. "Look at the shape. She's just added a periscope and propeller to it."

"But how could the rabbit have used Laura Lee's car again and again?" Rhonda asked. "I mean, I can see taking it once and her not noticing, but he must have used it several times. That seems pretty chancy."

"Not if it was someone Laura Lee knew," Katy said. "Someone she trusted. Someone who had his own set of keys."

Rhonda shook her head, looked back at the picture.

She saw Ernie and Peter Rabbit in the center of the island, Ernie smiling, holding the rabbit's paw. *Rabbit Island.* Rhonda imagined Ernie there right now, happy and warm in the sun. Maybe Rabbit Island was the place everyone who disappeared went to. Maybe, Rhonda thought in spite of herself, Lizzy and Daniel were there too. Perhaps, thought Rhonda as she touched the missing child's drawing, Rabbit Island was a place populated by all who were lost. She shook her head. *Be logical,* she told herself. *Look at the evidence.*

"So if the sub is the car, then Rabbit Island is probably an actual place, too," she said.

"A zoo maybe?" Warren guessed.

"Looks more like a park to me," Katy said.

Rhonda nodded. "Chances are it's not all that far away. When the rabbit took her for these rides, they couldn't have been gone long. He always got her back home before Trudy noticed she'd been missing."

"With all this water," Warren said, "it might be some place by the lake."

"Could be," said Rhonda. "The lake doesn't have any islands but there are plenty of small beaches and rocky outcroppings."

"There's another thing—something only the police know," Katy said as she looked up from the drawing. "For some reason or other, the rabbit had this weird name he called her."

"Weird name?" Rhonda asked.

"He called her Birdie," Katy said. "I heard my aunt tell my mom. Crowley found a card from Peter Rabbit tucked under Ernie's mattress. It was addressed to Birdie."

"Jesus," Rhonda said.

"Bizarre," Warren said, sucking in his lower lip and biting down.

"But you didn't hear the Birdie thing from me," Katy said, sliding the drawing back into the folder and sticking the folder in her backpack. "And if anyone sees I've got this, it'll go straight to Crowley. If my aunt catches me talking to you, she'll have a conniption. Maybe I'll see you guys later. If I can't come back this afternoon, I'll make it tomorrow."

"Take it easy," said Warren, smiling. "And thanks for lunch!"

"No problem," Katy said, practically glowing as she smiled back at him.

"So what do you think?" Warren asked as they watched Katy hop on her bike outside.

"I think someone's got a crush on you," Rhonda said.

Warren's face flushed. "I mean about the drawing and this weird bird name," he said.

"I don't know yet," Rhonda said, standing. "You want a candy bar?" Warren shook his head, started doodling on the paper in front of him. *Birdie*, he wrote.

Rhonda walked over to the rack of candy, picked out a Snickers bar and brought it up to Pat at the register. Pat looked up from the latest Ernie spread in the newspaper (in which a photo of Pat herself featured prominently) and gave Rhonda a huge smile.

"It's on the house, Rhonda. It's the least I can do to thank you for all of your work here. You know, what Trudy said wasn't fair and I'm sorry."

Rhonda shrugged.

"You keep your chin up, now," Pat ordered. "We mustn't start to lose hope. We've got to stick together and bring this little girl home." She gave Rhonda a robust pat on the shoulder. Maybe Warren had spoken up for her, and she was off Pat's list?

Pat came out from behind the counter and walked over to Warren.

"FYI, we have a new volunteer, Cecil Lowry, coming in around two. He used to be the fire chief but he's been retired for years now. He's still got a lot of connections, knows everybody. He'll bring a real sense of order to things here. He's a character alright—I think you'll like him."

Then she bent down and said something in a low voice to him. He glanced over to Rhonda, then away. He whispered something back, looking a little frustrated.

"Oh, for Christ's sake," Rhonda muttered to herself. So much for being off the suspect list.

She walked down the hall past the bathroom, office, and storeroom, and into the garage, where Jim was doing an oil change while he listened to the Red Sox game on the radio. There was no sign of Peter.

There was a metal desk in the corner, with a large appointment book taking up most of the surface. Rhonda saw no harm in wandering over and taking a look. It was opened to today's date, June 7. Peter was the one supposed to be doing the oil change. There were two inspections and a brake job scheduled for later that afternoon: things she knew Jim wasn't qualified to do. She flipped back through the greasy pages, glancing at the schedules over the past three weeks. Laura Lee's car had been in three times. Peter had installed a new fuel line and fuel filter back on May 15. The VW was in again on May 25 to have the rear brakes replaced. Then, on June 1, last Thursday, Peter had replaced some clamps and hoses. There was also a list of things he hadn't gotten around to: replacing the fan belt (he had to order the part) and fixing the latch on the passenger side door (a note in the book said Laura Lee reported the door only stayed closed if it was locked). Peter had penciled her in again for next Friday to finish the work. Doubtful she'd come now that the car had been impounded.

But it *had* been in last Thursday, which was, according to Katy, when the rabbit had given Ernie a ride home in his submarine.

Shit.

Rhonda closed the book.

"You doing our scheduling now?" Jim had come up behind her.

"Huh? Oh, no. Sorry, just looking. I was wondering when Peter worked next."

Jim nodded grimly. "Supposed to be here now. I don't know what's gotten into him lately. Shows up when he feels like it, I guess. Must be nice."

"I guess he's got a lot on his mind," she said.

"No excuse," Jim said.

"I guess not," Rhonda answered. "I better get back to the phones."

On the short walk back to the tables in the corner, Rhonda made up her mind not to tell Warren about seeing Laura Lee's car in the scheduling book. Like it or not, the evidence was stacked against Peter and proving his innocence was going to be tricky. She needed more clues. Rhonda peeked into Pat's office as she went by—empty. She stepped in and glanced at the clipboard on the wall next to the desk: the employee schedule. She flipped back to the week before and scanned the schedule for Thursday. Pat was working, along with someone named Carl. And Peter. Surely, if Peter drove off in Laura Lee's car for any length of time, someone would have noticed. She couldn't very well ask Pat, who would just see it as more evidence of Peter's involvement (and possibly Rhonda's too), so what she needed to do was find this Carl guy. She saw his name on the schedule later in the week. Perfect.

Rhonda hurried out of the office and back down the hall, and there he was: the suspect of the hour.

"Hey, Ronnie," Peter called.

He was standing next to Warren, holding the hair back from his forehead, showing off his scar. Warren, apparently, had remembered Laura Lee's instructions and thought to ask about the scar. Beside Peter was Suzy, dressed in a tie-dye shirt and cutoff shorts. Rhonda scanned the store quickly: no Tock. She practically bounded up to them.

"Aunt Rhonda!" Suzy said, "Daddy says I can come see Sadie again soon."

"Of course," Rhonda said. "Any time you like."

"Can I bring her some apples?"

"Of course, sweetie. She'd love that."

"What, you have a horse or something?" Warren asked.

Rhonda and Suzy giggled.

"A pig," Suzy told him.

He looked shocked.

"A guinea pig," Rhonda explained.

"Hey Ronnie, can you keep an eye on Suzy for a minute?" Peter asked. "I've gotta go patch things up with Pat and Jim. Tock and I screwed up our schedules and I've got Suzy all day. I had to bring her to the doctor's this morning."

"I had another storm," Suzy said.

"They changed her medication again. Freaking doctors. You'd think they'd have a clue what would work here. That's her third seizure in a week." Peter was already on his way across the store and into the garage. Suzy sat down at the table, flipped over a flyer with Ernie's picture to the blank side and began to scribble.

"So what's this guinea pig like?" Warren asked, directing the question more at Suzy than Rhonda.

"She's albino," Suzy said. "She's all white with red eyes. Like a ghost."

Suzy began to draw an octopus, counting the legs carefully.

"No kidding," Warren said. "How cool is that? When do I get to meet her?" Now he looked in Rhonda's direction.

"Anytime," Rhonda said before she had a chance to think better of it.

"Today? When we get out of here?" Warren suggested.

"Why not?" Rhonda said.

"She likes apples," Suzy told him.

"Well then I better go see if I can find one. I don't want to make a bad first impression by arriving empty-handed." He got up and walked over to the coolers to search for an apple.

"He's funny," Suzy said.

"Yeah, he is," Rhonda agreed. Had she really just invited Warren home? What was she thinking? Why did he even want to come? Maybe he was just an animal lover.

"Daddy says you're helping to find Ernie," Suzy said, looking up from her drawing. The octopus now had eight legs and had been joined by a smiling starfish.

"We're sure trying," Rhonda said. The reality was, they weren't doing shit. It seemed no one was. Forty-eight hours later, there was no sign of the little girl. It was like they disappeared into thin air, she and the rabbit in the submarine.

It could so easily have been Suzy, Rhonda thought as she stroked the little girl's hair. *It could have been any little girl.*

"Hey, Suzy? Did you know about the rabbit visiting Ernie?" Rhonda asked.

"Yep. He came to school."

"You saw him?"

"No. Only Ernie. She said she was lucky. That Peter picked her because she was special. I only met the *other* Peter."

Was Suzy drawing a rabbit there, hopping through her underwater scene?

"What other Peter?" Rhonda's heart began beating double-time.

No, it wasn't a rabbit. Suzy was drawing an angelfish.

"The stuffed one. Like a toy? Ernie said the real Peter gave her the stuffed Peter to keep her company. So she wouldn't be lonely when he couldn't be with her."

"So he gave her a stuffed rabbit?"

"Uh-huh. White and fluffy but it got dingy quick."

"Come on, Suzy Q, time to jump back in the saddle!" Peter called. He was walking stiffly toward them.

"That was fast," Rhonda said.

"It doesn't take long to get canned," Peter said, trying to sound casual, but Rhonda heard the faint tremor in his voice.

"What?" Rhonda asked.

"They fired me. Said my working here was bad for business."

"They can't do that!"

"Sure they can," Peter shrugged. "It's a small town. People talk." He drew in a breath, blew it out slowly, calmly. Only someone who knew him as well as Rhonda could read his face: he was seething.

"About what?" Suzy asked.

"A lot of nonsense, that's what," Peter said. "Now grab your latest masterpiece and come on. We've gotta get the shopping done and dinner cooked before your mama gets home."

"I DIDN'T KNOW guinea pigs were so talkative," Warren said as he kneeled on the floor of Rhonda's living room, stroking Sadie, who was showing off with whistles and coos.

"I think she's got a thing for you."

"She just loves me for my apple slices." He reached into the aquarium and fed her another. "Her pink eyes are kind of freaky."

"Some cultures believe that albinos have magical powers," Rhonda said.

Warren raised his eyebrows. "Don't tell me: that's why you chose Sadie, to help with your mojo?"

"Nope." Rhonda leaned in and stroked Sadie's head. "No magical powers here. Just a distinct lack of melanin. I rescued her from the lab at school."

Warren tossed in another apple slice, then stood up, wiping his hands on his shorts. Rhonda found herself staring at the fine hairs on his legs and wondered, for an instant, what it would be like to run her fingers lightly over them.

Get over it, she told herself.

Rhonda had dated in college. Not much, but enough to know that it always ended in disappointment. She'd gone out to the movies, dinner, even fooled around a little, but it never amounted to anything. No matter how nice the guy, how well he treated her or how much they had in common, he still wasn't Peter.

"You want a drink or something?" Rhonda asked, turning away from Warren and his legs. "I've got Diet Coke and beer. Or I could make tea."

"Beer would be great." He followed her down the hall toward the kitchen, stopping to study the dissection drawings.

"Did you do these?" Warren asked, finger hovering over the eviscerated rabbit, tracing the outline of its lungs and heart.

Rhonda nodded.

"They're really good. Kind of a sick thing to put up on the wall of your home—animals all taken apart like this—but they're excellent. Beautiful, even. You're an artist."

Rhonda shook her head. "I just draw what I see. An artist interprets and manipulates—I don't have that kind of imagination or ability."

"Yeah and I just film what I see too and they call it art. It's all about perspective, Rhonda."

She shrugged and led him to the kitchen, where they settled in at the table with a couple of beers and some mildly stale pretzels Rhonda dug out of the back of a cupboard.

"I've been thinking about this thing with Peter," Rhonda said. "I think it's shitty that Pat and Jim fired him. And it's probably not even legal."

Warren nodded. "Probably not."

"So I thought maybe you could talk to them. Convince them that firing him isn't the right way to handle things. It's just going to make everything worse. People are looking to Pat as a key player in this Ernie thing—she's had way more media exposure than Trudy and she's pretty much become the star of Pike's Crossing overnight. If she fires Peter, it makes him look even more guilty."

"I don't know, Rhonda. Jim's pretty easy. But Pat, once she makes up her mind about a thing, it's like trying to stir dried cement."

"Will you try?"

"Okay. I'll try. If you'll do something for me."

"What?"

"Consider that Peter might not be what you think. I'm not saying he's the one who took Ernie, I'm just asking you to look at the evidence and realize he might be involved in some way. He might not be the person he seems."

"I've known Peter since I was born!"

"I know. I know you have. But everyone has secrets."

She was about to open her mouth to say that she knew all of Peter's secrets, and he all of hers, but she was interrupted by the ringing phone. She excused herself and grabbed the cordless phone from the table in the front hall.

"Ronnie? It's Tock. Listen, Suzy just told me she was talking to you about Ernie this afternoon."

"Yeah, a little." Rhonda began to pace back and forth across the hall, studying the dissection drawings.

"She said you asked about Ernie and the rabbit." There was an edge to Tock's voice that made Rhonda cringe.

"I just wondered if she'd ever seen the rabbit," Rhonda explained. She looked at her own rabbit drawing, the layers of fur, skin, and tissue peeled back to reveal the bright, jewel-like organs inside.

Tock blew out a breath, hissing into the phone like some far-off snake. "She had one of her worst seizures ever last night. Did Peter tell you that? God, I can't believe he brought her into Pat's in the first place, all that Ernie stuff around . . . it's too much. She's a *little girl*, Rhonda. A very upset little girl with a serious medical condition that isn't being controlled very well at the moment." Tock's voice was strained. She sounded like she was on the verge of either crying or screaming.

"I'm sorry, Tock. God, I would never do anything to hurt or upset Suzy. I was just making conversation. I'm so sorry. I'll be more careful in the future." Rhonda stood with her back against the wall and let herself sink down, back sliding, until she was sitting on the floor.

"Thank you. That's all I'm asking."

"Of course," Rhonda said. "Thanks for calling, Tock. Thanks for telling me." She started to stand.

"Wait, there's something else. Did you stop by my mother's trailer yesterday?"

Rhonda took in a breath, let herself fall back to the ground. Shit. "Yeah. I just wanted to see how she was."

"And you brought some guy . . . some movie director or something?"

"I brought a friend. My friend Warren. He's not really—"

"My family's been through a lot these last couple of days. I don't know what it is you hoped to find by interrogating a sick woman and a little girl, but you're not the cop, Rhonda. It's not your job to go digging around in other people's lives. You're just a *witness*. A witness who did nothing, which, let's face it, is pretty fucking suspicious, isn't it?"

Before Rhonda could respond, Tock slammed the phone down, sending a smashing shriek across the lines, echoing inside Rhonda's already rattled skull.

MAY 31, 1993

TWO WEEKS BEFORE his birthday, Clem began sleeping in his study. There was a love seat there, and he'd lie down with his long legs draped over one armrest, his head forced up at an unnatural angle by the other. When he woke up in the morning, he'd emerge from his new lair in the rough shape of a question mark, hobble his way to the kitchen, and make coffee. By the time he was into his second cup, he'd straightened up again.

"Why are you sleeping in the study?" Rhonda asked after it became clear that this was to be an ongoing arrangement.

"My snoring was keeping your mother awake," he said.

"You snore, Daddy?"

He shrugged, turned the coffee mug in his hands.

Rhonda would watch him get ready for work (Clem was the boss at the sawmill those days—Dave Lancaster had retired) after one of his nights on the love seat, wondering what was really going on. She heard bits and pieces of arguments through the walls. Hushed conversations. She never picked up enough to know what the fighting was about—only that her mother seemed very angry with her father. And Rhonda knew enough to realize it sure didn't have anything to do with her father snoring.

She made up her mind to do something extra special for his birthday. She'd make him a drawing. A really nice one. She'd take her time and do a sketch of something he'd really love. But what? She made a mental list of the things her father loved: black coffee, unfiltered Camel cigarettes, German beer, and the Civil War. The war seemed like the best candidate for a good picture.

Her father spent nearly all his free time reading about it, studying battle plans and maps. One weekend a month, he got together with a group of other Civil War enthusiasts and planned reenactments. Clem had a scratchy wool costume and marched in parades with a musket, camped out at fairs, and reenacted battles all over the east coast. Rhonda didn't get her father's fascination, obsession even, with a war he'd had nothing to do with. She felt a little embarrassed for him when he dug his Union Army uniform out of storage and put it on, marching off to war in his Dodge pickup, Camel cigarettes and a cup of coffee by his side.

Maybe, Rhonda thought, she could do a drawing of one of the generals. She just needed to find a good photo to work from and she could draw just about anything. She resolved to sneak into his study when she got home from school, before he got out of work, and find a picture.

GRANT AND LEE stared up at her, along with endless photos of young men in uniform. None of them were right. She thought about trying to draw an old map depicting a battleground, but that seemed silly—a map is a drawing, anyway. Then, she found it. There in the pages of one of her father's books, her subject stared up at her: the *Hunley*.

The *Hunley* was a Confederate-built submarine powered by eight men turning hand cranks. While it was not the first submarine, it was, Rhonda knew from her father's Civil War rants, the first sub ever to sink a ship in battle. The *Hunley* itself sank in the waters near Charleston in 1864 after tearing a hole in the side of a Union ship. The Confederate camp nearby saw the blue light from the *Hunley* signaling that they'd been successful in their mission and were returning to shore, but something went wrong along the way. The submarine, and the crew that went down with it, were never recovered. What happened to the *Hunley* and its crew was, according to Clem, one of the greatest mysteries in United States history.

Rhonda spent the next hour studying old drawings of the *Hunley* in Clem's Civil War books, reading everything she could find about it, and decided to do a series of sketches—her own renditions of the submarine, a composite of all she had gleaned. The top drawing would show the outside of the *Hunley*, and the middle would be a cutaway view of the inside, depicting the soldiers working the cranks while the captain manned the controls at the front of the machine. The image at the bottom would be the same cutaway view, but without the men. Instead, Rhonda would carefully print the names and explanations for all the mechanical features of the sub: the water ballast tanks, sea cocks, steering rods, propeller, rudder, mercury gauge for measuring depth, even the candle that illuminated the controls, and warned when air was running out.

She found the submarine pictures she would work from and was flipping through a book, looking for one that showed a close-up of a Confederate uniform, when a photograph that had been stuck between the pages fell out. Rhonda leaned down and picked it up from the floor, assuming it would be some silly snapshot of her father and his Civil War dress-up pals.

It wasn't. It was a wedding photo. The groom in a tux, looking young and tan, was her father. Beside him, the bride smiled out from cascade of white lace and clutched a heavy bouquet like a club. But it was not Rhonda's mother looking out at her: it was Aggie.

He wishes this would never end. He imagines going away with her, living like this forever, being this happy. He wishes there was a real Rabbit Island, a place they could go and not be bothered. Where she could go on being his Birdie and he could be her Peter Rabbit forever.

But the rabbit understands the reality of the situation. He knows his days as a rabbit are numbered. But he doesn't want her to forget him. Not ever. He doesn't want her to be lonely. He gives her a gift: a fluffy stuffed rabbit. He puts a tag around its neck. FOR BIRDIE WITH LOVE FROM PETER, it says. He's taking a chance giving her the gift, but she is a careful girl. She understands that everything that passes between them is a secret. The little girl squeezes the soft, white bunny to her chest, then turns and hugs Peter. If she could see beneath the mask, behind the mesh eyes, she'd know he was crying.

JUNE 12, 13 & 14, 2006

ONE WEEK AFTER the kidnapping, Ernie had not been found, and Pike's Crossing was in an uproar. Lakeview Lodge, The Inn and Out Motel, and the two bed-and-breakfasts in town were booked solid with out-of-state media and volunteers. The little café down the street from Pat's did a booming business despite their lack of lattes. The streets, fields, and woods had been searched by dogs, helicopters, Boy Scouts, a group of National Guard volunteers, and citizens. The state police brought in divers and boats, and dragged Nickel Lake. Candlelight vigils were held at the Methodist church. And though people were worried that no trace of Ernie had been found, they recalled Ella Starkee: ten days in a hole with a tin can, worms, and beetles. Anything was possible.

Pat held another press conference, Trudy Florucci by her side, to say she'd enlisted the services of a woman who dowsed for lost children and pets with a forked willow branch. She introduced Shirley Bowes, who was old enough to be Pat's mother, and who looked, to Rhonda's surprise, like a farm wife. She did not wear a turban or long, flowing dress hanging with bells. The only jewelry Shirley wore was a plain gold wedding band. She had permed white hair and wore sensible, old-lady clothes. Shirley scuffed her shoes on the floor and smiled shyly at the cameras.

"You might remember," Pat went on, "last year Shirley found a toddler in an old dry well up in Swanton."

Rhonda remembered. The little boy had fallen into the deep hole and stayed there overnight, for nearly twenty-four hours. Nothing like Ella Starkee, who lost track of time down in her hole. She measured her days with crinkly cellophane butterscotch wrappers. She sang every song she knew. When she ran out of songs, she began talking to God.

"And he talked back to me," she told reporters later.

"What did he say?" the reporters asked.

Ella smiled bashfully. "He told elephant jokes."

"Elephant jokes?"

"Like, how can you tell an elephant has been in your refrigerator? Look for footprints in the butter."

Rhonda focused back on Pat's conference.

"Ernie's been gone too long and we're at a dead end. We've got to seek out new leads wherever we can find them," Pat said in her hearty voice. Pat the boss. Pat in her name tag that said STATION OWNER, to show who was in charge. Rhonda found an odd comfort in Pat's enthusiasm.

It was only in her moments off camera, when Rhonda caught Pat pacing nervously or muttering to herself, that she sensed Pat might be losing her grip on the situation—preparing to admit the possibility of defeat. Rhonda cringed at the idea that Pat still thought of her as a suspect. She also hated to think that this might be the true reason behind all the time Warren had been spending with her. And did he suspect her, too? Think she and Peter had conspired to steal the little girl?

"One more thing," Pat told the reporters. "Bonnie Starkee, the mother of little Ella, called Trudy this morning."

An excited murmur went through the room.

"What did Mrs. Starkee say?" asked one of the reporters.

"She said she's praying for Ernie. She told Trudy she mustn't lose hope. Now, there's no time to waste. Let's put Shirley to work!" Cameras clicked as Shirley stepped forward and asked, in a barely audible voice, to be given something that had belonged to Ernie. Trudy reached down into a wrinkled paper grocery bag at her feet and pulled out a stuffed bear with an embroidered heart on its chest. The dowser sat in the padded chair dragged from behind the register, clutching the pink teddy bear as cameras clicked and television stations shot footage for the evening news. At last, Shirley stood up, handed the bear back to Trudy, took out a map of the state, spread it on the counter, and dangled a clear quartz crystal on a thin silver chain over it. The pendulum hung still, not circling or swaying, a dead weight. When Shirley wasn't able to get a reading on the Vermont map, she spread out a map of the whole country. Still nothing.

Maybe Ernie was in outer space, Rhonda thought. Like the cow that jumped over the moon. Maybe that's where the rabbit took her in his submarine. Maybe Rabbit Island was up there somewhere, its own kind of heaven. Rhonda looked up, away from the pendulum and map, and tried to get her eyes to look right through the ceiling and roof—to look somehow beyond. She sensed Warren watching her and turned toward him. He looked unspeakably sad, defeated. Rhonda reached out to him, then pulled her hand back, hesitating. But wasn't it her own hesitation that got her into this mess in the first place? Her inaction was the very reason Ernie was gone, so lost even the dowser couldn't find her. For better or worse, she reached out and took

Warren's hand. He squeezed her fingers tightly, encircling her hand with his own.

"I'LL SAY ONE thing," Cecil Lowry mumbled as the press conference was breaking up. Cecil, the ex–fire chief, was a happily cranky old man who challenged everyone he met to guess how old he was, and, when people politely guessed a good ten years lower than they believed he was, would crow, *Eighty-four! Can you believe it? Ha!* They could believe it. "All this has put Pike's Crossing on the map. Don't tell nobody I said so, but in some ways, this kidnapping is the best thing that ever happened to Pike's Crossing. And you can't tell me all business owners who are raking it in don't feel just the same."

RHONDA'S HEAD WAS full of rabbits. She drew them on scraps of paper when she talked on the phone or puzzled over what little evidence they had. She scribbled out chains of rabbits, paws linked one through the other, and as she drew, she studied them for clues, thinking they might know the thing that all bunnies knew: the way to Rabbit Island. She stared down at her doodles like she half-expected the rabbits to dance off the page, doing the bunny hop all the way to Ernie Florucci. And maybe, if she was lucky enough, to Lizzy and Daniel too.

Among the rabbits, she scribbled notes on the few clues they had: Rabbit Island, Laura Lee's car, the name Birdie. None of it made any sense. But the doodling calmed her.

False leads continued to pile up: a gold bug had been spotted at a motel in Lyndonville, someone's bachelor uncle kept a rabbit suit in his closet, Ernie was seen buying a soda from a machine at a rest area in Massachusetts. Each time a new lead came in, a buzz of excitement swept through the Mini Mart, a jolt of hope.

The police followed every one, but they were all dead ends. When word filtered back down to the Mini Mart, a hush fell over everyone. Defeated glances were exchanged. There was nothing to do but wait for the phone to ring, for the next tip to come in that would start the cycle over again.

SHIRLEY BOWES HAD a friend, Marsha, a psychic. Marsha, a woman about Trudy's age, who'd recently moved from New York City, was called in, and held the stuffed bear. She closed her eyes and said, "I'm getting a picture." This woman had artfully sculpted hair, beautiful clothes, expensive perfume.

"Oh, she's alive," Marsha said. To Rhonda, her Bronx accent sounded almost fake. "She's in the woods. I see tall trees. Rocks. A cave. He's got her in a cave. That's where she sleeps at night."

Shirley tried dowsing again, and this time her pendulum circled over the state forest not far from where Ernie was taken. The area, Rhonda knew, Peter said he was hiking in that day.

Pat called Crowley, and, although he did not believe in psychics or dowsers, he agreed to help organize a search party of cops, civilians, and park rangers to go through the forest the next day. A dozen TV news crews followed the search party, and all the local papers sent reporters. Pat called everyone she knew in town—which amounted to essentially everyone in Pike's Crossing—to help comb the forest.

The rangers and guides insisted there were no caves in the park. But then Marsha the psychic said, "It might not be an actual cave, technically. Maybe a group of rocks that could give shelter—something a little girl might call a cave."

Shirley Bowes walked through briars and along hiking trails holding a wooden Y-shaped stick, letting it pull her this way and that. The stick tilted down and vibrated a little when she was supposedly on the right track. It looked to Rhonda like the stick was leading the poor old lady with the sensible shoes in circles. And right at her heels was Pat, Trudy Florucci in tow. And the cameras all around them clicked and flashed.

Trudy was looking a little the worse for wear. There were whispers that it was Trudy's own fault that Ernie was gone. What kind of mother left her six-year-old daughter alone in the car like that? Rhonda knew that Katy's mom was providing some kind of pills for Trudy. *Something for her nerves,* Katy had whispered. But it seemed that Trudy was taking more and more of them, and by the time they searched the park, she was all but staggering and drooling. At one point, Shirley was leading a small group up a rocky hill and Trudy lost her footing, twisting an ankle. She lay in the leaf litter, sobbing. Pat called for Warren to come and take her back to base camp, which consisted of a few tables set up with coffee, sandwiches, and maps next to the ranger station—and, of course, camera crews. Warren was having trouble guiding Trudy by himself, and called for Rhonda to come help.

Trudy's only protest was to narrow her eyes at Rhonda and say, "You!"

"I'm here to help," Rhonda said.

"You want to help?" Trudy gave a bitter laugh. "You wouldn't even know where to begin."

"Please, Miss Florucci, I . . ."

"*Mrs.* Florucci," Trudy corrected in a drug-slurred voice. "My husband, my husband, Sal, he lost his right arm in an accident just last year. He killed himself six months ago. He was a granite cutter, and his arm was crushed by a piece of rock.

"For weeks after the accident Sal woke up in the night swearing he could still feel his arm: *It feels tingly, like it's asleep,* he'd tell me. I'd turn on the light and he'd stare at the stump like he couldn't believe his own eyes."

Rhonda nodded, didn't know what to say. Trudy leaned into her, hobbling on one foot, Warren at her right side.

"At night, when I sleep, sometimes I dream none of this has happened, and Ernie's right there beside me. I wake up and lie still, sure I can feel Ernie tucked safely under my arm, spooned up against me. I can *smell* her, almost taste her." Trudy looked to Rhonda, her eyes full of rage once more. "And then I turn on the light."

They were nearly back to base camp now, and television cameras were pointed at them.

"Are you hurt, Trudy?" one of the reporters called.

"Have they found anything yet?" another asked.

Trudy hung her head, and Warren stepped protectively in front of her. "Give her some space, for God's sake," he snapped.

"You can dream all you want," Trudy whispered, her breath hot in Rhonda's ear. "But at some point, someone's gonna turn on the goddamn light."

THE HILLSIDES WERE searched all day and no sign of Ernie was found. Then, the next morning, a volunteer fireman discovered a pile of bones hidden in a cluster of rocks. The forensic team was called in and quickly identified the fragmented bones as animal: deer, most likely. The fireman had discovered the den of a coyote. The news cameras filmed a shaky Trudy with Pat clinging hard to her arm like she was keeping Trudy from floating away. The volunteers went home at the end of the day, everyone convinced that Ernie Florucci, wherever she may be, was not in the state forest.

RHONDA AND WARREN went back to Pat's to check if any new information had come in. The phones were being manned by a grouchy old Cecil, who had a bad hip and couldn't join the search team at the state park.

"Not a damn thing. Phone didn't ring once. The most exciting part of my day was when that little Katy brought me these god-damn brownies." He gestured spitefully at the tray of goodies. "I ate about half of them—*which* I'm not supposed to, with my sugar. Doc put me on pills, maybe I'll just take an extra tonight." He sighed, ruminating on his misfortune for a moment. "Oh, and she dropped this off for you." He handed over a manila envelope with WARREN & RHONDA scrawled on the outside in pink marker.

"Damn shame you didn't find anything in the forest. Watching it on the news at noon, I felt almost as bad for Patty as for Trudy. She's taking it real hard."

Warren nodded. "She's doing all she can."

"You know, I was on the fire department back when Rebecca was killed," Cecil said, rubbing the stubble on his chin. "I was one of the first on the scene. I'm the one who grabbed Patty and took her away. She didn't need to see her sister all messed up like a bunch of dog food."

"Rebecca?" Rhonda asked. Nothing about this story was familiar to her.

"My mom's and Pat's little sister," Warren explained. Rhonda remembered the photograph in Pat's office, the littlest girl on the end, her hair in ribbons.

"Hit by a logging truck back in '73. I'm no headshrinker, but know what I think?" Cecil asked. "I think Patty's always blamed herself. I mean, she was the only one at home that day with Rebecca. She was supposed to be keeping an eye on her. But little girls can be as slippery as snakes—weren't her fault and nobody ever said it were. Just the same, all these years later, here's a chance to save another little girl. And she jumps on it. Throws herself into it like it's her life's calling. Right?"

Warren nodded.

Two lost girls, Rhonda was thinking.

Cecil got up to leave. "She was holding one of Rebecca's little shoes when I found her. A white sneaker stained with blood. Wouldn't let it go." He pulled on an old VFD baseball cap. "Damn shame," he mumbled. They thanked Cecil and watched him go.

"I can't believe I never heard the story of Rebecca," Rhonda said.

"It was a long time ago," Warren said. "And one of those things people don't talk about, like cancer or something. I barely know the story myself and it was my own family."

Rhonda nodded, thinking of the secrets in her family.

"So, what do you think?" Warren asked. "Is it worth sticking around or should we go for beer?" He opened the envelope from Katy and shook it to let the paper fall out.

"I vote for beer. It's been a hell of a long day and it's not like the phones have been ringing off the hook."

She glanced down at the paper on the table. It was a color photocopy of Ernie's drawing of Rabbit Island. Attached to it was a sticky note: *Worried the original might get confiscated, so I made a copy. Thought you might want one too. I still say it's some kind of park with a stone garden or something. K.*

Warren turned the drawing to face him, and Rhonda was looking at it upside down, and only seeing it from this unfamiliar perspective did she recognize Rabbit Island for what it was.

"The beer's going to have to wait," Rhonda said. "Come on, we're going for a ride."

JUNE 12, 1993

PETER HAD HIS scripts printed and everyone was ready to go. He decided they would start at the beginning: with Peter Pan arriving in the nursery and taking the children away. Little Jamie O'Shea was playing Michael, and his brother Malcolm played John. The O'Sheas were quiet, red- haired boys from the end of the street, who had to be coached constantly to say their lines louder.

"What?" Peter yelled after one of them had spoken. "Speak up, John! Speak up, Michael! Or I'll feed you to the crocodile!"

But the problem was, they had no crocodile. Not yet. The lost boys, Indians, and pirates were all younger kids, summer kids whose folks owned cottages on the lake. They came back year after year, making their way to the woods to shyly ask Peter if they could try out for the play. Anyone who tried out got a part, even if it meant having to write in a new character.

The summer kids couldn't make it to every rehearsal, because their families took them swimming, boating, and fishing. None of these kids wanted the role of the crocodile. All the girls wanted Tiger Lily or Tinker Bell, but some were made pirates, others lost boys and Indians. The littlest girl of all, Natalie, played Tinker Bell in her pink bathing suit with wire wings draped in gauze.

Peter was perched in the window of the nursery, about to make his entrance, when, suddenly, Jamie O'Shea screamed.

"What is it now?" Peter demanded.

"A bee stung me!" Jamie yelled. "Ow! It got me again!"

Then Malcolm joined in: "OW!" And grabbed his butt.

Peter jumped down from the window into the nursery and looked around. "I don't see any bees."

Rhonda got up from the cot she was lying on and looked around, agreeing. There were no bees. Not so much as a mosquito or a blackfly.

"None of the stinging buggers here, matey," called Lizzy, watching from the deck of her pirate ship that was actually the hood of Clem's old car. A couple of the younger pirates sat in the backseat, sharing a bag of chocolate-covered peanuts. There were half a dozen other kids milling around, dressed as Indians and lost boys, waiting for Peter and the Darling children to fly off to Neverland so they could do the next scene. Panic sets in quickly among the bored.

Jamie slapped frantically at his neck, screaming, "Bees!" as he ran in circles around the stage.

"There must be a nest," Malcolm cried to the group of kids assembled. "Everyone run!"

And before Peter could stop them, there went his entire cast, with the exception of Rhonda and Lizzy, running wildly through the woods, screaming about killer bees.

Then came the laugh from the top of the trees. They looked up and there was Greta Clark, BB gun in hand, legs wrapped around the top of a white pine.

"Greta!" Peter shouted. "You could have put someone's eye out with that thing!"

"Buzz, buzz, buzz!" she shouted back.

Greta lived in a trailer near the lake with her kooky mother, Laura Lee Clark, who claimed to have been in just about every movie made in the seventies. There was never any confirmation of what might have happened to Greta's father, who might or might not have been Warren Beatty, according to Laura Lee.

Greta Clark was twelve and carried a homemade bow and arrows and a BB gun that she used to shoot squirrels. She wore a red felt cowboy hat meant for a kid much smaller than her, and it just perched on the very top of her head, the chin strap pulled tight to keep it in place.

Greta fought mean and dirty. She would challenge a kid to a bicycle race, and halfway through, his front wheel would come loose or his tire would go flat because of a tiny pebble jammed up inside the valve. During a fistfight (of which there had been many over the years), she would throw sand in her opponent's face, or, if he was a boy, grab his privates and squeeze as hard as she could until he lay moaning and puking in the dirt, kicking like a bug stuck on its back.

There was also a rumor at school that she was a lesbo.

"Your play sucks shit!" Greta called down.

"I think we should kick her ass," said Lizzy. She was perched on the roof of the car, waving her coat hanger hook through the air, wooden sword drawn. She had on black satin pants tucked into an old pair of her father's motorcycle boots. They were way too big for her feet, so she wore them with lots of pairs of socks. She had a ruffled white shirt with a wide lapel and an old red velvet jacket that she'd sewn some gold trim to. On her head was the big splurge, an actual black pirate hat from the costume shop up in Burlington.

Peter shook his head. "We've gotta get to Clem's birthday

party anyway. We'll round up everyone tomorrow and have a real rehearsal." He jumped off the stage and started to walk down the path to Rhonda's house.

"You're not gonna do anything?" Lizzy asked when the girls caught up with him.

"What, you mean to Greta?" Peter asked.

"Well, yeah! She just ruined our first rehearsal," Lizzy said.

"What am I supposed to do, climb the tree and drag her down?"

"Something like that," Lizzy said. "I'll let her have it with my hook!" She waved her coat hanger hook through the air menacingly.

"Nah," said Peter. "The best thing we can do is ignore her. She just wants attention."

Lizzy leaned into Rhonda and said, "Maybe she's harassing us 'cause she's got a crush on you!"

"No," Rhonda said. "It's *you* she wants. She must have heard you singing 'Achy Breaky Heart' and fell head over heels!"

They both cackled.

"But you know I was singing for you, Wendy," Lizzy said.

"Oh Captain Hook," Rhonda swooned, "you're so romantic." She grabbed Lizzy's hand and coat hanger hook, dancing a few steps until the hook came off in her hands, which prompted Lizzy to sing a few lines of the old Patsy Cline song "I Fall to Pieces" in her booming pirate voice. She finished with a high kick, and one of her huge motorcycle boots went flying off, crashing through a stand of striped maple. Both girls convulsed with laughter again.

"Would you guys grow up?" said Peter, glancing back over his shoulder at the figure high up in the tree.

THE GRILL WAS crammed with burgers and hot dogs, and the picnic table was laid out with potato and pasta salads and a sheet cake that said HAPPY BIRTHDAY CLEM in Justine's careful script. There were two bowls of punch, one of them for the kids, and the other one was having another cup of dark rum added by Aggie, who insisted it was still too weak.

Some of the men who worked at the mill were there with their wives, talking about pulp wood prices and the Red Sox and whatever else it was men talked about. Rhonda was only half-listening. She was watching Peter sneak three cups of rum punch.

"I don't want any," Lizzy said when he handed her a paper cup.

"Oh, come on! What kind of a pirate are you?"

She accepted the cup, as did Rhonda. The girls took tentative sips. Peter took a long gulp. "Ahhh!" he said. "Shiver me timbers, that's good. It'll put hair on your chest, me mateys!" He left the girls and went sidling up to where Daniel stood talking with a group of men from the mill. Daniel put a hand on Peter's head and Peter laughed at some dumb joke about the president, which Rhonda only half-heard.

"Do you think Wendy's in love with Peter Pan?" Lizzy asked.

"What?"

"I mean it's pretty obvious, isn't it? She loves him, but he doesn't love her back."

Rhonda took a big sip of punch. "I think he loves her back. He just doesn't know it."

Lizzy shook her head. "Stupid! It's not like they're going to end up together. To get married and everything. It's impossible."

Rhonda took a long sip of punch, reached into the pocket of her white Wendy nightgown, and touched the photograph of her father and Aggie that she carried to rehearsal every day. She wanted to show Peter and ask him what it meant. Ask him if it was possible that her father and his mother were once married. But she could never bring herself to do it.

As she let the rum seep into her, she knew what she had to do. It wasn't Peter who'd have the answers. It was her father. She'd simply show him the photo and ask for an explanation. And today, she decided, was as good a day as any. She finished her punch in two big glugs, left Lizzy, and ran off into the house. She'd seen Clem head inside just minutes before. She went straight to her room and pulled the *Hunley* drawing from its hiding place in the suitcase under her bed. Her mother had taken her to the art store in St. Johnsbury and paid to have it professionally matted and framed. Rhonda had wrapped it in blue paper with silver stars. She tucked the drawing under her arm and went searching for her father. He was not in the kitchen or the living room. She turned left and went down the hall to his study. The door was open a crack and she pushed it the rest of the way, holding out the present in front of her while she yelled, "Happy birthday!"

And there was her father, kissing Aggie, their arms moving over each other like they were one giant pulsating octopus.

SHE DIDN'T KNOW where she was going. She was running through the woods in her white Wendy nightgown and bare feet. She'd dropped the drawing on the study floor and heard the glass crack like a gunshot before she turned and ran out. She raced through the party, past Peter and Lizzy and her mother, who was putting out more clam dip. She felt like she was underwater. Sounds didn't reach her the way they should. The landscape was blurry and strange. Even her feet weren't listening to what her head told them to do. She stumbled, ran into the trees. But on she went until the path led her to Martin Cemetery; then she slowed to a walk. Her feet were cut from sharp rocks. Her lungs wheezed. She walked beside the cast-iron fence and found the opening. She hadn't been yet this year. She made her way to the back of the cemetery, to her favorite stone: a simple square marker that said only: HATTIE, DIED DECEMBER 12, 1896, AGED 7. Rhonda collapsed in front of the marker, over the place where she believed Hattie to be, and let herself cry. She was facedown, letting her tears soak into the grass.

Her father was still in love with Aggie. He was secretly married to her. Maybe, just maybe, her mother and father weren't really married at all. There were no wedding photos. No proof. And if her parents weren't really married, what were they? And where did that leave her?

Suddenly, she felt a hand on her shoulder. Had her father followed her to explain, to make up some lie that was supposed to make her feel better when she'd just seen the truth with her own eyes?

"Go away," she said, not looking up.

"What happened?" The voice was not her father's. It was Peter's.

Rhonda kept her face against the ground, wondering what to tell him.

"You tore out of there like someone was trying to kill you," he said.

Rhonda sat up, still not daring to look at Peter. If she looked, he might be able to see it in her face; he'd somehow know what she'd seen.

"Ronnie, talk to me," he said.

But what could she say? *I just saw your mom making out with my dad?* The very thought of it made her feel guilty, like it was her fault somehow.

Rhonda cleared her throat. "I wonder how she died."

"What? Who?"

"Hattie," Rhonda said, running her fingers over the name on the marker. "She was seven years old."

"I don't know," Peter said. "It could have been anything, I guess. Back then, you died if you, like, stubbed your *toe*."

"It's just really sad," Rhonda said, and she began to cry again. Peter turned her to face him and held her, stroking her hair.

"Shhh. It's okay. You know what I think?" he asked. "I think I shouldn't have given you that rum punch. It made things all topsy-turvy."

"I guess," Rhonda said.

"Come here," he said, lifting her chin. And then he kissed her. A gentle, dry kiss on the forehead. Then another, just as gentle, on her lips.

"You know you're my girl, right?" he asked quietly. She nodded. She hadn't known that she knew—but she knew. She felt very still inside. She reached up and touched the crown of leaves he was still wearing. And then, over his shoulder, she saw it: Lizzy crouched behind a tombstone, watching them. Feeling suddenly guilty and caught, Rhonda pulled away from Peter and said they'd better get back to the party.

THE WROUGHT-IRON FENCE that surrounded Martin Cemetery was rusted and leaning. The front gate hung open and was guarded on either side by two gnarled hydrangea bushes still covered with the crispy brown bunches of last year's flowers. Out-of-control lilacs lined the front of the cemetery. Rhonda drove her car up into the little pull-off in front of the gate and looked at the drawing in Warren's hand. *Rabbit Island.*

"This is it! I'm sure of it. Look at the neat rows of stones. The way the black fence goes all the way around. And it's the perfect place to bring a kid. It's isolated, but not far from the school. No one ever comes by here. And even if they did, you can't see through the bushes." Rhonda bounded out of the car and through the gate, Warren behind her, clutching the drawing like a treasure map.

The air was thick with the sweet, heady scent of lilacs. Crickets sang. The grass needed to be cut and was full of red clover. Bees flew drunkenly from flower to flower, filling the cemetery with the sound of their low, droning buzz.

"Damn," he said. "You're right. Look at these hills in the background. And that row of pines there. This is definitely the place! So what now?"

"We look around, I guess."

"For what?"

"A clue. Evidence. I don't know, something to go to Crowley with."

Warren headed off across the cemetery, Ernie's drawing in hand. Rhonda stood for a minute, scanning the landscape, squinting, trying to imagine she was a little girl who'd just landed her sub on Rabbit Island.

The stones were old, the most recent of them was from the 1930s. Carved on the headstones were weeping willows, angels, skeletal-looking faces with wings. Some of the stones had eroded to the point of being illegible. Some leaned to one side, or lay flat on their backs—tipped over by time, or maybe kicked over by bored teenagers drunk on warm beer. Rhonda hadn't visited Martin Cemetery since she was a kid. Now, as she had back then, she began by searching for her favorite stone, the one tucked in at the northwest corner, the small marker that said HATTIE, DIED DECEMBER 12, 1896, AGED 7. She made her way across the cemetery and had the tiny monument in sight when something caught her eye: a little glimmer in the too-tall grass. Cigarette foil? Aluminum can?

No. She reached it and looked down, unable to quite believe what she was seeing. It was a key ring with a bottle opener and a white rabbit's foot, which was missing fur in places—worn down, Rhonda imagined, by Peter trying to increase his luck.

She scooped the keys up, stuck them in her bag, heart thudding.

"Hey, there's a path back there," Warren called. He was jogging toward her, weaving in and out of the old gravestones. She closed up her bag, pulled it against her side protectively. She knew she wouldn't tell Warren. If she did, he'd insist they go to Crowley. And wasn't that the right thing to do? Wasn't this evidence? How far was she willing to go to protect Peter?

She remembered the long-ago kiss in the cemetery, in that same exact spot.

You know you're my girl.

"Yeah," she told Warren. "I used to follow that path to get here."

"Where does it go?" He was right in front of her now, his forehead beaded with sweat, his eyes lit up, like an excited little boy.

"Through the woods a ways. It goes by Peter's mom's house, our old stage, my parents. If you turn off, it takes you down to the lake. That's how we used to get down to our swimming spot at Loon's Cove."

"People must still use it," Warren said. "It's been kept clear."

"Kids, probably." She was kneeling in front of the little marker now, still clutching the bag to her side. *Or rabbits.*

"That's sad," Warren said, pointing down. "Seven years old. What do you suppose happened to her?"

"Could have been anything," Rhonda heard herself say. "People died of any little thing in those days—children especially."

"Cemeteries are so intriguing," he said. "Each stone its own little mystery, right?"

"I used to come here all the time when I was a kid," Rhonda confessed. "I'd sit right here, over Hattie, and try to make sense of the world." *But that was in another time, when I was Wendy and Peter was a boy dressed in a suit of leaves, who promised never to grow old, not a suspect in the kidnapping of a child.*

"I can picture it now," Warren said. "The young philosopher." There was that grin. He stepped forward and Rhonda didn't retreat. Instead, she reached out her hand and he took it.

"I wish I could have met you as a little girl," Warren said, giving her hand a barely perceptible squeeze.

Rhonda laughed. It may well have been the nicest thing any guy had ever said to her.

"No. I was such a weird kid. And I had this god-awful retainer that made me sound like a drunk gopher."

Warren laughed. "Just my kind of girl," he told her.

They walked out of the cemetery hand in hand. And for those few brief and wonderfully luscious moments, she forgot all about Peter. All about the key ring in her purse that spoke of terrible possibilities. There was only the comfort of Warren beside her, and for the first time in months, years maybe even, Rhonda felt light and floaty, like if she took a step forward, she might just leave the ground.

THAT NIGHT, RHONDA dreamed of submarines. She was in a small spherical submarine, operated by hand cranks. She was propelling herself through the water, toward another submarine she saw in the distance. When she got close enough, she could make out Ernestine Florucci and the rabbit in the other long, narrow sub—the *Hunley*. She worked the cranks madly. At last, she pulled up alongside. A third face peered out at her through a porthole—it was Lizzy, her long-lost twin. Lizzy at eleven, the year she lost her voice. She was dressed in her Captain Hook costume, and through the porthole, Rhonda could see the coat hanger sticking out of the end of her sleeve.

Rhonda chased them through the sea, but couldn't keep up. Her arms turned to rubber. The candle in her tiny submarine flickered, showing her oxygen was running out. But she couldn't remember what she needed to do to surface. She yanked levers, struck buttons, but just kept sinking. The candle went out and through the portholes was nothing but black.

"WHAT DO YOU think it means?" Rhonda whispered into the phone. It was seven in the morning, and she had rolled over in bed and called Warren on his cell phone.

"I don't know. But I think you should listen to your dream. Study it. Write it down. Draw it. You're an artist. Make a picture showing what happened."

"And this is going to help how exactly?"

"Maybe it'll take you deeper," Warren said.

"Deeper where?"

"Down the rabbit hole," he said.

JUNE 16, 1993

THEY WERE ON the wooden stage. Peter was leading Rhonda and the O'Shea boys out the window of the bedroom, yelling at the boys to *Speak up, damn it!* and sprinkling fairy dust on them, which was actually gold glitter. The kids from the lake were not around (much to Peter's frustration), so they went over the nursery scenes again and again while they waited for the lost boys, pirates, and Indians to wander in, no doubt to be reprimanded for choosing boating with their families over *Peter Pan*.

Lizzy was on a nearby stump, holding a mirror while she practiced her pirate scowl and drew on a thin, curling mustache with one of Aggie's eyebrow pencils.

Before rehearsal, Rhonda had found Lizzy in her room, hanging upside down from the bar in her pirate costume. Her hat was lying on the ground beneath her. Lizzy had barely spoken to her since the day she spied on Rhonda and Peter in the cemetery.

"Away with you, lass, or I'll take an eye out with me hook!" Lizzy threatened.

"Are you mad at me or something?" Rhonda asked.

"And why would I be mad at you, Miss Wendy Darling?"

"I don't know. About me and Peter?"

Lizzy reached up with the hand that didn't have the hook, grabbed hold of the bar, and unhooked her legs, dropping to the floor. Her huge boots made a loud thump when she hit the ground.

"Ah, Pan," Lizzy said through gritted teeth. "One day, he'll get his. I'll smite him. You mark my words, my wee lass!" She reached down and got her hat off the floor, carefully placing it on her head, then stopping to eye herself in the mirror on her closet door. She gave herself her best pirate sneer.

"Do you like it?" she said to Ronnie, in her own voice now. "I've been practicing."

Rhonda nodded. "It's good. Very piratey."

"It's still missing something," Lizzy said. "I think what I need is a mustache."

Rhonda followed Lizzy down the hall to her parents' bedroom, where she rummaged through Aggie's makeup on the dressing table until she found an eyebrow pencil. She also took a gold hoop earring.

"Wanna see something?" Lizzy asked, once she'd put the earring in her left ear. She reached into the pocket of her pants and pulled out a little drawstring bag. She opened it up and pulled out a stack of coins. Silver dollars. About ten of them.

"Where'd you get those?" Rhonda asked.

"They're my pirate treasure," Lizzy explained. "Look how shiny they are. I polished them with toothpaste. It's just as good as silver polish." She spat on a coin, shined it up on the sleeve of her jacket, then returned it and the others to the pouch. Then she was off, wooden sword drawn as she raced out of the house and

into the woods, shouting lines to the trees in her pirate voice—
"Make them walk the plank! Aye, matey!" Rhonda followed si-
lently behind.

PETER, RHONDA, AND the O'Sheas were just about to jump off
the stage and start flying when the arrow hit.

It was a huge wooden dowel, three feet long, and at the tip
was a ball of flames made from gauze soaked in lighter fluid. It
hurtled through the air from above, missed Malcolm O'Shea's
head by a few inches, and landed on one of the fold-up cots they
were using for the children's beds. Both the O'Sheas hit the floor,
screaming. Rhonda, who had been perched in the window frame,
ready to jump, froze, desperately trying to comprehend what had
happened.

"Holy Christ!" Peter yelled. He rushed to the flaming cot
and began flailing at it with his wooden sword. The sword itself
caught fire. He waved it through the air, which only fanned the
flames. At last, he threw it to the ground and stamped on it, the
O'Sheas up and screaming, "Do something! *Do* something!"

The sword was extinguished, but the flames were spread-
ing cheerfully along the cot. Peter yelled, "Get water!" and the
O'Shea boys took off like lightning. Lizzy, who had dropped
the mirror, the eyebrow pencil, and even her hook, in the dirt in
all the excitement, led the red-headed boys through the woods,
shouting, "Water, mateys! The ship's burning!" The O'Sheas
seemed relieved to be sent a safe distance away should any more
flaming arrows come from the sky.

Rhonda jumped out of the window at last, grabbed a wool
blanket from the other cot, and threw it on top of the fire. The
smoke was black and thick, and Rhonda and Peter choked on it,
but the flames stopped. Billows of dark smoke filled the stage. It
smelled of smoldering wool, like a singed animal.

Peter walked to the edge of the stage, waved his blackened sword at the tree tops in the most threatening gesture he could manage.

"Greta!" he bellowed, his eyes red and watering. "Show yourself!"

They heard a cackling from a nearby white pine. Rhonda squinted up through the thick cover of pine needles and saw a flash of red.

"Greta Clark, get your chickenshit ass down here!" Peter yelled.

"Come get me!" she taunted.

Peter tucked the sword into his belt, jumped down from the stage, and ran to the tree. He hoisted himself up on one of the bottom branches and began to climb.

"You could have burned down the damn stage! The whole forest could have caught fire!" he yelled up as he climbed.

"Better luck next time!" she called down. Greta began to climb too, making her way up toward the top, slowly and surely, with Peter scrambling beneath her.

"You're sick!" shouted Peter.

"And you're the worst actor I've ever seen!"

Peter paused a minute to catch his breath and plan the rest of his route up.

"And I suppose you could do so much better!" he shouted up at her. "What with your mom being a Hollywood movie star and all!" He was nearly to her first perch now, but she was all the way at the top, swaying as she clung to the thin peak.

"As a matter of fact, I can. I could act circles around you."

Lizzy and the O'Sheas came running into the clearing then, carrying buckets of water and squirt guns. They stopped at the base of the stage and looked up into the tree, to the same spot Rhonda was squinting at.

"So why don't you prove it then?" he asked. "Be in our play."

Peter was just below Greta now, and the top of the tree bent and swayed with their weight. Greta was quiet for a moment, perhaps securing her grip.

"Peter!" Lizzy screamed up. "What are you doing?"

"Yeah, she can't be in our play. She just tried to kill us," said Malcolm, running his hand through his hair, checking to see if it had been singed by the arrow.

Rhonda just held her breath, wondering what might happen next.

"Why would I want to be in your sucky play?" Greta asked.

"To prove what a great actress you are! To rub it in our faces. You could be one of the Indians. God knows you can shoot an arrow okay."

Greta frowned and looked through the branches at Peter. "I don't want to be a dumb Indian!"

"What do you want to be?" asked Peter.

"I want to be able to kill someone!"

"But no one gets killed in our play. Only Hook at the end. He gets eaten by the crocodile."

Greta thought for a moment, reaching up to adjust the small hat on her head. She wore her bow slung with the string across her chest and ran the fingers of her free hand down from her hat to the string, plucking at it like an instrument.

"Then I'll be the crocodile!" she called out.

And that was that.

They climbed down from the tree, as the O'Sheas dumped water on the still smoldering cot, and they went back to rehearsing. Peter told Greta she had to make her own costume and she agreed, seemed eager even. She practiced being the crocodile, crawling around on her belly, circling the stage.

"I was thinking that maybe you hide in here," Peter explained, showing her the trap door, and Greta Clark practiced crawling up through the trap door. She snapped her jaws at Lizzy, who sneered her best Captain Hook sneer, but Rhonda thought Lizzy couldn't help looking a little afraid.

"Another thing," explained Peter. "The crocodile swallowed a clock and so when we see you, you have to call out 'Tick tock, tick tock, tick tock.'"

Greta nodded and from then on, she practiced all day. In fact, she seemed to take her role quite seriously.

"Tick tock!" she called out when she left to go home for lunch. "Tick tock!" she hollered an hour later, as she walked back through the woods, snapping her arms like jaws, like she was warning of her approach. Like maybe, Rhonda thought, you always needed to be on guard for Greta Clark, for the tick and tock, and she was giving you a fair chance.

JUNE 15, 2006

THE STORY WENT something like this: There was once a woman named Queenie Benette, who gave her sweetheart, George Dixon, a twenty-dollar gold piece for luck. George Dixon would one day become captain of the *Hunley*. Before that, on April 6, 1862, he was shot in the leg at the Battle of Shiloh. He happened to have the gold piece in his pocket, and the bullet struck the coin, saving his leg (and possibly—so the story goes—his life). The bullet left its impression in the gold. Lieutenant Dixon carried that gold piece with him for the rest of the war, a good luck charm. If the story was true, Dixon had the coin in his pocket the day his luck ran out, and the *Hunley* went down.

Clem had always loved this story and even now, as he told it to Rhonda for what was easily the hundredth time, there was a glint in his eye. Justine sat beside Rhonda on the couch, absorbed in her crossword puzzle. Clem was pacing around the living room, gesturing with his coffee cup as he spoke. The bagels Rhonda brought over were on the kitchen table along with cream cheese, jam, and peanut butter.

"Everyone has something like that gold coin, some little piece of protection, some tiny thing with the potential to save them, whether they know about it or not," Clem said.

Rhonda sat, sipping coffee, half-listening, gazing down at the framed *Hunley* pictures she'd done for him years ago, in a whole other lifetime. What Rhonda was most interested in, what she had driven all the way to her parents for, was to reacquaint herself with the mechanics of the submarine: how the cranks worked to turn the propeller, how water was taken in, then expelled to make the craft rise and fall. She needed these details to work into her new drawing. She wanted to make sure the rabbit had all the right switches and gears.

It felt good to have something to focus on other than Ernie's kidnapping. Tock had been right: it wasn't Rhonda's job to go poking around in other people's lives like some stout, bumbling version of Nancy Drew. She was a witness, that was all—in the wrong place at the wrong time. Or maybe the right place at the right time—despite what Trudy said, without Rhonda, no one would even know about the rabbit taking Ernie.

So Rhonda decided to take Warren's advice and spend the day working on a drawing of a scene from her dream—poking into nothing but her own subconscious. She was excited at the thought of drawing again. It had been her great love throughout childhood, and as she grew older, she let it go, using her skills only when they were required, like for the biology classes. She'd been so busy with school and her work study job as a lab assistant (which was really little more than a glorified cleaning job) that she had time for little else. Drawing for the sake of drawing felt indulgent, and to give herself a whole day for it—decadent.

Gazing down, Rhonda saw that the one thing she hadn't put

in her father's *Hunley* drawing, the thing she'd carefully left out, was any emotion. The faces of the soldiers were blank—they were like mannequins or robots; more like machines than men—no sense of danger, fear, or imminent death in their expressions.

And what must it have been like the last moments aboard the *Hunley*, trapped in an iron coffin, the smell of sweat making the thin air seem heavy? Rhonda stared at the faces of the soldiers, searching them for any trace of a sense of what was to come—for just the faintest hint of fear or sorrow.

The *Hunley*, she knew from her father's daily lectures, was finally found in the waters of Charleston Harbor on May 4, 1995. Dives showed that it appeared to be intact. It took five years of planning and preparation, of discussion and debate, but on August 8, 2000, the *Hunley* was raised—pulled out on straps with a crane and carried to land. It was placed in a tank of cold water to keep it preserved. Over the months that followed, the submarine was opened and the sand and silt sifted through. Clem checked the Internet every day, sometimes several times a day—a man truly obsessed, not wanting to miss a single detail. He told Rhonda each time something new was found: a wallet, a canteen, a sewing kit, buttons, a tobacco pipe. But what Clem and Rhonda were waiting for, what they both held their breath in anticipation of, each day, was the bodies. Eventually, they would find the remains of those men. And they did.

At first, it was just three ribs. Then leg bones. Skulls. Bone by bone, scientists discovered the bodies of the crewmen. The placement of the remains suggested that the crew remained in their stations right up until the end. Turning the hand cranks, pumping away as they sank. *Right up until the end,* Rhonda thought as she studied the drawing she'd done when she was ten. Then she looked up at her father and wondered what the one thing that could save her might be.

On May 21, 2001, the remains of the captain of the *Hunley*,

Lieutenant George Dixon, were found at the front of the sub. He too had stayed in his place, held his position until the very end.

On May 25, 2001, Dixon's legendary gold coin was found inside the sub, the dent from the bullet clear. One side of the coin had been sanded down and given a scratched-on inscription in Lieutenant Dixon's cursive: *Shiloh April 6, 1862 My life preserver.*

Clem had tears in his eyes the day they found the coin. The day he learned the story was true. *My life preserver*, scratched into a piece of gold carried in Dixon's pocket the night he drowned. It made Rhonda think of how you could hold off the inevitable with dumb luck and good timing, but in the end, when your time came, it came. The submarine would sink. The rabbit would snatch you. Whatever happened, you'd go down, life preserver or not.

JUSTINE'S SWEAT SUIT today was pastel blue.

Rhonda had inherited her mother's straight brown hair, her plump face and body. When Rhonda looked at her mother, she thought to herself, *This is how I will look in thirty years*, and the thought somehow comforted her. Justine at fifty-six, Rhonda thought, was pretty in a frumpy, housewife kind of way. She wore her shoulder-length hair cut in a pageboy. She had it colored to cover the gray. The lines on her face had grown deeper over the years, but were the same lines that had always been there: the wrinkles around her eyes that showed when she smiled and the ones around her mouth that showed when she didn't. She was ten years older than Clem but looked younger than he.

"I need a six-letter word for deceive," Justine said, not looking up from the puzzle on her lap. She put the end of the pencil in her mouth, nibbled on the eraser.

"Mislead," said Rhonda.

"That's seven letters, dear."

"Delude," said Clem, not looking up from his own puzzle.

"That's it!" cried out Justine. "That's the one. Thank you, sweetie." She began penciling busily.

"I'm going to go look for the photo albums," Rhonda announced. She'd told them she was working on a new drawing and wanted some old photos to work from.

"I think they're mostly in our bedroom closet," Justine said.

"I might have moved them," Clem told her.

"I'll go check," Rhonda offered.

Past the closed door to her old bedroom, now used only for storage and the rare overnight guest, and into Clem and Justine's room, Rhonda made her way to the large closet and pulled back the folding slatted door. The left side was her father's, the right, her mother's. Marriage is full of such cut-and-dry arrangements, Rhonda thought, then felt that small ache she sometimes got at the back of her skull—the one that told her she might be alone forever, not a fate that she chose but rather a fate that seemed to have been chosen for her. Then she thought of Warren, of holding hands in the cemetery. Dare she even hope that this might go somewhere? Did she really want it to?

She found the leaning stack of photo albums on the shelf above her father's Civil War costumes, which were hung in plastic bags from the dry cleaners.

"Found 'em!" she hollered over her shoulder, not realizing Clem was right behind her. He helped her get them down. They were mostly bound in cracked and stained fake leather with *Family Photographs* and *Memories* embossed in curly gold script.

"What is it you're looking for?" Clem asked as he helped her carry the albums down the hall and into the kitchen, where there was better light.

"Pictures of Lizzy, mostly."

Clem smiled weakly. His already ashen face lost whatever hint of color it may have had. Her father, Rhonda thought, looked terribly old.

He was still tall and trim, his hair gone to a distinguished salt-and-pepper. But his breath had a whistling rasp to it and he coughed often. Smoker's cough. The hollow hack of a man twenty years older.

Over the years, both Justine and Rhonda had begged him to give up cigarettes. He tried a few times, half-hearted attempts, really just to placate his wife and daughter. But he would end up sneaking cigarettes in the garage, at work—making up lies for reasons to duck outside for a smoke. He took the trash out twice a day, went to the store for milk when there was still half a quart left. He was fooling no one. Just going through the motions.

"Why the interest in Lizzy all of a sudden?" he asked.

"I had a dream about her. A friend suggested I do a drawing of it," she explained.

Clem nodded grimly.

Rhonda decided they should get it over with quickly, close the books back up and tuck them away in the closet, laying the past to rest again, all but forgotten, gathering dust on a shelf. She carried them out to the kitchen table, where her father settled into the chair next to her.

"Did you ever reschedule that interview at the science center?" he asked.

She shook her head.

"Have you sent out any more résumés?"

"Uh, no," she admitted. "This Ernie thing has been taking all my time."

"But you're not exactly getting paid for it," he reminded her. And she knew he was right. What little money she had in savings was quickly dwindling, and those student loan bills would start arriving soon. But she couldn't think about that now. She put it out of her head and opened the first photo album.

The first photo album starred Rhonda—Rhonda as a scrunchy-faced infant, Rhonda in Clem's arms, Rhonda in her high chair, covered with grape jelly, grinning. Toward the end of the album, around the time the photos began to feature Rhonda on her own two feet—Rhonda picking a dandelion, Rhonda with arms out-stretched to a blurry Clem—Daniel, Aggie, Peter, and Lizzy started appearing in the pictures. There were photos of them all celebrating the Fourth of July, with Peter wearing a cardboard party hat, blowing out a cake with four candles. They were all there at Rhonda's first and second birthdays, and there were two cakes, one for her, one for Lizzy. There were no pictures in the album of her parents before Rhonda came along. No photos of their quiet wedding performed by a justice of the peace. Of their honeymoon trip to Pennsylvania Dutch Country. It was like their real life started once the baby was born.

In later albums, there were pictures of Lizzy, Rhonda, and Daniel in the teacups at Disney World, the two girls looking impossibly small, wearing Mickey Mouse ears with their names stitched across the front in red cursive; all three kids meeting Davey Crockett at Wild West World—Peter, who looked to be about eleven, wearing a matching coonskin cap. The Farrs and the Shales spent nearly every holiday together, like one big extended family: here was a picture of everyone but Justine, surrounding a monstrously huge Thanksgiving turkey, and another of them sitting in a sea of festive crumpled paper and ribbons on Christmas morning. Justine was the photographer of the family, so she was in few of the photos. Clem hated pictures—hated taking them and having them taken—so there were many shots of him turning away: a blurred profile, a raised arm, a fuzzy, unidentifiable ghost of a man.

RHONDA OPENED ANOTHER album, thumbed through the plastic-covered pages, traveling forward in time, and found the pictures her mother had taken the last night they performed *Peter Pan*. There was a shot of all of them lined up in their costumes, holding hands, taking bows. There was Daniel carrying Lizzy in her Captain Hook costume high up on his shoulders. Daniel sword-fighting with Peter after the play. Daniel and Clem standing together drinking beer. Daniel dancing with Laura Lee Clark, who wore a slinky sequined gown. Rhonda searched the photos, searched Daniel's face for a sign of his leaving, of his having had enough somehow. All she noticed that was different on Daniel's face was his lack of mustache. He was clean-shaven that night, a sign, maybe, that he was ready for a change.

He chose some other life, Rhonda thought as she ran a finger over his smooth face. And then Lizzy, her secret twin, Captain Hook, stopped speaking, and eventually joined her father, leaving for school one morning never to return.

These are the choices people make, Rhonda thought, trying to convince herself such a simple explanation could account for such loss.

"God," Rhonda said, pointing to the photo of Daniel and Laura Lee, "look how dressed up she is! Like she was going to the Oscars or something." Then her eye was drawn to something else: "Check it out, Dad—he's got his hand on her ass!"

Clem nodded. "I think Daniel's hand was quite familiar with Laura Lee's derriere."

"Were they sleeping together?"

Clem nodded again. "It wasn't exactly a secret. Actually, Aggie always thought Laura Lee had something to do with what happened to Daniel."

"What do you mean?"

"Like maybe Laura Lee was pressuring him. Maybe she told him she was pregnant. Of course, Aggie had all kinds of . . . theories."

"Jesus, I had no idea," Rhonda said.

She flipped backward again and came across a photo she hadn't remembered. She and Lizzy wearing matching powder-blue windbreakers. They had their arms around each other and were standing in front of Lizzy and Peter's house. She and Lizzy must have been about nine or ten. It was fall—there was a pile of freshly raked leaves behind them. They had the same haircuts, same face shape, they were even dressed like twins. Twins in rumpled clothes. Plump, scarecrow girls with big, haunted eyes. They held on to each other tightly, like their young lives depended on it. They were smiling, but it seemed a forced smile, a *give a big smile for the camera, stop looking so sullen and say cheese* kind of smile. She wondered who took the picture—Aggie, Daniel? Through her own smile, she saw a glint of metal that must have been her retainer.

She let her fingers touch her lost friend's face.

"Can I keep this one?" Rhonda asked her father.

"Take the whole album, Ronnie. Your mother and I don't look at them much anymore. In fact, I think I even have that old video of *Peter Pan* if you want it."

Rhonda nodded. She'd forgotten there was a video. Clem shuffled back into the bedroom and returned in a few minutes, videotape in hand.

He looked relieved to see it all go; like if you took away the proof, you could imagine whatever you like—even erase Daniel and Lizzy from the landscape of their lives.

Could it be that easy?

LAURA LEE HELPED Greta with her crocodile costume, and when she showed it to everyone at last, they were all quite impressed. Even Peter was pleased, and he was not one to give compliments easily.

"You're some crocodile," he acknowledged with a wide grin.

The costume was made from a series of cardboard boxes. The largest box was the torso, and it was where Greta hid inside and crawled around. Another long, narrow box made up the head, and a series of boxes attached to each other with string going from largest to smallest made up the tail. The crocodile's feet were made from four small boxes stapled to the body. The whole thing was painted bright green, and covered (everyone figured this must have been Laura Lee's touch) with silver foil scales. The narrow box up front had round egg-carton eyes and a painted-on toothy grin that sparkled in the light (the teeth were made from glued-on tin foil also). Greta navigated through a small slit cut in the front of the body, just above the head.

"Tick tock, tick tock, tick tock!" she cried out, her voice muffled as she clambered her way around the stage, chasing Lizzy, cardboard tail dragging, foil scales and teeth gleaming.

Even out of costume, she chased Lizzy. Greta took great delight in sneaking up on poor unsuspecting Captain Hook during breaks, or popping out from behind a tree first thing in the morning.

"Tick tock!" she snarled, snapping her arms menacingly as Lizzy jumped back.

"See," Rhonda whispered when the others were out of earshot. "I told you she had a crush on you."

This got Rhonda a strong thump on the shoulder from Lizzy's hook, which got caught in her nightgown, ripping it.

"Hey!" Rhonda shouted, fingering the rip. "I'm gonna make you sew this." But Lizzy had walked away and was standing with the crocodile.

GRETA, AFTER PUTTING so much effort into the costume, was angry that she wasn't in more scenes.

"Tick *tock*," she snapped at Peter. "Shouldn't the crocodile be there during the war with the lost boys, pirates, and Indians?"

"I don't know, Tock. I guess I could stick you in here and there."

Greta smiled to show she was pleased with both the plan to put her in more scenes and the new nickname.

She sat lurking at the edge of the action in nearly every scene, making her clock sounds, watching, just like she had done from the trees, only this time she had a front row seat. She was a part of things.

RHONDA HAD BEEN studiously avoiding her father, using the play as an excuse to be away from home as much as possible. She would run in for meals, let her mother heap tuna sandwiches or pork chops on her plate, while Rhonda sat in her white night-gown and told them little details about her day, like that Peter had let that awful Greta Clark join the play. But she couldn't avoid her father forever.

"I think it's time you and I had a talk," he said to her after dinner, when her mother had cleared the table and was running water in the sink. Rhonda nodded. "Come into the office. You haven't even seen where I hung your picture."

So, reluctantly, Rhonda followed him into the office and saw her drawings, tucked behind the new sheet of glass, hanging on the wall beside her father's desk.

"They're beautiful drawings," he told her. "I look at them all the time. You got every detail just right, right down to the buttons on the uniforms."

Rhonda nodded.

"It's the best birthday present I ever got."

She nodded again.

"Ronnie, about what you saw . . ."

"It doesn't matter," Rhonda said, staring down at her sneakers.

"Of course it matters. And you deserve an explanation. I made a mistake. And you caught me. But it's not a mistake I'm going to make again. Do you understand?"

"Not really," Rhonda mumbled.

"What is it you don't understand?"

"How you can be married to two people at once," Rhonda said.

"I'm not. I'm married to your mother. And I'm going to stay married to her."

"But you *were* married to Aggie."

Clem reached into his shirt pocket and took out a cigarette. "Yes," he said. "I was once married to Aggie. A long time ago. Before I met your mother."

"Does Mom know?"

"Of course."

"Why didn't you tell me?"

"I was waiting until you were old enough to understand. And now you are."

But Rhonda *didn't* understand. She didn't understand how you could marry one person, then another. Once you got married, it was supposed to be forever. If she married Peter, she would make sure it lasted. But now, she wasn't sure she could marry Peter, because, it dawned on her, the fact that his mother and her father had once been married might make them related after all. Her head spun. She had to get out of the office.

"I'm late for rehearsal," she told her father.

"I didn't think you rehearsed after supper," her father said.

"Peter says the opening scene still isn't right, so we're going to work on it," she lied.

Now it was her father's turn to nod, and she left him there in his office, sitting in his swivel chair, staring into the eyes of the men on the submarine who were going down, whether they knew it or not.

AS RHONDA JOGGED out to the stage, she was sure she could smell a hint of cherry tobacco smoke in the air. There was a muffled rustling coming from beneath the trap door and she snuck up onto the stage, walking on tiptoes, yanking the door open quickly to surprise him. She surprised them both.

Peter was there in the hole along with Tock and was, Rhonda quickly saw, kissing the crocodile. So much for the lesbo rumors.

Tock's hat had slid to the back of her head, the string holding it tight around her neck. Her BB gun was leaning against the dirt wall and beside it was Peter's still smoldering pipe.

Peter pulled away from Tock, but she kept a hand on his shoulder as Rhonda looked down.

"We were working out some details about the play. About how the crocodile should enter," Peter said. He seemed startled, but not particularly ashamed. He made no move to shake the girl's hand from his shoulder. Tock just smiled.

Rhonda's face burned, her hands ached from being clenched into fists so tightly, ached with the need to hit someone. But Rhonda was not a fighter. And she knew she didn't stand a chance against sand-throwing, arrow-shooting Greta Clark and her BB gun. She wanted to hit Peter, but what if he kicked her out of the play? The idea that she couldn't play Wendy scared her almost as much as the idea of losing Peter to Greta. So Rhonda let her hands fall open.

"Your mother and my father were married," she said.

"I know," Peter answered, like it was no big deal at all.

Tock laughed.

Rhonda reached down and grabbed the trap door, meaning to slam it, but instead closing it softly over their upturned faces.

THAT IS ONE fucked-up picture."

It was the first thing Peter said after a long silence. His brow was wrinkled, his eyes searching, straining as he squinted at the picture taped to the wall above Rhonda's bed. It was the same way he'd studied those postcards from Lizzy years ago.

And there was Lizzy, his long-lost sister, looking back at him from Rhonda's drawing. Lizzy at eleven. Lizzy the year of *Peter Pan*. The year she lost her voice. "That's Ernestine Florucci with her," Rhonda explained. "I only had the photo from the flyers to work with."

"I knew who it was," Peter said.

He pulled a pack of cigarettes from his T-shirt pocket and lit one, still squinting at the drawing like the images were off in the distance somewhere.

Rhonda had spent the entire afternoon on the drawing, an

image from her submarine dream. As soon as she was finished, she called Peter. It felt important to her that he see it. She hadn't imagined how he might respond to seeing a picture of his sister—if she'd thought it through, she would have realized she was running the risk of having him shut down. Lizzy was another topic never mentioned, not quite as taboo as Daniel, but close.

It had gotten to the point where Rhonda rarely let herself think of Lizzy. It was like shutting a valve somewhere—the Lizzy pipeline—a trick she'd learned from Peter. But now, here was her once-upon-a-time twin. Back again, the valve broken by that damn rabbit.

When Lizzy stopped talking after Daniel left, nobody took it very seriously at first. She was upset, naturally, and if she was reacting a little dramatically, well, she'd always been dramatic, hadn't she? She'd talk when she was good and ready. Aggie herself was so distraught about Daniel, she barely seemed to notice Lizzy's new silence. Eventually, though, there were doctors' visits—a speech therapist, a psychiatrist, even a pediatric neurologist over at Dartmouth, who ruled out a physical cause and called it "elective mutism." But the diagnosis was essentially the one the laypeople of Pike's Crossing had already made: Lizzy would talk when she was good and ready.

Months went by, and then years, and she continued to choose muteness. Then one morning, two weeks after they'd started high school, Lizzy disappeared. Peter had offered her a ride to school, but she waved him on. He was the last one to see her, her book bag slung over her shoulder, as she made her way down Lake Street.

But the Lizzy in Rhonda's drawing was from a time well before that. It was the Captain Hook Lizzy she'd put in the submarine, just as it had been in her dream. The Lizzy who hung from her closet for fifteen minutes each day, trying to make herself grow.

The one whose voice was good and strong as she belted out crazy songs or threatened to make you walk the plank. The girl who wanted, more than anything, to grow up to be a Rockette.

The drawing was done in pencil first, then gone over in thin black pen lines. She used cross-hatching to shade the submarine, making it a few shades lighter than the dark sea. Rhonda had used a blotchy, swirling ink wash for the water, and filled the ocean with terrible, nightmare creatures whose features could barely be seen in the wild, writhing water. It was like one of those drawings she'd been given in school years ago—a landscape where you were supposed to find the hidden images: a wheelbarrow, a clock, a shovel, and a tea pot. Only in Rhonda's ocean, monsters lurked. A giant squid, a toothy shark, a dragon with fins. And there were ghosts in the waves, horrible phantoms, their bodies lacking true form, only open-mouthed screaming faces.

Through the portholes of the submarine, the rabbit and two girls could be seen looking out into the dark sea. The rabbit, huge and looming with paws the size of the girls' heads, stood at the front, working the controls. His eyes twinkled with mad fury as he urged the submarine on. The girls looked like they'd resigned themselves to fright, like they'd given up on being saved.

"So what's it supposed to mean?" Peter asked, brushing hair back from his face, showing his scar, the mark that bound him to her, as he turned away from the drawing to look Rhonda in the eye.

Her heart rose up into her throat, filling it, rendering her unable to speak. She wanted so badly for Peter to understand the drawing. She half-hoped he would tell her what it meant. But he looked a little irritated about the whole thing, like it wasn't worth him driving all the way into town for. She wondered what he would tell Tock about it. If he'd speak in patronizing tones—

Poor, crazy Rhonda. Rhonda and her fucked-up drawing. Rhonda who can't let shit go. Poor thing.

"It's just a drawing, Peter," Rhonda managed to blurt out, her words crisp and defensive. "Just a picture."

She wanted to remind him how he used to love her drawings. How he had once encouraged her artistic endeavors. When they were kids, he would pose for her, usually in one of his costumes. How well she knew his body then, each contour, each tiny imperfection. She filled sketchbooks with pictures of him. She could do entire pages of just his nose, trying to perfectly capture its gentle slope. Or his mouth—the thin lips, the slight gap between his two front teeth, which he could whistle through.

Afternoons when they'd go swimming at Loon's Cove, Rhonda would connect the dots of the freckles on his back and shoulders, now untouchable to her, and tell him they were like constellations, then describe each picture she saw there. Sometimes it seemed his whole life was laid out there in the pictures on his back, and it was up to her to read it, to discern the meaning of each image like some early astronomer or a gypsy reading tea leaves at the bottom of a cup.

As he lowered himself down to sit on the edge of her bed, she wondered how so much could have changed, thought how unfamiliar his body seemed to her now. His stomach hung over his jeans, his shoulders slouched forward. When did he start to slouch? He had always stood up so straight, so defiant. He crushed out his cigarette in her glass ashtray like it was an effort.

He leaned back and laid himself down on her bed, his arms clasped behind his head. His faded black T-shirt was tucked into jeans with holes at the knees. He wore basketball sneakers, black canvas high-tops, the kind he'd worn all his life. It was like he'd worn the same outfit through boyhood and it was just now wearing thin at the edges, the fabric finally giving from years of growth.

Sometimes, like right then, as he lay on her bed, she imagined he was flirting with her—teasing her, reminding her of the power he still held over her. Some days, she flirted back in her own awkward way—allowing herself to touch his arm, laugh a little too loud at something he'd said, brush the hair away from his forehead and place a finger on his scar. But it always made her feel pathetic, second best.

"I'm glad you're drawing again," he said, his voice barely above a whisper. "It's just a little weird, ya know? A strange choice of subject matter. Couldn't you do a bowl of fruit or something?"

"Do you think it really looks like Lizzy? Did I get it right?" Rhonda asked, studying the drawing taped to her wall.

"You got it right. I knew just who it was." Peter looked up at her as he spoke. There was such tenderness in his face. He looked so at ease, there on her bed. She let herself imagine, for an instant, that it was his bed too. That he was just getting into bed after a long day, into their bed where they slept night after night.

"Don't you ever wonder about her?" Rhonda asked, letting herself look down at Peter's face again. "Don't you ever hope that maybe someday she'll come back and explain everything?"

"What is there to explain?" Peter asked, shifting his weight, sounding a little exasperated.

"I don't know . . . why she left, I guess. What she's been doing with herself all these years. Maybe she's married and has kids. You could be an uncle! Don't you ever wonder what she does every day, what she sees each morning when she gets up?"

"Of course I wonder, but it's her choice that we don't know."

Her choice. Rhonda thought about the different choices they had all made—how much conscious decision had gone into any of them?

"Doesn't that seem unfair to you?" she asked him.

"Ronnie, a lot of things are unfair. What happened to Ernestine Florucci was unfair." He looked up at the ceiling, breaking eye contact with her. "Lizzy wasn't kidnapped by a rabbit though. We lost her, but not like that. That's what I don't get about the drawing."

"Loss just feels like loss," Rhonda said. "Maybe that's what the drawing is supposed to be about. How easily one loss just blurs into the next." She bit her lip, stared down at him—him, Peter, perhaps her greatest loss of all.

"Do you remember," Rhonda asked, "how much Lizzy wanted to be a Rockette? How she was always practicing that high kick and doing all this crazy stuff so that she'd grow tall enough?"

Peter nodded.

"Maybe she's a dancer?" Rhonda said.

"Ronnie, I don't think any of us grew up to live the life we dreamed we'd be living. Did we?"

Rhonda thought a moment. "Tock did," she said.

"And what was it Tock wanted?" Peter asked, shaking his head.

"You," Rhonda said. "She wanted to grow up and be with you."

Their eyes met and Peter took in a breath like he was going to say something, but instead, he held it. Rhonda looked away.

"Tock's really pissed at you, you know?" Peter said finally.

"She's overreacting, Peter, can't you see that? I didn't set out to traumatize Suzy. She's a smart kid, it's not like she hasn't noticed what's going on. Jesus, it's probably *good* for her to talk about it."

"And what were you doing at Laura Lee's?" he asked.

"Just visiting," she said.

"Right." Peter narrowed his eyes.

"Anyway," Rhonda said, desperate to change the subject, "what have you been up to? Are you working?"

"I've been fixing up my mom's place. We've decided to put it on the market."

"You are not!"

"It's not like Mom's ever going to use it again. And Tock and I have our house. Seems a shame to have a perfectly good house just sitting vacant. Besides, the taxes are killing us, and we could use some cash." Rhonda nodded. "Speaking of cash, have you done anything about a job yet?"

"God, you sound like my father!" Rhonda moaned.

"Maybe he's got a point," Peter said.

"Yeah, I know. He's right. You're both right . . ." Rhonda trailed off. "Peter, can I ask you something?"

"What?"

"Why did you decide to take the day off to go hiking? You know, the day Ernie was kidnapped?"

Peter blew out an exasperated breath. "I don't know, Ronnie. I guess I figured I needed some alone time. So I packed some trail mix, put on my hiking boots, and headed for Gunner's Ridge. What's the big deal?"

Rhonda bit her lip. "I thought you said you were at Sawyer's Pond. When Tock and Suzy went to find you, your truck wasn't at the trailhead by Gunner's Ridge."

"What I meant was," Peter said, sounding more than a little flustered, "I headed for Gunner's Ridge, then decided at the last minute to do something different. Christ, can't a guy be spontaneous?"

What, Rhonda wondered, would Peter say if she asked him about the missing keys she found in the cemetery? The keys were in the pocket of her jeans, and she stuck her hand in, stroked the rabbit's foot as Peter lay sprawled out on her bed. *Another day,* she decided.

Peter laid his head back on the pillow, let out a little sigh. Then he frowned.

"What's this?" Peter said, twisting, sliding his hand under the pillow. He withdrew a claw hammer with a worn wooden handle and nicked, black-painted head. Peter regarded it with the same look he'd used for her drawing and Lizzy's postcards—squinting, confused. He turned the hammer in his hand, as if it was an object he was unfamiliar with. As if he were not a mechanic but a man from another galaxy.

Rhonda stepped back, alarmed at first. Then she remembered, and her face flushed. As she spoke, the story sounded made-up, even to her ears.

"Oh, that!" She gave a nervous little laugh, looked away. "Uh, I had a bad dream last night . . . after the submarine dream. The, um—" she flapped her hand at the hammer, "made me feel safe. I guess it worked, just knowing it was there. I fell right back to sleep."

Peter turned the battered old hammer in his hands, felt its weight. He gave her a look she knew well. It was his worried look. His *poor, pitiful Rhonda* look. He stood up from the bed and walked out into the hallway, taking the hammer with him. She watched as he put it back where it belonged, in the kitchen drawer.

"Want my advice?" he called back to her as he came out of the kitchen and turned to leave. "Stick to drawing fruit. You'll sleep better."

Rhonda stood in the doorway to the bedroom, watching the front door to her apartment close, listening to his footsteps on the stairs. She heard the motor of his truck turn over, the engine revving a little too hard and fast as he put it in gear, the tires squealing. Peter never had been good at good-byes.

She turned around and eyed the drawing above her bed from a distance, pitying the girls trapped in the submarine. She stared hard at the ghost faces swirling, dancing around the submarine. And—was it her imagination?—the largest face, the cruelest, the one that hovered, looming large over the submarine, staring in at the girls, giving them an evil, screaming wink, looked an awful lot like Peter.

JUNE 30, 1993

I SAVED MONEY ALL through high school for this car," Clem told her. They were side by side in Clem's abandoned convertible beside the stage. The car had been turned into a pirate ship complete with a painted skull-and-crossbones flag that flapped from a pole lashed to the middle of the front seat. Clem had the wheel and was turning it gently with the remaining three fingers of his right hand. Rhonda thought that maybe bodies held memories; maybe when he put his hand on the wheel, he could feel all his fingers there, just as they'd been the summer after high school, when he cruised the open roads with the top down.

"A '61 Impala. A true classic. When I got it, it was a wreck. Daniel and I worked nights and weekends on it, restoring it. I'm telling you, Ronnie, when we were through, it was a beauty. I was so proud of this damn car."

Rhonda nodded, fiddled with the glove compartment. Usually,

she loved it when her father told her stories about his past. He got all dreamy-eyed and lost in his own memories, and sometimes he'd seem to almost forget she was there. It made her feel special; like there was a secret window into her father's past and Rhonda was the only one he'd open it up for. Her mother wasn't much of a talker. She preferred to read Rhonda stories out of books: fairy tales about handsome princes and fair maidens. Not much different from the romance novels she lost herself in each day.

This time was different, though. Clem was going to tell her something she wasn't sure she wanted to hear.

"I used to take Aggie for rides. Back when I first met her. When she worked at the mill. Daniel would come along, too, sometimes. We'd go fishing. We'd all three sit around a little campfire by the stream, frying up trout, drinking beer, smoking cigarettes, thinking, *This is as good as it gets.*" Clem gave a wistful little smile that made Rhonda's stomach ache. This was not *her* story, but the story of what might have been, and how Rhonda almost wasn't. It was the story of a time when Clem had imagined his life whole and perfect without either Rhonda or her mother in it.

"I was nineteen years old when I asked Aggie to marry me. I took her out to the middle of Nickel Lake in this old aluminum canoe I had. Water had pooled there and soaked through my pants. I pulled the ring in its velvet box from the pocket of my fishing vest. I couldn't believe it when she said yes."

When Rhonda was a very little girl, one of her favorite stories was how her parents met. Clem took a trip to Hanover, New Hampshire, in the spring of 1981 to go to a forestry conference. Justine was the desk clerk at the hotel. She was ten years older than Clem and he was immediately taken by her green eyes and the faint lines around them. He thought she looked patient, kind, and wise. When she asked if he needed help getting his bags up to his room, he winked and said only if she promised not to drop them. This made Justine laugh, and it got Rhonda laughing too, hearing the story told and re-told when she was a little girl. Justine called a bellhop to help with the bags, and Clem asked if she would join him for a drink later in the hotel lounge. By the end of the week, he'd talked her into going away with him the next weekend. She got to pick where. She picked Niagara Falls, and he proposed to her there, two weeks after they'd met. *Love is love*, he told her, down on his knee.

"HOW LONG WERE you and Aggie married?" Rhonda asked.

"Not long. Less than two years."

"When was this?"

"A long time ago. Before I met your mother."

"But what year?"

"Aggie and I were married September 9, 1978."

Rhonda frowned as she did the math.

Peter and Lizzy came crashing through the woods, up the path from their house, arguing.

"There's no way to make it work," Lizzy was saying.

"Come on," Peter said. "I'm Peter Pan. If I say I want to fly, I'll find a way."

"I guess I should get out of here and let you kids rehearse," Clem said, putting a hand on Rhonda's knee before jumping out over the stuck door.

1978, Rhonda was thinking. *And then Peter was born in July of 1979, which means . . .*

"We'll talk again later," Clem promised.

Are you Peter's father?

DANIEL'S IDEA THAT spring and summer, the latest scheme that was going to make him rich, was coffins. His own father had died over the winter (no one had been very upset about this, least of all Peter and Lizzy, who were never allowed to see their grandfather), and Daniel had been appalled when he was shown the coffins in the funeral home—the expense, the luxury. Daniel insisted that his father would have spat in his face if he'd been laid to rest in creamy, cushioned satin. So Daniel had his father buried in a simple pine box he built himself. (With sufficient bullying, the funeral director admitted that, strictly speaking, there was no legal requirement that Mr. Shale be interred in one of the elegant, affordable caskets available from Arceneaux and Sons Funeral Home.)

Daniel felt sure he was onto something, an untapped market. Vermonters in particular would surely want to save money and maintain their dear departed loved ones' dignity with a handmade, unpretentious casket. He made himself a sign, using a router and a slab of pine—SHALE COFFINS—and hung it on the shed. He put a few flyers up in town. He got two orders right away, one from a college student who wanted to use the coffin as a coffee table, another from an old widower who wanted to have things all prepared when he went. Daniel built coffins all spring and summer, stacking the finished ones in eerie rows on the cement floor of the shed. He waited for the rush of orders. He waited, and every afternoon, he diligently went out to the shed and got to work building more. This was where Peter and Rhonda found him that afternoon—bent over the table saw, tool belt strapped to his waist, radio turned up loud to a classic rock station.

"Hiya, Dad," Peter shouted.

Daniel looked up, smiled, flipped off the saw.

"What brings you to the mad scientist's lab this fine afternoon?" Daniel asked.

"We want to fly," Peter said.

"Fly?"

"For the play," Peter explained. "We want to be able to fly."

Daniel nodded. "I could make you some wings," he said.

Peter grinned. "Would it work?"

"Of course," Daniel said. He looked around the workshop. "Ronnie, hand me one of those two-by-twos piled up there. And Peter, we're gonna need that heavy-duty roll of plastic we bought to cover the windows in the winter. Go get it from the basement, would you?"

"Yes, sir," Peter said.

"Where's your sister?" Daniel asked as Peter turned to go.

Peter shrugged. "She and Tock took off on their bikes. She said figuring out a way to fly was impossible."

Daniel grinned. "Well, we'll show her, won't we? Now go on and get that plastic."

DANIEL WORKED ON the wings all afternoon, and just before dinner, they were finished. They looked a little like bat wings. Daniel had cut thin strips of wood for the frame and covered it in plastic, stapled on. They attached to Peter's body with a crude harness made from an old belt of Daniel's.

"That should do it," Daniel said, slapping Peter on the back. "I'm gonna go grab a beer." He turned and loped back toward the house, where they watched him head in through the cellar door—Daniel kept a second fridge in the basement, for the sole purpose of beer storage.

"It's not going to work," whispered Lizzy who had just pulled up on her bike and stood watching, dressed, as usual, in her Captain Hook outfit. It seemed that Lizzy never changed out of it anymore. She even slept in the shirt with the puffy sleeves, the satin pants tied at the waist with a gold rope that had once held curtains open, her wire coat-hanger hook resting carefully on the bureau beside her. She was, she explained, living the life of a true pirate, getting deeper into her character every day. She swore and spat and refused to bathe or brush her teeth, claiming that pirates were notoriously filthy. Whenever they complained about her smell, there was Tock to back her up: *She's a pirate, for Christ's sake! She's supposed to stink!*

"Besides," continued Lizzy, "Peter Pan doesn't have wings—he flies by magic."

"These are real wings!" Peter said. "I bet they'll work just like a hang glider."

Lizzy laughed. "You wish."

"Dad said they would!" Peter told her.

"Well, Dad says lots of stuff," Lizzy said. She toed the ground with her scuffed black motorcycle boots. Then she cleared her throat and spat.

"Come on," Rhonda said. "Let's get back to the stage. You can try jumping off."

"I'll never get enough wind under me for it to work right," Peter said.

Rhonda watched in horror as Peter grabbed a stepladder from the workshop, positioned it against the building, and climbed, pulling himself up onto the shingled roof of the garage.

"What are you doing?" Rhonda asked. "Come down!"

"You're going to crack your skull, matey," Lizzy said, though she didn't sound too worried. "Your brains will ooze all over the driveway!"

"God, you are sick," Rhonda told Lizzy.

Peter walked to the front edge and looked down, then backed up all the way to the other side to get a running start.

"Walk the plank, matey!" Lizzy called up to him.

"Would you shut up," Rhonda hissed at her. "Peter, don't do it!" Rhonda yelled up. It was a stupid stunt just to prove allegiance to his father, who probably wasn't his real father after all.

A sick feeling washed over her like a polluted wave, toxic waste and biohazardous needles in the current. She was in love with her own brother, which was not only disgusting but probably illegal.

"Climb back down and I'll tell you a secret," Rhonda promised.

"What secret?" Peter asked.

"A really good one. Just climb down and I'll tell it to you. Please." Would she tell? And if she did, would it ruin everything?

Lizzy came up behind Rhonda, leaned in, and hissed, "What's the big secret, Ronnie? That you love Peter? It doesn't matter, matey, 'cause Pan has fallen for the crocodile. He's slipping it to her every chance he gets."

Lizzy's breath was sour and fishy. She took her cheek in her fingertips and pulled it in and out fast, making disgusting wet, smacking sounds.

"You don't know what you're talking about," Rhonda said. She stepped forward, turned her hand into a visor to keep the sun out while she squinted up at Peter on the roof. Rhonda was beginning to feel like there were two Lizzys: a good one and a bad one. The good one was the Lizzy she'd known all her life, the one who wanted to grow up to be a Rockette and sang goofy songs. The bad one stank and used expressions like *slipping it to her*, complete with sound effects, and the whole thing was just plain gross and definitely not true.

"Oh don't I?" Lizzy asked, snickering.

"Please, Peter!" Rhonda called up.

Daniel shuffled back out of the basement then, open beer can in his hand. "Hey there, Rocket!" he called to Lizzy. "Where've you been hiding all afternoon?"

Lizzy didn't answer, but once Daniel was out in the yard, he turned to see what the girls were looking at up on the workshop roof.

"What the devil are you doing, Peter?" he called up. "Get your ass back down that ladder! Now!"

Peter hesitated. Looked down at the ground, then at his father.

Daniel set his beer can down and started for the ladder. "Don't make me come up after you! You *know* you'll be sorry!"

Rhonda cringed.

Daniel started up the ladder. Peter crept to the back corner of the roof. Rhonda held her breath.

"You get away from him!" Aggie was hurrying from the house toward the garage.

"Damn fool's gonna bust his head open," Daniel explained from his perch halfway up.

"Don't you touch him!" Aggie said.

"I'm not gonna hurt him, I'm just gonna get him down!"

"He can get himself down," Aggie said.

"I think he's got himself stuck up there like a goddamn cat," Daniel said.

Aggie grabbed a shovel from its resting place against the side of the garage.

"Get down from that ladder or I'll knock you down!"

She was wielding a shovel like a medieval weapon.

Daniel backed slowly down the ladder and stood with his hands raised in surrender, calmly coaxing her, "Put it down, Aggie."

Aggie brought the shovel up, slugger-style, and came toward him, swinging. Daniel ducked.

"What the fuck are you doing?" he screamed. She took another swing, barely missing as he jumped away.

"Mom!" Peter cried from the top of the garage. "Mom, stop!" Peter had scrambled to the edge and crouched there like a boy-gargoyle. But Aggie raised the shovel again. Daniel was backed up against the garage and was inching his way to the left, his eyes on the metal spade.

"Aggie!" Clem called. He had come running around the other side of the garage, which was weird, because it meant he must have come from Peter and Lizzy's house. "Put it down, Ag. Easy now, just put it down."

Aggie lowered the shovel but held on to it tightly.

She started to cry.

"You fucking crazy bitch," Daniel muttered. Up went the shovel again, but Clem was too fast. He reached her before she had a chance to swing, and grabbed hold of the wooden handle, prying it from her fingers.

Then they all held their positions, none of them seeming to know what to do next: Rhonda in the driveway, palms red from digging her fingernails into them; Peter crouched on the edge of the garage, wings rising up behind him; Aggie sobbing, her face buried in Clem's shirt; Clem holding the shovel high in the air, out of Aggie's reach; Daniel, back pressed against the garage, a look of utter disbelief on his face; and Lizzy, who hadn't moved since her father started climbing the ladder, just stood with her hook raised in the air like a kid at school waiting to get called on, her eyes blank and glassy, matted hair sticking out at crazy angles from under her black pirate hat. Then she began to cry in soft sniffles. She covered her mouth with the hand that didn't hold the hook. It took Rhonda a minute to understand that the crying sound coming from Captain Hook wasn't crying at all—Lizzy was laughing—and the more she tried to stop herself, the harder she cackled. All eyes were on her as she laughed so loud and hard, so hysterically, that she wet her pants there on the driveway and the realization of having done this only made her laugh harder still.

The time has come. He knew it would. She's been telling people about him. Drawing pictures of their secret places. Carrying the stuffed bunny to school and showing him off at show-and-tell.

The rabbit isn't angry. Only sad.

He picks her up in his submarine for the last time. Touches her shoulder. Thinks there are some things gestures cannot convey.

He turns away from her. Grips the wheel. He knows what has to be done. He has a plan. And she trusts him so completely, it will be easy.

And when it's over, they'll all live happily ever after, just like a real-life fairy tale.

JUNE 16, 2006

IT WAS TEN A.M. when Rhonda found herself underneath the parrot wind chimes once more, calling Laura Lee's name. Behind her, a motorboat started on the lake. A loon called—its song a haunting vibrato. There was no response from Laura Lee.

"It's Rhonda Farr!" she yelled. "You home?"

She heard only a low moan, then the sound of breaking glass.

"I'm coming in!" Rhonda shouted, pushing the unlatched screen door open.

The kitchen was even filthier than it had been during her last visit. Piles of moldy dishes sat undone in the sink. Flies buzzed. Rhonda moved through the kitchen and into the living room, where she saw Laura Lee sprawled out on the floor, bleeding from the hand. The remains of a shattered highball glass and its sticky pink contents were on the coffee table.

"You okay?" Rhonda asked, getting down on her knees.

"Just a little tipsy, lovie. Nothing to worry over. I have low blood sugar, you know," Laura Lee said. Rhonda helped her to her feet.

"Steady now," Rhonda said. "Let's get you into the bathroom and clean up that cut."

Rhonda found some peroxide, a roll of gauze, and some surgical tape in the medicine cabinet. Laura Lee sat slumped on the toilet while Rhonda administered first aid. The cut wasn't very deep and Laura Lee seemed to be feeling no pain.

"Where's your boyfriend?" Laura Lee asked.

"Warren? He's not really my boyfriend."

"What are you waiting for, Ronnie? You're not getting any goddamn younger. When a good one comes along, you hold on. Understand what I'm saying?"

"Maybe you should lie down," Rhonda suggested.

"A fine idea. First, let me refill my glass. What *did* I do with my glass?"

"Let's get you another one, okay?"

Rhonda settled Laura Lee in on the couch under the afghan, with a plastic tumbler full of sangria. "Can I ask you something?" Rhonda asked. "You don't have to answer if you don't want to."

"How intriguing. Ask away, love."

"Did you and Daniel have an affair?"

Laura Lee smiled. "Who on earth told you that? Oh never mind, it's not important. It's ancient history. And for the record, yes: we were fucking like rabbits."

Rhonda cringed.

"You're not shocked, are you?"

"No. Not at all. I was just wondering if you might know where he went?"

"Honey, if I'd known that, I would have hightailed it after him. I was *in love*. God, he was a wreck. But what a goddamn *handsome* wreck." Laura Lee sighed grandly. "I truly don't know what happened. He was in so much goddamn trouble that summer. He owed *a lot* of money to people. And he and Clem had some horrible blowup."

"About what?"

"I don't know, Ronnie. He never told me. He was a broken man. I think that at the very end, I was the only thing he felt he really had. But evidently that wasn't enough. Ain't that just the story of my goddamn life?"

RHONDA DROVE BACK to Pat's only to find she'd be working the phones alone. Pat and Warren had gone up to Burlington to hand out flyers and Pat was going to be the guest on a cable access show. Jim was in the garage and a greasy kid named Carl was running the register. Carl, Rhonda remembered, was the one who'd been working last Thursday, when someone picked Ernie up from school in Laura Lee's VW.

Pat's Mini Mart was dead. No phone calls, no one stopping in for gas. Rhonda was trying to figure out how to check the e-mail from the Find Ernie Web site on the laptop when Carl sauntered over, hitched up his voluminous jeans, and went to work opening a stick of beef jerky he'd helped himself to.

"Not much action, huh?" he said. Rhonda shook her head.

"Carl, I saw that you were working last Thursday."

"Was I?"

"Your name's on the schedule."

He studied the beef jerky in his hand. "Guess I was here, then." His eyes were red and glassy—he was wasted.

"Pat and Peter were working," she reminded him. "Laura Lee's Volkswagen was in the shop."

He nodded. "Shit, that car was always in the shop. But," he jabbed his beef jerky at her and narrowed his eyes shrewdly, "I know the exact day you're talking about, 'cause that cop Crowley asked me about it."

"He did?"

"Yeah, he wanted to know if I saw Peter take off in the VW."

"And did you?"

He contemplated the beef jerky again. "Nah. I didn't see shit. I was here by myself and we were slammed. Some Little League bus stopped off with like six hundred kids all paying for their fucking soda and candy bars separately with their little piles of change. Jee-*sus*."

"Where was Pat?"

"Search me," he shrugged.

"And Peter was in the garage?"

"Guess so. He comes and goes. I don't always see him leaving and I can't tell when he's back there." He ripped at the plastic on the beef jerky with his teeth. "It's bullshit about Peter getting canned," he said, spitting a corner of wrapper onto the floor.

"Yep," she agreed. "It sure is."

"And the cops riding his ass like they are . . . it's not right. He didn't take that girl." He took a bite of the jerky and chewed hard.

"I know," Rhonda said.

"Yeah, I know it, too," he said, mouth full. "I know it for a *fact*. I saw him that afternoon and it wasn't a little girl he had with him."

"You mean you saw him hiking?"

"Hiking? Not hardly. I saw him pulling into the Inn and Out Motel around three. He was driving his truck and he had this real hot girl with him. Dark hair, makeup. She looked like a model. It sure as shit wasn't Tock. So I went to him a few days later, offered to go to the cops, tell them what I saw. Give him an alibi, you know? And you know what he said? It wasn't him!" Carl put on a prissy, uptight voice: "*You must be mistaken.*" He shook his head. "But there wasn't no mistake. Now, if he wants to fuck around on Tock, more power to the dude, I could really give a shit, right? But in the meantime, everyone thinks he did the crime of the fucking century, and he's cool with that? Dude really wants to keep a secret."

A customer came in then, went straight to the counter for cigarettes, and Carl went back to work, beef jerky stuck in his mouth like a cigar, leaving Rhonda dumbstruck.

THE INN AND OUT Motel was up on a hill overlooking the highway and had only a dozen rooms, one of them with an efficiency kitchen. The remains of the continental breakfast were spread out on a low table against the back wall of the small lobby, not looking terribly continental: a few doughnuts drawing flies, the dregs of a pot of coffee, and a couple of black-spotted bananas. The girl behind the desk looked about sixteen—seventeen, tops. The tips of her auburn hair were dyed black and she had a pierced nose. She was staring at the computer screen, clicking away with the mouse and muttering to herself. The girl didn't look up when Rhonda cleared her throat.

"If you're looking for room, we're full up," the girl said. As an afterthought, she added, "Sorry."

"No, actually, I was hoping you could help me out with something," Rhonda said.

The girl repressed a sigh, gave a few final clicks of the mouse, and turned to Rhonda.

"What?" she asked.

"See, a friend of mine was staying here a couple weeks back. An old girlfriend. We lost touch after high school . . ."

Rhonda improvised while the girl looked on, bored and unimpressed by her story. Her eyes kept going back to the computer screen.

"We were best friends in school, you know?"

The girl nodded.

"Then she goes off, goes to college, gets married, and we lose touch. She looked me up when she was back in town on June 5. We went out for drinks, talked about old times, old boyfriends, the crazy shit we used to do, you know?"

She had the girl's attention now.

"But here's the thing: she wrote down her name and address, but we were out drinking and I lost it. I could kick myself in the ass. I don't even remember her married name. It kills me to think I've lost her all over again. Do you think you could just check and tell me what she goes by now?"

The girl nodded, hit some keys on the computer. "I'm not supposed to give out addresses, but I don't see why I can't give you her name. She was here on the fifth?"

"Yes, the fifth."

"And what's her first name?"

Shit. "Um, it's Lisa, I mean she goes by Lisa, but that's really her middle name. Her real first name is something kind of weird, I can never remember it."

"No Lisa on the fifth, but I've got a C. Hook who checked in that day. From Seattle. That's gotta be her, right? I actually remember, it was right before we got so busy—you know, from the kidnapping?—so I remember. She was here with a guy. I think this is his car in the computer: a Toyota with license number DKT 747."

Peter's truck. Rhonda nodded in what she hoped was a calm yet grateful manner.

C. Hook . . . Captain Hook?

Lizzy? Could it possibly have been Lizzy? Rhonda had that moving-underwater feeling.

"Cornelia," Rhonda heard herself say. "Her real name's Cornelia. After her grandmother."

The girl shivered. "Ughh! I'd use my middle name, too."

"So you were working that day?" Rhonda asked.

"I'm here most evenings. I'm not supposed to work mornings, but Jennifer called in with a migraine today." The girl rolled her eyes. "I remember your friend. Nice lady. Real pretty. And such a sweet little girl."

"Little girl?" the words knotted in Rhonda's throat, came out sounding more like a croak.

"Yeah, she and the guy, they had a kid with them. You didn't meet her?" The girl looked at Rhonda suspiciously.

Rhonda shook her head. "No, I . . . Lisa, she said she had a daughter, but the kid was off with her uncle when we went out for drinks. I forgot all about her, actually. I wish I'd had a chance to meet her. What did . . . um, what did the little girl look like?"

"Like her mom: dark hair and eyes. Maybe six . . . seven years old."

YOU SMELL LIKE old piss," Peter complained.

It was the night of Peter's fourteenth birthday party, and he, Rhonda, Lizzy, and Tock had ridden their bikes to the lake to watch the fireworks. They arrived at the beach as it was getting dark, and waited. They lay on their backs in the sand, looking across the water toward the center of town, listening as the band played and people laughed and applauded on the other shore.

They were the only ones at the little beach called Loon's Cove, which was really more of a boat launch, but it's where they always went swimming. There were people out on the water in canoes, kayaks, and paddleboats. Motorboats weren't allowed on the water after sundown.

"And you smell like Tock's snatch, matey," Lizzy said back in her pirate voice.

"What the hell is wrong with you?" Peter asked. He looked

like he'd been slapped. He got up and moved down the beach, or-
dering Tock to come with him. Tock stayed where she was, next
to Lizzy, who did reek of old pee and sweat. Rhonda was on the
other side of Lizzy. A mosquito landed on her arm and Rhonda
let it drink. She watched it get so fat with her blood that it could
barely take off again.

"I think you smell good," Tock said to Lizzy.

"Christ!" Peter yelled. "Are you going out with me or my
sister?"

"Asshole," Tock muttered, but she got up and went to him,
lying down next to him in the sand.

The evening had started out so well. Everyone was getting
along. Clem and Daniel had grilled steaks, Aggie and Justine
made potato salad, corn on the cob, coleslaw. Then, there was
Peter's birthday cake, Aggie's creation: a rectangle decorated in
red, white, and blue, to look like the flag. And in the center, a
ring of fourteen silver sparklers, not candles. They flashed and
sizzled, leaving their ashes scattered on the frosting. The whole
cake tasted like discharged ammunition.

Rhonda lay on the beach, thinking about the painted rocks
out in the middle of the lake. Each winter, when the lake was still
covered in clusters of ice fishing shacks—tiny villages of men
with propane heaters and flasks of whiskey, watching for a tug on
their lines—when snowmobilers raced from one side to the other,
the Pike's Crossing Volunteer Fire Department would tow a big
rock spray-painted in Day-Glo colors, with the year marked on
top, right out to the middle of the lake. Everyone paid a dollar to
guess the date the rock would fall through in the spring. There
was a different prize for the Ice Out contest each year: a month of
free coffee and doughnuts from Pat's Mini Mart, a dinner for four
at the Lakeside Diner, a fly rod from B&D Sports.

Rhonda thought of all those luridly painted boulders at the

bottom of the lake, each carrying the weight of a whole year, the numbers sprayed across them. 1982, the year she was born. Below it, 1978, the year her father married Aggie. On top of them all was this year, 1993, the year of *Peter Pan*. A pile of years sunk in the sand and muck, covered with algae, a playground for fish and snapping turtles.

THE FIREWORKS SEEMED to end only minutes after they began. Toward the end (which Rhonda thought must be the middle), she took her eyes off the sky and turned to her left to see Peter and Tock kissing, their faces flashing green, blue, and red. Then she turned to her right, to see Lizzy counting the silver dollars from her little treasure bag and humming to herself, not even looking at the fireworks, which, by the time Rhonda looked back up, were over. It was hard to make out in the dark, but it seemed like Lizzy had more coins than last time, and she'd stacked them into two piles.

"*What* are you singing?" Rhonda asked.

Lizzy raised her voice and sang so Rhonda could hear: "I'm too sexy for my shirt, too sexy for my shirt, so sexy it *hurts* . . ."

Rhonda looked at her friend in her piss-scented rumpled pirate clothes. "Right," she said. Peter and Tock were already on their bikes.

"Are you guys coming, or what?" Peter asked.

They rode home in a pack, Tock making the turn to the trailer, saying "Tick tock!" back to them when they called out their good-nights. Lizzy pulled ahead, racing down the street, her pirate shirt billowing out behind her. She kept singing about how sexy she was, in her Captain Hook voice, laughing between verses. Soon, she was so far ahead of them that all they could see was a speck of white, like the tail of a deer, then nothing.

Rhonda was supposed to spend the night at Lizzy's and now

she was dreading it. Who really wanted to spend the night with a smelly old pirate captain?

Peter and Rhonda took their time riding home from Nickel Lake. When they pulled into his driveway, Lizzy's bike was there, resting against the garage. The lights in the house were all off, which meant everyone was still in Rhonda's backyard, their parents no doubt fully plastered by then.

"I have something to show you," Peter said, heading toward the garage.

"I bet," said Rhonda and stayed put. How pitiful did he think she was? He came back and took her hand, pulling her to the old garage Daniel used as his workshop—the one Peter had nearly jumped from in the homemade wings just days ago. His grip was firm and Rhonda had no choice but to follow.

Peter dragged Rhonda into the dark workshop and led her to the row of coffins in the back.

"We're not supposed to be in here when your dad isn't," Rhonda said. "If he catches us . . ."

"See this one," Peter said, pointing to one of the coffins. "Check out the lid."

Rhonda bent down and focused on making out the carved letters in the dark. Initials: DLS. And an inscription: IT'S BETTER TO BURN OUT THAN TO FADE AWAY . . .

"Who's it for?" Rhonda asked.

"My father. He built his own coffin."

Rhonda shivered. "Creepy."

"Yeah, but you know the creepiest part?"

Rhonda was about to ask what the creepiest part was when Peter put a finger to his lips and hissed, "Shhh!"

Outside, they heard arguing. Two voices getting closer. Daniel and Clem.

Peter lifted the lid of one of the coffins.

"Get in," he ordered.

Rhonda shook her head. No way was she getting in there.

"You really want him to find us in here?" Peter whispered. "Now get in. It'll be fine. Trust me."

Trust me. How many times had he said those words to her? And how was she supposed to go on trusting him now? He'd kissed her, said she was his girl, then chosen Tock.

Rhonda remained silent and crawled into the coffin and lay down, arms at her sides, ever obedient. Peter set the lid down gently. Rhonda lay in the darkness, smelling pine, listening to Peter climb into the coffin beside her—Daniel's coffin. They were quiet for a while, lying there in the dark, playing at death.

She listened as Clem and Daniel argued outside the door then came into the workshop. The light went on and spilled through the crack around her coffin lid.

"For Christ's sakes, Daniel, it's a lot of money!" Rhonda heard her father say.

"But you'll get it all back tenfold. It's an investment. The coffins are gonna take off, I'm telling you," Daniel was explaining.

"Like the peanuts?" Clem asked.

"Fuck the peanuts!" Daniel replied. "This is bigger than that. This is the real thing."

Rhonda remembered the peanuts. The year before, Daniel decided to buy a peanut cart. At a buck a bag, he was going to get rich off tourists in Burlington, where vendors already sold chocolates, tacos, and jewelry (but, as yet, no peanuts) from carts. He ordered cases of peanuts, but the cart deal fell through. The peanuts sat in the garage for months, growing rancid, being invaded by mice, until Daniel finally loaded them into his pickup and took them to the town dump.

"I don't get it," Clem said. "You have all the tools you need. You're doing fine with what you have."

"But I'm talking *production*, Clem. I need better tools to up production, increase the profit margin."

Clem was silent for a moment, and then, flatly:

"I don't believe you."

"Well what the fuck do you believe?"

"I believe you need the money to pay Shane or Gordon or someone else you owe it to."

"Fuck you!" Daniel said. "You don't have the slightest fucking idea what you're talking about."

"I won't give you the money unless I know what it's for."

"A better table saw, a band saw, a drill press . . . I already told you. I showed you the fucking brochures!"

"How much trouble are you in, Daniel? Is it really ten thousand? More? Less?"

"You know what? Forget it. I don't need your fucking help! Just consider yourself no longer a financial partner in Shale Coffins. When the money starts rolling in you get shit, my friend."

"Daniel, look at yourself. You keep digging yourself into these holes. The gambling. The half-assed business plans. Aggie's worried. She says she's afraid one day you're gonna get in so deep there won't be any way to pull you back out."

"Aggie's worried, huh? Isn't that sweet? Isn't it great that she can come to you with this shit? You're such a fuck of a good guy, aren't you?" There was silence for a few seconds and then a sudden smacking sound—Rhonda knew Daniel was slapping the work bench with his open palm, a classic Daniel-in-a-rage move.

"*Aren't* you?" Daniel's voice was raised now, angry. "You stay away from my wife! Don't think I don't know what's going on!"

"I won't talk to you when you're like this," Clem's voice was calm, patient, low.

"Stay the fuck away from her!"

"Good night, Daniel. We'll talk in the morning."

There was the sound of metal hitting the concrete floor of the shed. Daniel had thrown something, some tool.

"Get the fuck off my property!" he shouted after Clem, his

voice flaming with rage, the echo of metal hitting concrete still in the air.

The light went out and the door to the garage slammed. Rhonda lay still, breathing pine. Peter got out of his coffin and pulled the lid off of Rhonda's.

"You okay?" he asked, giving her a hand and pulling her up.

Rhonda nodded. "You?" she asked.

Peter didn't answer. He just led her out of the workshop in silence. She never got to ask what the creepiest part of Daniel building his own coffin was.

HAD LIZZY REALLY come back? Was it possible? Why would Peter keep something like that a secret? And the dark-haired little girl at the motel . . . it couldn't be Ernie, could it?

Every question Rhonda asked led to new questions, and she felt she was spinning her wheels in sand.

Maybe, Rhonda thought, she'd been focusing on the disappearance of the wrong girl. Somehow or other, Lizzy was tied into it, and in order to understand what happened to Ernie, maybe Rhonda needed to start with Lizzy.

Safely ensconced in her apartment, Sadie on her lap and an open bottle of beer on the coffee table, Rhonda picked up the remote for the VCR and pressed PLAY.

The camera scanned the crowd before the opening act. There were Clem and Justine. Laura Lee in her silver gown. Daniel next to her, dressed in jeans and a red T-shirt, no bags packed beside him, no bus ticket sticking out of his pocket. And there was Aggie, tumbler of gin in one hand, cigarette in the other. Everyone looked young and healthy and like they'd be around forever.

Then Rhonda and the O'Shea boys were on the stage, tucked into their tiny beds, when outside the window, the audience heard a crow. There he was—Peter Pan lighting down on the window, crawling through like a cat burglar, a thief of children, a fairy king. He moved like water. He was that graceful. His body all elastic energy. Peter at fourteen. Rhonda leaned forward for a better look, wanting so badly to crawl into that scene, to be back on the stage, to remember what it was like.

"Second star to the right, and straight on till morning," she found herself mumbling. How many times had she caught herself mouthing these words as if it were some magic incantation?

The pounding on the door made her jump. She pushed PAUSE, held Sadie in her arms, and went to see who it was.

"I told you to stay away from my mother," Tock stormed into the apartment, her gray eyes nearly black. "Who the fuck do you think you are? What the hell do you get out of harassing some sick old lady? What is it you think she's going to tell you?"

"Nothing . . . I . . ."

"Do you seriously think she could have *anything* to do with what happened to Ernie?"

Rhonda took a step back.

"Do you?"

"No, but she might know something . . ."

"Know what? What might she know, Ronnie? The perfect sangria recipe?"

"Sometimes," Rhonda said, "people have clues that they don't even know are clues."

"Oh, that's very fucking profound. Here's a clue that it's time you picked up on: if you don't stay the fuck away from my mother, I'll have the cops arrest you for harassment. Everyone wants to give poor little Rhonda a pass because she's so fragile, so innocent. I'm over it, Rhonda. You need to grow the fuck up and move the fuck on and take some fucking *responsibility*."

Rhonda squinted at Tock. What she saw in the other woman's eyes wasn't simply rage: it was fear. "You think she might know something, too, don't you?"

"Jesus, Rhonda!"

"Maybe part of you wonders if Peter is involved. I mean, it's clear he wasn't hiking in the park that day, right? And if he lied to you about that . . ."

"Peter doesn't lie to me."

Rhonda thought of telling Tock about the girl in the motel, about finding Peter's keys in the cemetery. But then Tock looked past Rhonda into the living room and saw the frozen image in the TV screen: Peter bending over Rhonda in her cot.

"You are *pathetic*," Tock said. "Stay away from my family." She turned and left, slamming the door. Sadie jumped in Rhonda's arms.

"It's okay, girl," Rhonda cooed to the little white pig, her own voice shaking. "Everything's just fine."

But that was a lie. In the past eleven days, Rhonda's entire life had been turned upside down. She'd let a girl be kidnapped and come to question everything she thought she knew about Peter. Now Tock hated her, which probably meant she'd never see Peter again. She stared at the image of fourteen-year-old Peter on the screen.

Second star to the right, she thought.

But she couldn't go back. She could only move forward.

Rhonda sat back down on the couch, but didn't press PLAY. She picked up the phone instead and dialed the number for the Find Ernie hotline. Warren picked up on the first ring.

"It's Rhonda," she said. "I was hoping you could get out of there and meet me for a beer. I'm going a little crazy here."

"Sure," Warren said. "Name the place."

Rhonda laughed. There was only one bar in town. "The Silver Dollar. It's out on Route 6. Past the state forest."

"I know where it is."

"Good. Bring your cowboy hat and your singing voice—it's karaoke night. Two-dollar drafts and an order of wings on the house if you buy a pitcher."

"Hot damn! I'm there!" he said.

NOT LONG INTO their second pitcher, Rhonda told Warren about how she'd spent her entire life pining away after Peter.

It was a relief to be honest about her feelings for once. To have someone to tell the whole story to. She thought that maybe, if she talked about it, if she got it all out, she'd be purged. And ready to move forward at last.

Warren nodded, chewed his lip. "So you're in love with him?" He looked away from her and down into his beer. Beer he wasn't technically even old enough to be drinking, but like any resourceful college student, he carried a fake ID. Behind him, a string of Western lights with little plastic lassos, hats, and horses glowed against the rough wood paneled wall. They were shouting to hear each other over the noise of the other patrons and the guy on stage murdering an old Hank Williams song.

Rhonda laughed, shook her head. "I've decided it's not even really Peter I'm in love with. It's the *idea* of Peter. But I'm not even sure what that means anymore. I think he might be involved, Warren."

"Involved?"

"In taking Ernie. He was working on Laura Lee's bug in the shop when Katy said the rabbit picked Ernie up from school. And I found his keys in the cemetery."

"What? When?"

"That day you and I went. I hid them. I just couldn't tell you then. I couldn't believe Peter might have had anything to do with what happened to Ernie. It wasn't the truth I was working so hard to find, but my own twisted little version of it. Just like it's not the real Peter I've been in love with, but an eleven-year-old girl's idea of a boy who's half real boy, half Peter Pan."

"Have you shown anyone the keys? Peter? Crowley?"

"No one. You're the first person I've told. But there's more. Carl, who works at Pat's, saw Peter on the day of the kidnapping at a motel in town. I think he was with Lizzy . . . and that they may have had Ernie."

"His *sister* Lizzy? I thought you said she'd run away or been kidnapped or something when you were still kids?"

Rhonda nodded. "I think she came back."

"But why would they take Ernie?"

Rhonda blew out a frustrated breath.

"I don't know. None of it makes any sense. But there's one way to find out. I'm ready for the *real* truth, this time. I'll just tell him that if he doesn't level with me, I'm going straight to Crowley with what I have." She stood up, swaying, and reached to steady herself on the table, sending their glasses tottering.

"Whoa there, cowgirl," Warren stood up, placed a steadying arm around her. "I don't think you're in the shape to go confronting anyone. It'll wait till morning. I'll go with you. We'll get to the bottom of it, I promise. In the meantime, I'm gonna take you home."

RHONDA WAS NOT a drinker, and the beer had made her feel brave and floaty and like she could do or say anything.

"I should go," Warren said. He was hovering in her doorway.

"Why's that?" Rhonda said.

"Because you're a little drunk."

"Actually, I'm a lot drunk. But I know what I'm doing. I want you to come in." She held out her hand. He took it, and she pulled him into the hall and kissed him. She staggered backward, taking him with her, the kiss uninterrupted. She hit the wall, her head landing beside her drawing of the eviscerated rabbit. Warren pulled away.

"I need to go," he said, his voice a husky whisper, his eyes moving from her face to the dissected bunny beside her.

"Stay, Warren. I really want you to stay." She kissed him again.

"It's not that I don't want to," he said, pulling back. "You have no idea how much I want to. It's just that . . ."

"You've got a girlfriend, right?" It was Rhonda who pulled away now. "Waiting for you back in Pennsylvania?"

"No," Warren said. "That's not it. I don't have a girlfriend."

"Is it because of everything I told you about Peter? Because if that's it . . ."

"That's not it."

"Let me guess," Rhonda said, smiling, drawing him to her, her fingers hooked in the belt loops of his jeans. "You're a monk and you've taken a vow of celibacy?"

He shook his head, smiling as she pulled him down the hall toward her bedroom.

"Is it our age difference? Am I like an old lady to you?"

"Definitely not," he said.

"Remember what you told me . . . how everything happens for a reason? Maybe this is it. Maybe this is part of why I was there in that parking lot when Ernie was taken. So I would meet you."

"Rhonda, it was—" She put a finger on his lips.

"Shhh."

Warren looked slightly worried.

"What do you feel right now?" she asked him.

"Too much," he said.

"Good," she told him. "That's just perfect."

She started to unbutton his shirt. Then she switched over to her own. Only when they were naked on the bed, kissing, did she tell him the truth.

"I've never done this before," she whispered.

Warren pulled away. She guided him back on top of her.

"I want you to be the first," she said.

"Are you sure?" he asked.

She was sure.

WHILE WARREN SLEPT naked beside her, Rhonda dreamed of the rabbit. In the dream, she was a child again, chasing the giant white Easter Bunny through the seemingly endless woods behind her house. Brambles scraped at her face. She twisted her ankles on roots and loose stones. The rabbit ran ahead of her, stopped and waited until she'd nearly caught up with him, then bolted off through the trees. Soon, she was lost—unsure of the landscape around her. Then she looked up just in time to see the rabbit jump down into a hole, and eagerly, without fear, she followed.

The rabbit hole was a moist, earthy tunnel that smelled of worms and grubs, deep underground smells. *Here,* she thought, *here is where I will find what I'm looking for,* but in the dream she couldn't recall just what that might be.

Peter! Rhonda cried in her dream, there in the dark of the cave, in the heart of his burrow, where she hoped the hidden rabbit would hear her and take pity. *Peter.*

And then, he appeared. Not the rabbit, but *her* Peter, only he was young again—thirteen or fourteen maybe—and he was dressed in his costume from their play, covered in his green suit of leaves, a ring of them woven like a crown around the top of his curly head. When he appeared in the cave, it filled with light, as if he was imbued with the power to dispel darkness, to banish fear. She studied each detail of him, her beautiful Peter, running her fingers over the scar on his forehead just above his right eye. Even though he shouldn't have had the scar yet, the cut came later, in the dream she didn't question it. And there at the bottom of the rabbit hole, she threw her arms around him, thinking him a miracle. She let herself kiss him, her mouth fumbling against his in the half light, so happy to be rescued, so happy that she had realized that this was just what the rabbit was supposed to lead her to, this was where she was meant to be, now and forever. But then she pulled back and saw that he had blood on his hands and face. His cut was open again, and he was bleeding from the forehead. In his hands, he held tiny pieces of crumpled paper.

Our fears, he whispered. *Do you remember?*

JULY 4, 1993

AFTER PETER AND Rhonda left the coffin workshop, they walked across the driveway to his house. Daniel was nowhere to be seen. Aggie was doing the dishes in the kitchen, scrubbing at the cake pan, the big plastic bowls that held the salads. Peter called, "Night, Wendy," and walked off to his room. Rhonda found Lizzy in her own room, stretched out on top of the covers in her Captain Hook outfit, pretending to be asleep. Rhonda could tell she was faking, but didn't feel like talking anyway. Lizzy had laid out a nightgown for Rhonda on top of the extra bed. They'd planned all week for Rhonda to spend the night, and although Rhonda wanted more than anything to go home, she didn't want to deal with the inevitable questions from Justine—*Did you have a fight? Are you okay?* Lately Justine always asked a million questions anyway whenever Rhonda got back from a night at Lizzy's: *What did you do? How late were you up? Was Aggie there? Peter? Daniel?*

Rhonda slipped on her nightgown, lay down in the twin bed next to Lizzy's. The room glowed from a rocking horse nightlight plugged into the outlet next to the closet. Rhonda could see the pencil lines and dates Lizzy had scribbled on the frame of the closet doorway to measure her growth. She could see the last measurement was from July 1. So Lizzy hadn't given up on being a Rockette. This gave Rhonda hope. She lay there listening to Lizzy's fake snore, wondering if, once the play was over, she'd get the good Lizzy back. The door to the bedroom creaked open, then closed. Rhonda turned. No one was there. She shut her eyes and fell asleep, dreaming of a Lizzy so tall that she bumped her head on the ceilings.

She woke up later to find that Lizzy had crawled into bed next to her and had placed the hook on her pillow, next to Rhonda's head, so that it was the first thing she saw when she opened her eyes. The next thing she noticed was the foul smell coming from Lizzy: a mixture of body odor, stale urine, and breath as bad as any dog's she'd ever smelled.

"I have a secret," Lizzy whispered, her fetid breath hot on Rhonda's face. "Do you want to hear?"

Rhonda closed her eyes and turned so that she was facedown, being comfortably smothered by the pillow. She waited, playing possum, wondering if Lizzy would tell her secret anyway, but she didn't. Rhonda's cheek was pressed against Lizzy's hook, and when she awoke the next morning, she had a red mark there, like a scar.

JUNE 17, 2006

R HONDA WOKE UP and wrapped a blanket around herself. She watched Warren as he slept, tempted to wake him and tell him her dream about the rabbit hole.

Instead, she stood, put on her robe, padded gently out of the bedroom, and made a pot of coffee. Then she sat on the couch with the first cup in her hand. She found the remote and pressed PLAY. There was Peter again, struggling with his shadow, about to wake Wendy from her innocent slumber, and ferry her off to the Neverland.

"Hey," Warren said, as he leaned over the back of the couch and kissed the top of her head. "I smell coffee."

"I thought you didn't drink coffee."

Warren laughed. "I drink it on special occasions."

"Well, I'm honored, then. There's a pot in the kitchen. Cream's in the fridge. Help yourself." She watched as he sauntered into the kitchen in his boxers, seeming perfectly at ease.

I could get used to this, she thought, but then stopped herself. Who knew where this was going?

"What are you watching?"

"A video one of the parents shot of our last *Peter Pan* performance. Tinker Bell's father, I think."

"No way!" Warren said, settling in on the couch. "Rewind, I want to watch from the beginning."

He snuggled up to her and she pointed out the key players, the best scenes, the details of each costume.

They studied the few minutes of footage that followed the play: the parade of cast and audience through the woods, up the narrow path to Rhonda's yard, then shots of the party in the backyard lit with luau lights and tiki torches. The camera panned the yard— the feast laid out on the picnic table; the players and audience mingling, drinking, laughing. There was Rhonda in her white nightgown talking with Aggie—Rhonda looked both embarrassed and terrified by whatever Aggie was saying. And then the camera caught Peter and Lizzy having a quiet argument. Peter's hand was wrapped around her arm and he was leaning in, whispering something in her ear. Lizzy shook her head, the only audible words Rhonda caught were Lizzy saying, "I can't." She watched as Peter tightened his grip on his sister's arm, giving it a slight twist. "You will," he told her. Then the camera zoomed in on Tinker Bell eating cake, frosting covering her tiny nose and chin.

WHEN THE VIDEO was over, Rhonda told Warren about her dream. "I feel like, one way or another, I've been chasing that rabbit for years," she said.

Warren nodded. "Maybe you'll catch up to him one of these days. What were the slips of paper in your dream?"

Rhonda reached up and touched the scar on her forehead. "It's silly, really. We had this . . . this pretend funeral in the woods that summer. We buried this stuffed bogeyman. And Peter had us write down our fears on little scraps of paper, then dump them in on top of him. It was like we were having a funeral for fear."

"Do you remember what you wrote on your paper?" Warren asked.

"No."

"You've given Peter an awful lot of power, both in your life and in your dreams."

Rhonda nodded. "I convinced myself he was innocent. I believed it so much that I refused to look at the evidence. But now I see that we can't just go around creating whatever truth happens to suit us."

Warren nodded grimly and fell silent.

"Say something," Rhonda begged.

"I think . . ." He hesitated. "Rhonda?"

"What?" she asked, taking his hand.

He bit his lip. "I think you're right. We can't just invent truths that don't exist. We have to face the reality of the situation, no matter how grim."

Rhonda nodded. "That's why I'm going to Peter with what I know."

Warren shook his head. "No. I think you should wait."

"Wait for what, Warren? I've spent my life waiting for shit that doesn't happen. What if Peter knows something? What if he's got Ernie locked up somewhere?"

"Then you should start with Crowley. Tell him what you know."

"No. I need to talk to Peter first. I mean, what if I'm wrong?"

"And what if you're not? He could be dangerous, Rhonda. At least let me come with you."

"No," said Rhonda. "I need to do this alone. The one thing I know for sure is that there are things he's not telling me. If we both go, he'll feel cornered and shut down. I might have a chance of actually finding out something if I go alone. Can I meet you later?"

"Of course. I'm going to go back to Jim and Pat's and get cleaned up, then I'll be at the Mini Mart. Why don't you head over when you're through with Peter?"

"It's a date," Rhonda said.

"We can have microwave burritos and Twinkies for dinner. My treat," Warren said.

"Ooh, so romantic."

"You ain't seen nothing yet," he promised, taking her in his arms and kissing the top of her head.

In spite of everything, she was happy. But still, a little voice in the back of her head warned her not to get used to it, that the rabbit wasn't finished with her yet.

JULY 21, 1993

"GO AHEAD, LOOK," Peter instructed, pointing to the dark space under Lizzy's bed.

Lizzy and Rhonda had turned eleven the week before, and the remains of Lizzy's balloons were tied to her bedpost, hovering sadly, half-deflated. The Rockette video, leg warmers, and the dancing doll she got were all sitting on her dresser, still in their packages. Rhonda had bought Lizzy a goldfish in a bowl with blue marbles and a little sunken pirate ship at the bottom. The fish died the third day, but the bowl still sat on the dresser, growing stagnant and giving off a foul odor.

Lizzy shifted from foot to foot, played nervously with her coat hanger hook.

"C'mon, you can do it," Tock said. "Captain Hook's not afraid of anything."

"Who said I was scared?" Lizzy asked.

But that was the trouble. Lizzy *was* scared. And that's why they were all there: to cure her.

For weeks she'd been afraid, and it was getting worse. She wasn't sleeping at night, and the dark circles under her eyes made her look like a much more sinister Captain Hook. When she did go to bed, she left the lights in her room blazing. She claimed the bogeyman was out to get her. She stuffed coats and clothing under her bed so he couldn't hide there. Then she started to be afraid in the daytime, too. It was like the bogeyman could be anywhere: in the old garage, the trunk of a car, the hole under the stage.

"Get down there and look!" Peter ordered.

"Maybe this isn't such a great idea," Rhonda suggested.

"Go on, Lizzy, you'll be fine," promised Tock.

"You don't have to if you don't want to," Rhonda said, placing her hand on Lizzy's shoulder. But Lizzy shook it off and very gingerly got down on her hands and knees. When she peered under the bed, she let out a scream that made the hairs all over Rhonda's body stand up, giving her skin a prickly feel.

"Pull him out," Peter said.

"No!" Lizzy wailed.

"Help her," Peter ordered the other two girls.

Rhonda and Tock got down on their hands and knees to help Lizzy drag the body from under the bed.

Rhonda nearly let out a scream herself when she saw the large black eyes looking back at her. She was afraid, at first, to reach out her hand to grab it. Lizzy was crying quietly beside her.

Peter had made a stuffed man out of his father's old clothes filled with rags. His head was a nylon stocking filled with stuffing from an old pillow. Peter had glued huge felt eyes on the front of his face, like an owl. The bogeyman's face was all eyes, big black felt ovals, no nose or mouth.

"He's scary as hell," Tock admitted once they'd got him out into the light.

Peter handed Lizzy a kitchen knife, and she looked at the knife, then at the bogeyman, then at Peter.

Peter said, "Kill him, Lizzy. Kill the bogeyman."

At first, she hesitated, then she fell on him. She stabbed and stabbed, plunging the knife in, stuffing coming out of his head. The knife went through his body into the floor.

She stabbed until she was exhausted and out of tears. She collapsed on the floor. Tock went to her and stroked her knotted, greasy hair.

"You did it, Captain," Tock whispered.

"The job's not done yet," Peter explained. "Now we have to bury him."

They dragged the body out to the woods—they had to keep stopping to collect bits of him—and had a long funeral. Peter dug a deep hole next to the stage and they dumped the body in.

"Get rocks," Peter said. And they all collected stones, large and small, and threw them into the hole, on top of the bogeyman. "This is so he can't rise again," Peter explained.

They were all sweaty and smeared with dirt. Rhonda's hands hurt from hauling rocks. Lizzy had taken off her hat, hook, and boots and looked a little more like her old self and less like a pirate.

Peter gave each of them a piece of paper and pencil.

"Write down the things you're most afraid of," he instructed. Rhonda's mind went blank. Then she scribbled: *That Peter's my brother. That he'll stay with Tock. That Dad loves Aggie more than Mom. That Lizzy's going truly crazy.*

She looked over, trying to see what Lizzy had written on her paper, but Lizzy covered it up with her hand. And what, Rhonda wondered, had Peter written? And Tock? Surely, she wasn't afraid of anything.

They each folded up their papers and dropped them into the hole, on top of the bogeyman.

"Good-bye, fears," Peter said.

They all helped fill in the grave, then did a wild dance, waving their arms, doing Rockette kicks, laughing and howling, sure that Lizzy was cured, that they all were. There was nothing to be afraid of anymore.

IT WAS NEARLY three by the time Warren left. Rhonda took a shower, did the dishes, then lay down on the couch to rest. She fell asleep and had another fuzzy dream about chasing the rabbit and falling down the hole. This time, at the end of the dream, it was Lizzy she found down in the hole. Lizzy in her Captain Hook costume, only instead of the hook for a hand, she had a bloody hammer sticking out of her sleeve.

Rhonda snapped open her eyes and looked at the clock: it was almost seven.

"Shit!" she said, scrambling for the phone and punching in Peter's number.

"Ronnie, I was just on my way out the door."

"We need to talk, Peter."

"Well, maybe we can meet tomorrow. I'm free in the afternoon."

"No. This won't wait."

Peter let out an exasperated breath.

"I've got a realtor coming to look at my mom's place in the morning and I've got a shitload of work to do. I'm on my way over there now. Whatever you have to tell me is going to have to wait until tomorrow. I'll call you then."

"I could meet you there," Rhonda said.

"No. I'll call you tomorrow." Even as he spoke these words, he was moving the phone away from his mouth to hang up, his voice fading out like a far-off AM radio station broadcasting from a place Rhonda may have heard of, but had never been.

RHONDA PULLED INTO the driveway of Aggie's house, parking behind Peter's Toyota pickup, which was in front of the one-car detached garage Daniel had used as a workshop. She noticed the door to the garage was padlocked closed, the windows boarded over. She glanced up at the roof, shingles loose and moss-covered now, and remembered the day Peter had nearly jumped off to prove his father's wings would work. She thought of the rows of coffins and wondered if they were still inside—she didn't remember Aggie getting rid of them. What on earth might the real estate agent make of those?

Rhonda turned from the memory, made her way up the front steps onto the porch of the old house. The floorboards sagged beneath her weight. Paint was peeling. The corners were full of spiderwebs. To the right of the door, an enormous orb weaver was making its way to the center of the web, where a fly had become entangled.

Rhonda knocked. There was no answer. She turned the knob and pushed the door open.

How many times had she come through this door, running, laughing, chasing after Peter and Lizzy, shouldering a knapsack full of Barbie dolls and pajamas, costumes from whatever play they were working on?

She stood in the front hallway, facing the closet. On a whim, she opened it. A few moth-eaten coats of Aggie's. Daniel's red-and-black checked hunting jacket. After all these years, his jacket hung waiting for him. Beside it, the matching hat that Peter had worn on that egg hunt long ago.

Where's Lizzy? Aggie had asked.

Still in the woods with the rabbit.

Rhonda shut the closet door.

"Peter?" she called. She heard a bang upstairs. Footsteps. A dragging sound.

Something didn't feel right here. She suddenly regretted not bringing Warren along. But it was, she told herself, simply being in the old house that put her on edge. "Peter?" she called again, her voice a little weaker this time. She made her way into the living room. Same plaid couch and matching recliner. A TV covered in dust. On the wall above the fireplace, the velvet Elvis painting Daniel was so proud of. She and Lizzy had played a game called "Elvis Is Watching You," in which they tried to find hiding places where the all-seeing eyes of Elvis couldn't find them, and would end up chasing each other around the room laughing hysterically. In the end, Elvis always knew just where they were.

Where is she now? Rhonda longed to ask the dusty garage sale relic. And what about little Ernie? Could Elvis's all-seeing eyes spot her as well? Could he see all the way to Rabbit Island?

More dragging upstairs, this time just above her head. Lizzy's old room.

She took the stairs slowly, quietly. Her body remembered where each squeaky spot was, and carefully avoided them. She got to the top and made her way down the carpeted hallway, past the collages of framed studio portraits and school photos of Lizzy and Peter. She passed Daniel and Aggie's room. The door was open and she glanced in to see a mountain of clothing piled on the bed. Empty cardboard boxes scattered around the floor.

The next room was Lizzy's. The door was open. Rhonda put her back against the wall and slid sideways, like a cop on television, thinking she could spin around once she got to the doorway, draw her gun, and yell *Freeze!* But this was no cop show. And she had no gun. And it was only Peter she was going to face, not some boxy-jawed criminal. She turned slowly and peeked into the room. Peter's back was to her. He was doing something at the foot of the bed.

Rope.

He was coiling a long piece of coarse rope.

She inhaled sharply. He heard her and turned.

"Rhonda? What the fuck? You just about gave me a heart attack! Why'd you sneak up on me like that?"

"I called your name. You didn't answer. I heard funny noises. I guess I was kind of freaked."

"Well that makes two of us, now. Shit! What are you doing here?" He held the coiled rope in clenched hands.

"I thought I'd drop by. See if I could give you a hand."

Peter tossed the rope down on the bed. "Maybe you can help me get this thing out of here." He nodded at the immense dresser that had once belonged to Lizzy. "It's oak. It's been in my mom's family forever. Tock thinks we should keep it. Pass it on to Suzy."

Rhonda nodded, stepped into the room. She went toward the closet. The metal rod Lizzy used to hang from was gone and the frame had been repainted. But there, through the hastily applied coat of paint, Rhonda could still see the ghosts of Lizzy's pencil marks. Rhonda bent down to study them and saw the last date: August 10, 1993. The day they did their last performance of *Peter Pan*. It was as if Lizzy had stopped getting taller, refusing to grow up along with Peter and the lost boys.

"It's a bitch though," Peter said, slapping the top of the dresser with his open palm. "Weighs ten tons. Come on, grab a side."

Rhonda went around and grabbed the left side of the dresser. It was nearly five feet high and four feet wide. She lifted with a grunt, and got it about an inch up, then set it down. "We've got to get the drawers out," she said.

They pulled out empty drawers. Found a mothball. A couple of pennies. A single brown button. Rhonda picked up the button and held it, thinking it was the saddest, most lonely object she could imagine. A lost button from a lost girl. Rhonda slid it into her pocket when Peter wasn't looking, then went back to her side and lifted again, nodding at Peter.

"So what did you want to talk to me about so bad?" Peter asked, lifting his own side. Together, they did a slow shuffle walk with the dresser, Rhonda going backward, aiming for the doorway. With the dresser raised, they could barely make eye contact over the top.

Rhonda took in a breath, unsure of where to begin. She'd rehearsed in the car on the way over and she decided to stick to her script. Begin with the motel, with Lizzy. Then show him the keys. But when she opened her mouth, that's not what she started with.

"The night we did *Peter Pan*, you and Lizzy had a fight. You asked her to do something she didn't want to do. She was scared. What was it?" Rhonda set her end of the dresser down. A few more steps and she'd be to the doorway.

Peter narrowed his eyes. "I don't remember."

He was lying.

Rhonda picked up her end and lifted again. Peter followed her lead and they resumed their shuffle walk.

"I went to the Inn and Out Motel," she told him, her eyes meeting his over the flat surface of the dresser. It was time to stop playing games. Throw something at him that he couldn't lie his way out of.

They were at the doorway now and Rhonda backed herself through. It was tight fit, and when they got to the middle, the dresser jammed. They wiggled it, but it wouldn't squeeze through. Rhonda caught the back of her hand on a jagged edge of the metal strike plate on the doorjamb, ripping the thin skin there.

"Jesus Christ!" she said, dropping her end and pulling her hand up to inspect the cut. Peter, still in Lizzy's room, set his end down as well.

"Shit," he mumbled. "If it came in through the door, it's gotta come out." He wiped sweat from his brow with the back of his hand.

Rhonda, who had brought the hurt hand to her mouth, was determined to stay on track.

"Peter," she began, the taste of blood fresh on her tongue, "I know you were at the Inn and Out Motel the day Ernie was kidnapped. And I think you were there with Lizzy."

He looked disconcerted. "I was hiking in the state forest."

"No," she told him. "You were there. The license plate of your truck is listed on the registration for the room. You were there with Lizzy—or some other young, dark-haired woman from out of state who happened to register as *C. Hook*, for God's sake—and a little girl. A little girl who I think may have been Ernestine Florucci."

"You can't be serious."

"Just tell me the truth, Peter. It's time."

"But *I am* telling the truth," he insisted. "I had nothing to do with what happened to Ernie. The first I even heard of it was when you called me that day."

"But you were at the motel," Rhonda said.

"Shit, Ronnie. Let's not do this. Just let it go, okay?"

Rhonda turned and walked down the hall toward the bathroom.

"Where are you going?" he asked.

"To wash out my cut."

"And what am I supposed to do?" he asked, peering at her over the jammed dresser. "I'm kind of stuck here."

"I don't know, Peter—figure out how we're going to get the dresser out. And while you're at it, you can think about telling me the truth when I get back. This is *me*, Peter. The one you used to tell everything to, remember?"

The cut itself wasn't too bad, but the metal strike plate had been covered in some kind of black grease that Rhonda assumed probably didn't belong in an open wound. She turned on the hot water and found a cracked sliver of soap. The water stung, and she watched it turn pink in the bowl of the sink as it mixed with her blood. Then she looked down and gasped.

There, resting on the floor, tucked against the cabinet the sink was mounted on, was a pair of tiny red sneakers. Rhonda turned off the water, dried her hands, leaned down, and picked up one of the sneakers. It was dirty, the boxy white rubber toe scuffed to gray, the untied shoelaces broken and tied back together haphazardly. Ernie's sneaker. Rhonda's hands began to tremble.

"You okay in there?" Peter called from the bedroom. "You're not bleeding to death or anything, are you?"

"I'm fine," Rhonda said. "The soap stings, that's all."

Think, Rhonda, think.

If her shoes were here, then that meant Ernie was. Or had been at some point.

"Oh my God," she mumbled as the reality of the situation finally hit her.

She patted Peter's keys in her pocket—the keys she'd found in the cemetery, which was only a ten-minute walk from here. And Aggie's house was abandoned. He could easily keep a little girl in a place like this. The closest neighbors were Clem and Justine, and a quarter mile of thick woods separated them.

"Are you gonna help me move this thing, or what?" Peter called.

"Coming," Rhonda shouted.

What next? She had to get help. Her cell phone was in the car. She'd get to it quickly, make the call, then come back in and stall for time. Ernie could be here, right here, somewhere in the house.

She went down the hall and opened the door to Peter's old room. Checked the closet. Under the bed. Only dust bunnies. Had she seriously expected to find Ernie that easily?

"What are you doing?" Peter called.

"Looking for a Band-Aid! I think there's one in my car." She moved to Daniel and Aggie's old room, throwing open the closet door. Nothing. Cardboard boxes and abandoned clothing.

"Rhonda, what's going on?" Peter called from behind the dresser in the doorway down the hall.

"I'm just gonna run to my car," she told him. She heard the scrape of a chair. Then a shuffle and slide.

Shit. Peter was scrambling over the top of the dresser.

She ran to the stairs and bounded down them, two at a time.

"Rhonda, slow down. Talk to me. Are you hurt?" He was after her now.

She got to the bottom of the stairs, tripped on the toy bear there. Hadn't the rabbit given Ernie a white stuffed animal? A bear, right? No. It was a bunny. Of course it was a bunny. Rhonda picked up the plush animal. Tiny rounded ears. Big brown nose. Definitely a bear.

Peter was nearly at the bottom of the stairs, coming slowly, steadily.

"Why's the garage padlocked, Peter?"

"I have no idea."

"What's in it?"

"I don't know, Rhonda—tools, coffins—the same shit that's always been in there."

She backed her way to the front door and put her hand on the knob and turned. She raced outside, Peter right behind. She got to the garage, pounded on the locked door. "Hello?" she called. "Can you hear me?"

"What do you think you're doing, Ronnie?" Peter asked.

"Unlock the door, Peter!"

"I can't. I don't have the key."

She reached into the front pocket of her jeans, pulled the key ring with the rabbit's foot out, and tossed the keys in his direction. They landed on the front porch with a dull clank. He doubled back and picked them up.

"Where did you get these?" he asked. He looked horrified, as if she'd thrown a severed hand at him.

"Open the door to the garage," she demanded, trying to keep her voice calm and level.

"I told you, Ronnie, I don't have a key. Never had one. My mother must have put that lock on years ago." He was talking slowly and calmly, as if to an unhinged person. He jogged down the porch steps and came toward her. She saw the old shovel leaning against the garage and picked it up, as Aggie had done to Daniel years before.

"Jesus, Ronnie! Put the shovel down." He raised his hands in surrender but took another step toward her.

"Come any closer and I aim for your head," she told him. "I mean it, Peter." Her hands were shaking. She backed up and slowly made her way to her car. Peter followed, making sure to keep just out of shovel range.

"You can't leave here like this," he said.

"Watch me," she said, throwing the shovel at him. He dove and it missed him by an inch. She got in her car and locked the doors. He came forward, tried the door handle, pounded on her window while she fumbled with the keys in the ignition.

"Wait!" he yelled. She threw the car into reverse and Peter lost his balance, falling in the driveway. She peeled out onto the road. Checked her rearview mirror to see Peter running after her. She floored it.

"Fuck!" she screamed, pounding the steering wheel. "Fucking think!" She could go to her parents, but what would they do? The police. She had to call the police. She grabbed her cell phone, but dialed the Find Ernie hotline instead of 911. Pat picked up.

"Find Ernie hotline. Do you have a tip for us?"

"Pat, it's Rhonda. I need to talk to Warren."

"He's not here."

"Where is he?" Rhonda's voice was frantic.

"I don't know, Rhonda. I haven't seen him all day. Or last night for that matter. He might be at home with Jim."

Rhonda turned left, toward town. Pat and Jim's house was on the way to the Mini Mart. She'd stop by there first and find Warren.

"Pat, listen to me. I think Peter has Ernie at his mother's house. Out on Lake Street. I think she's in the garage."

"*What?* Are you sure?"

"I saw her shoes, Pat. I'm going to hang up and call Crowley right now. Peter knows I know. He may move her. Or worse."

*I*t's all come crashing down. The rabbit suit is unpacked from its secret hiding place in a box at the back of a closet no one would ever think to look in. A faux fur pelt. Enormous ears, pink inside. Oh, the secrets those ears have heard! The heady secrets of little girls, whispered in soft, sugary breaths.

One last time, the rabbit suit will be worn. One last time, Peter Rabbit will come to life.

AUGUST 10, 1993

THEY HAD DONE the play the past two nights and tonight's performance would be the last and greatest. Rhonda floated across the stage, saying her lines as if in a dream she hoped she would never wake up from.

"Do you know," Rhonda, as the now elderly Wendy, said as she sat in the rocking chair by the window, peering out into the night, "I sometimes wonder if I ever did really fly."

Over the past weeks, she had sensed change was coming. She sensed it each time she heard Peter speak, calling out directions, throwing them their lines. It was there in the way his voice was starting to crack when he let out his crow through the woods. She heard change in the tilt and tremble, the slight squeak of his call; felt its powerful presence looming like a monster under the trapdoor, waiting to ruin everything in the final act.

In the last days leading up to the play, they addressed each other in character all day long, losing track of their old selves as easily as Peter Pan lost his shadow.

But shadows, as Rhonda showed Peter on stage, can be sewn back. And after tonight, Rhonda wondered, would they put their old selves back on? Would it really be that simple?

"And I wonder," Rhonda as Wendy said, "if I would now remember the way."

The final scene in their version of the play, the one Peter wrote, had Wendy as an old woman (Rhonda wore a gray wig and drew wrinkles on her heavily powdered face) trying to remember just where it was Peter Pan lived and what it had been like there. Finally, after a great struggle, after trying to remember if Peter sang or crowed, if he had really taught them to fly, if he was even real at all, Rhonda, as Wendy, had a flash—a line that came to her, and it was the last line of the play. She stood up slowly from her chair, hobbled over to the window with her cane, pulled back the curtain, and remembered out loud, "Second star to the right, and straight on till morning."

Rhonda, there on the stage that night, had a sudden vision of herself as an adult, saying that line quietly on some far-off night as she stared up at the sky, like it might help bring her back. Back to Peter, to that summer. To Lizzy, her once upon a time twin. To her character Wendy who she was afraid of becoming, because Wendy forgets, little by little, and Rhonda did not want to forget, not one tiny piece. Not the way Peter looked in his green outfit they'd sewn felt leaves to. The way he smelled green all summer, like trees and roots, like growing things. She didn't want to forget Lizzy, who truly became Captain Hook, running through the woods with a bent wire coat hanger sticking out of her sleeve, a real felt pirate's hat on her head, cocked sideways. The way Lizzy got to die at the end of the play, tossed to the crocodile, who gobbled her up as she screamed.

She did not want to forget the toothy crocodile, played by

Tock Clark, who had been their worst enemy forever and then suddenly wasn't anymore. Tock Clark whom they all had hated, Peter most of all, until something changed, as big things always do when you're young, but as an adult, you can never remember just what it was. All you can do is pull back the curtain, thinking you half-remember the way back. *Second star to the right, and straight on till morning.* And there, through the window, at the edge of the horizon, is the crocodile's smile, Peter's crow, and his adamant line—*I shall never grow up!*—called out in a voice cracking with change.

"Second star to the right, and straight on till morning," Rhonda said there in her Wendy nightgown, and she also heard herself say it in some alternate universe, where she was a grown woman trying to find her way back.

Rhonda spoke the last line and the crowd was up on its feet, applauding. Hooting, whistling, screaming, "Bravo!" Rhonda looked out into the rows of chairs set up in the clearing. Every one of them had been filled. There, in the front row, were her parents, and Daniel and Aggie. Next to them was Laura Lee Clark in a sequined gown. Some of the men her father worked with were there, and all of the parents of the lost boys, pirates, and Indians. There were children too young or too shy to have been given roles. Tinker Bell's parents recorded the entire play with a video camera.

Rhonda was joined on stage by the entire cast, and, arms around each other, they took their final bow.

THE PROCESSION THROUGH the woods to Rhonda's house was noisy and chaotic. The pirates and lost boys were sword fighting. Tock was snapping imaginary crocodile jaws at everyone. Laura Lee was telling a story about Sandy Duncan.

The two picnic tables in Rhonda's yard were covered in dishes everyone had brought. There were four different pasta salads, a frightening-looking Jell-O mold, a cake shaped like a pirate ship complete with mast and sails, shish kebabs, burgers, and hotdogs, chips and dip, a tray of Swedish meatballs being kept warm by a can of Sterno, pigs in a blanket, coolers full of beer and soda, and two bowls of punch with fruit floating in it.

Daniel was sword fighting with Peter and Lizzy. Peter, still in character, looked very serious and fought hard against his father, like he was out for blood with his wooden sword.

Tinker Bell was riding high on her father's shoulders. "I'll make you a copy of the video," her dad promised Justine, who smiled, said, "That would be lovely," and heaped more Swedish meatballs on his plate.

As the evening progressed, the punch flowed freely. Daniel and Clem had dragged the stereo from the living room, then cranked up Van Morrison. People started dancing. Clem danced with Rhonda. Daniel and Laura Lee swung each other drunkenly through the crowd. Justine stood by the food table, tapping her foot in time with the music. Aggie danced by herself, going in circles around a tiki torch, eyes closed, arms stretched out toward the sky. At one point, when Rhonda passed in front of her on her way to get more cake, Aggie said, "Rhonda, you were marvelous! It's such a sad ending, though, don't you think?"

Rhonda shrugged.

"I mean, Peter and Wendy don't get to be together. She grows old. He doesn't. He gets to live out eternity in Neverland with that little fairy. And Wendy has nothing."

"But it was what she wanted," Rhonda said, her voice sounding squeaky and defensive. "To go home, I mean."

Aggie looked up over Rhonda's shoulders.

Peter was calling to Rhonda from across the table and Rhonda excused herself from Aggie, forgetting all about the cake she'd meant to get.

Peter passed out cups of rum punch to Rhonda, Tock, and Lizzy, urging them to drink up. Clem went and spoke to Aggie, who laughed, closed her eyes, and kept dancing, spilling punch but seeming not to notice or care. When Clem returned to the food table, Justine snapped at him, words Rhonda couldn't hear, and he hung his head like a beaten dog. Justine turned and marched into the house, slamming the door. Clem, who rarely drank, poured himself a cup of punch and downed it in two gulps. Aggie opened her eyes again and beckoned him over with seductive waves of her fingers. Clem stood his ground and poured himself another cup of punch.

"Dance with me," Aggie called.

He shook his head.

"Suit yourself," she said, and began to dance alone, her arms circling slowly at first, then fast like a windmill. She came forward and bumped against the picnic table, losing her balance. She put down her arm to steady herself, and her hand went right into the tray of Swedish meatballs.

"Shit!" she screamed, waving her burned hand wildly through the air. The meatballs had fallen off their metal stand and knocked over the Sterno. The paper tablecloth caught fire. A pile of napkins and paper plates went up in flames.

Aggie laughed. "Someone call 911," she cackled. Around her, people began batting at the fire with paper plates and dumping cups of punch on it. There was much staggering and laughter as pineapple and maraschino cherries flew through the air, landing on the flaming table like little meteorites. Clem dashed to get the hose at the side of the house, but it was in tangles and wouldn't reach the table. He began the slow process of unknotting it, cursing the whole time, yelling, "Stay back!"

In the midst of the chaos, Rhonda watched Peter and Tock slip away into the woods. She looked for Lizzy, but Captain Hook was nowhere to be seen.

JUNE 17, 2006

PATCHES. THAT WAS the name of the border collie who found her. The farmer and Patches were just out for a walk when Patches began to whine, sniff, and dig at the dirt. The dirt moved away and the farmer saw the sheet of plywood. He pulled it back. When Ella Starkee looked up at him, the sun blinded her and she saw only his tall shadow. She thought he was God and waited for an elephant joke. When he didn't tell her one, she thought maybe it was her turn.

"What's big and gray and goes around and around in circles?" Ella asked.

"I see a ladder here," the farmer said. Patches whined.

"An elephant stuck in a revolving door," Ella said.

"You're okay," he told her as he lowered the ladder. "I'm going to get you out of here."

———

WARREN'S CAR WASN'T in the driveway of Pat and Jim's tiny modular home. Rhonda jumped out of the Honda and pounded on the door anyway. While she waited, she reached into the pocket of her jeans, found Lizzy's abandoned button, and worked her fingers over it. Jim answered, looking more scruffy and disheveled than usual, like she'd just interrupted a nap on the couch.

"Warren's not here?" Rhonda asked.

Jim shook his head. "Try the Mini Mart. He left for there a couple hours ago."

"No. He's not there, and he's not answering his cell phone. I've really gotta find him."

"Is there news?" Jim asked.

Rhonda told him about her discovery and the call she'd made to the police. "Crowley and his guys should be there by now. They might have found Ernie already. God, wouldn't that be something?"

Jim nodded. "It sure would be good for all this to be over. Poor Pat's been through the wringer. She doesn't eat. Doesn't sleep. She's just been . . . consumed."

"You know, I heard about her sister—the one who was killed when they were kids."

Jim shifted in the doorway. Rubbed his eyes. "She doesn't talk about it much. But it's a hell of a thing for anyone to go through—to see your baby sister hit and dragged like that. And they were close. Real close. She and Birdie were inseparable."

The name hit Rhonda in the solar plexus, knocking the air from her lungs, rendering her unable to speak for several seconds.

"Birdie?" she asked at last, a whispery gasp.

Hadn't that been the name the rabbit called Ernie, the one on the hidden note Katy told them about?

One of the many clues that had never made any sense.

"Her sister Rebecca," Jim explained. "That's what Pat always called her. 'Cause when she was born she'd peck her little head just like a bird."

AUGUST 10, 1993

RHONDA LEFT THE chaos of the burning picnic table, the laughing and screaming adults spilling punch, her father dousing the flames with the garden hose he'd finally managed to untangle with Rhonda's help.

She slipped away quietly, down the path back toward the stage. It was dark, but the moon was out. It didn't matter though; she knew the way by heart. She could make the five-minute walk along the narrow trail blindfolded and not bump into a single tree.

The path dipped. Her nightgown rippled in the breeze, making her feel more like a ghost than a girl.

Ahead of her, she heard crying. Behind her, the loud thump of Van Morrison.

She hurried into the clearing and there, in the moonlight, she saw the three of them on the stage. Peter with a hammer. Tock with her arms wrapped around Lizzy, who was collapsed on the floor beside the trapdoor, sobbing.

It looked, to Rhonda, like they were rehearsing a scene from a play Rhonda didn't recognize.

"What's going on?" she called out.

"You're just in time, Rhonda," Peter said.

"For what?" she asked.

"We're going to tear the whole thing down," he told her. "Now come up here and give me a hand."

I T WAS QUARTER of nine by the time Rhonda pulled into the Mini Mart. The gas signs were off and the store and garage were dark, but Pat's car was there in the lot.

Rhonda got to the front door and found it unlocked. Slowly, she opened it, hearing the little electronic ding-dong that went off at the registers as she entered.

She did a quick scan of the Mini Mart. No Pat. No Warren.

"Hello?" she called, her voice squeaky, hesitant.

She went back to the front door and looked out across the parking lot toward the road. No one. Nothing.

How could she never have considered Pat a suspect before? Pat knew Trudy and Ernie. But it still didn't make sense. Pat had been so earnest in her search for Ernie. She so desperately wanted to find the little girl.

Had Pat and Peter been in on it together? Or was Rhonda wrong about Peter?

Rhonda had never been alone in the Mini Mart before. She'd never noticed the low droning hum of the coolers and air conditioning. The place was full of barely audible clicks and whirs. At each new noise, she turned to look over her shoulder.

She was sure she could hear breathing.

"Pat?"

Rhonda walked through the store, around the racks of snack cakes and chips, finally stepping behind the register, where she flipped the wall switches, making the store blaze with light. She looked up at the rows of cigarettes, the warnings about selling tobacco and alcohol to underage kids, which included a visual guide to acceptable photo IDs. The counter was covered in scratched Plexiglas and, under it, was a list of prices for beer, soda, coffee, and dairy products. She heard a low rumble in the back corner—just the soda fountain machine making ice.

She made her way to the abandoned volunteer table. Notepads, telephones, and the laptop were scattered across the surface. And there was a Styrofoam cup nearly full of hot chocolate. Rhonda picked it up—still warm.

"Rhonda."

The voice behind her made Rhonda jump, spilling the warm cocoa on the leg of her jeans. "Jesus!" she yelped, spinning around to face Pat.

"I didn't mean to startle you," Pat said. "I was doing some work in my office and thought I heard a noise."

"I . . ." Rhonda stammered. "I just wondered if there was any word yet."

Pat shook her head. "Not yet." She eyed the cup of hot chocolate in Rhonda's hand.

"Looks like maybe Warren showed up?" Rhonda asked.

Pat gave a slow nod. "He's in my office, actually. I think he's got some things to explain to you."

Rhonda set the Styrofoam cup down, wiped her hands on her

jeans, and looked across the store and down the hall that led to the office.

"It's time he told you the truth," Pat said.

"Truth?" Rhonda murmured. Pat gestured toward the back hall, reminding Rhonda of the way the white rabbit had guided her through the woods that Easter long ago.

Now Warren was the basket of candy.

Hesitantly, with Pat half a step behind her, Rhonda made her way to the office. She opened the door and stepped inside.

"Where is—" Rhonda said.

Pat slipped in and closed the door behind them, standing with her back against it. Next to the door, a large crowbar leaned against the wall. Pat bent and picked it up in one quick move.

AUGUST 10, 1993

WHY?" RHONDA SAID. "Why would you want to wreck our stage?"

"Because it's over," Peter said.

"What is?" Rhonda hoped he meant things with him and Tock. Maybe Tock and Lizzy *were* secretly in love. Right then, up on stage, Tock spooned against Lizzy, whispering in her ear, they looked like two people in love. Rhonda was almost embarrassed for them. But jealous at the same time. Whatever this big thing was that was happening between them, Rhonda wasn't a part of it and she had been a part of everything in Lizzy's life up till then.

"Do you trust me, Ronnie?" Peter asked.

She nodded.

"Then help me do this." He held out his hand and Rhonda joined him on stage. Together, they grabbed the sheet with the painted scene of the Darling children's nursery and ripped it down. Behind it were the blue water and palm trees of Neverland.

"But Peter—" Rhonda began.

"We need more tools," Peter said, jumping off the stage, running behind it to the box where they kept a few basics. He returned with a crowbar and saw.

"It's time," Tock whispered, pulling Lizzy up. Lizzy picked up the hammer Peter had been holding and started hitting the floorboards, cautiously at first, then using all of her force. Tock picked up the crowbar and began ripping floorboards up, the rusty nails screeching.

Peter was sawing at the two-by-four frame of the wall that held the backdrops. "It's over," he said, more to himself than anyone in particular. Lizzy dropped the hammer and started to cry.

"Lizzy?" Rhonda said, walking over to her friend, putting a hand on her shoulder. "What happened, Lizzy?"

"Let her be," Tock warned, coming toward them with the crowbar in her hand. Rhonda backed away.

"Ronnie, I need you over here," Peter called. He was pushing on the left side of the backdrop frame, making it sway. "Grab the other end."

Rhonda went over and wrapped her hands around the two-by-four, imagining it was Tock's neck.

"No one ever has to know," Tock whispered to Lizzy.

Know what? Rhonda screamed inside her head. *What did you do to my best friend?*

"Pull!" Peter shouted.

The back wall didn't budge. Rhonda jumped up, grabbed hold of the board that ran across the top of the frame, and swung there, the Neverland landscape behind her: blue water, even bluer sky, the shoreline of their island.

I sometimes wonder if I ever did really fly . . .

She thought of Lizzy hanging from the closet, trying to stretch herself, to grow taller. She could just hear the music pumping out of the speakers back in the bright chaos of her yard: "Brown-eyed Girl." Van Morrison crooned, *Do you remember when we used to sing* . . .

There was a cracking sound and the wall broke free, tipping, sending Peter and Rhonda down, a pile of boards and the tangled sheet with the painted island on top of them, a searing pain in Rhonda's forehead, like everything in there—all her memories of Lizzy and Peter, and all the random things she'd learned, like lines from their plays and the shape of buttons on the uniform of a Confederate soldier—was trying to find a way back out. She closed her eyes. Let the shoreline of Neverland cover her, hold her, threaten to never let her go.

PAT HEFTED THE crowbar and rested it on her shoulder casually. "He was just supposed to take her to the woods. Leave her there. She would've stayed put and we would've found her in a few hours."

Rhonda nodded, took a step back, bumping up against the large metal desk. "Who?" she asked.

"Little Ernie, of course. I was going to find her. It was all arranged."

It made sense in a horrible sort of way. Pat's guilt over what happened to her sister. An opportunity, years later, to redeem herself. To be the hero. Even if it meant staging a kidnapping. She'd have her fifteen minutes of fame. Be redeemed. The whole town would benefit, really. It would be Ella Starkee all over again.

But if it wasn't Pat in the rabbit suit that day, who was it? Had she talked Peter into taking the little girl? Blackmailed him somehow?

"It was you who visited Ernie all along, right? You wanted to be the one to develop the relationship. To build trust."

Pat stared, stone-faced.

"You picked her up in Laura Lee's car. I bet she liked it. It must have made her so happy, to see the rabbit waiting for her, ready to take her to the cemetery."

Pat gave a wistful little smile. "Rabbit Island," she whispered, relaxing her grip on the crowbar.

"Right, Rabbit Island. I saw one of Ernie's drawings," Rhonda said. "She made it look like paradise."

"Yes. She loved it there. She loved *me*."

Rhonda nodded. "Who did you get to wear the suit that last day, Pat? Who took her? Where is she now?"

"You're a smart girl." Pat's eyes blazed now as she spoke. "I thought you'd have it figured out by now."

Rhonda shook her head. She put her hand back on the desk and felt around. Her desperate fingers found only papers. Magazines. A pen.

"Warren," Pat said, the name an angry hum through her clenched teeth. "It was Warren. Warren killed her."

"No," Rhonda almost laughed. "He wasn't even here. He was in Pennsylvania."

"I offered him money. Five hundred dollars. An easy job for a college kid. Just pick her up, drive a few miles, and drop her off. I drew him a *goddamn map*."

"You're lying!" Rhonda said. "Where is he? What did you do to him?"

Pat continued: "Then he'd lie low and tell everyone he'd come up to help out the next day. Driven all night, that was the story. He heard about the kidnapping and wanted to help. Such a good boy."

Rhonda reached back, stretched her arm across the desk until her fingers found the cool, smooth edge of the granite stone, felt the indentations of engraved letters: PAT HEBERT, STATION OWNER

AND MANAGER. She grabbed it. Heavy. Seven or eight pounds maybe.

"Good boy, my ass!" Pat hissed. She clenched the crowbar. "He killed her. He took my little Birdie and he . . ."

"No!" Rhonda raised the stone and aimed for Pat's temple. She made contact, and the force of it vibrated through her arm and into her chest. The crowbar slipped from Pat's hands, clanking on the ground. Then Pat herself went down.

Rhonda, gripping the granite stone in her hands, stepped carefully over Pat and opened the door.

"Shit, shit, shit," she whispered, trying to calm herself. What had she done?

"I didn't have a choice," Rhonda whispered, trying to convince herself. "Warren?" she called out.

She peered carefully left, toward the store, and right, down the hall toward the garage. No one. Quiet. She tiptoed across the hall and into the dark storeroom, felt for the switch, and turned on the lights, only to find herself face-to-face with a tall man in sunglasses and a baseball cap. She swung and knocked him flat.

"Fuck!"

She'd knocked down a life-size cardboard cutout of a race car driver advertising motor oil.

"Good shot, Farr," Rhonda told herself. Her hands were shaking.

She backed out of the storeroom, keeping the light on. She wanted every corner blazing.

Adrenaline buzzed through her body. She turned and faced the metal door leading to the garage. EMPLOYEES ONLY, warned a red-lettered metal sign.

She looked for a light switch to the garage outside the door leading to it. No such luck. She'd have to go in and feel her way around. Still clutching the heavy PAT stone in her hand, she pushed the door open and stepped into the garage, where she smelled burned rubber, oil, and exhaust. An engine was running. The metal door swung closed behind her with a loud thunk. After the fluorescent bright hallway, her eyes could make out nothing in the inky black garage. The air was hot and thick, full of exhaust. She turned and felt along the wall for a switch. There was one to the right of the door: four switches, all pointed down. Using her index finger, she flipped them all up and turned around.

Rhonda's heart jackhammered. She dropped the stone, which hit the cement floor and cracked, the words PAT HEBERT breaking off from STATION OWNER AND MANAGER.

There, in the far bay, was Warren's car. The rabbit was strapped into the driver's seat. The car was running, and a length of hose ran from the exhaust pipe to the back window cracked open.

"Shit!" Rhonda leaped forward, hurried to the car. She pulled the hose from the exhaust pipe and went around to the driver's side. Locked. "Shit!"

Back to the tool bench, where she found a small sledgehammer. Two swings and she'd shattered the front passenger side window. She reached in, pushed the button to unlock the doors, then returned to the driver's side and opened the door. The rabbit was leaning back, seat reclined like he was just taking a little bunny nap. She leaned over him, turned off the car, then found the button to release the seat belt.

He was heavy. Dead weight. No, she thought, not dead. Can't be dead. Can't be a killer.

She dragged him from the car. Laid him down on the cement floor of the garage.

Air. She had to get air. She unlatched the lock on the overhead door of the left bay of the garage and yanked it open. She took a deep breath, then crouched beside the rabbit. She placed two hands on the mask, and gently, ever so gently, she pulled it off.

A sob escaped her lips. She snatched her cell phone from her pocket and dialed 911.

While Rhonda waited for the ambulance, she thought about Ella Starkee—how the Magic Man was found dead in his living room the day Ella was rescued and was able to describe him and his car. He was a thirty-two-year-old janitor, described by coworkers and neighbors as a helpful, friendly man. Later, in a televised interview, Ella had only this to say about his death: "It's sad, really. Sometimes, a person does a bad thing but it doesn't make them a bad person. Sometimes . . ." she paused here, twirled her hair in her fingers, then looked straight at the camera, "sometimes, what a person needs most is to be forgiven."

AUGUST 15, 1993

DANIEL HAD BEEN gone for five days. Aggie was pacing in Rhonda's living room, talking to Clem and Justine. Rhonda hovered in the kitchen, out of their line of sight, but where she could hear perfectly. She heard Aggie's footsteps, the fevered pitch of her speech.

"Something's happened to him," Aggie insisted as she rattled the ice cubes in her empty glass, a not-so-subtle hint for one of them to pour her another gin and tonic.

"Ag, you're overreacting," Clem told her. "He's just lying low. Guaranteed he'll be back any minute now hungover and all fired up about some cockamamie money-making scheme."

"He's never been gone this long," Aggie said. "A night or two. But not this long. Do you know what I did today, Clem? I even called up Laura Lee."

Clem cleared his throat. "What did she say?"

"She claimed not to know a thing, but I think she was lying."

"Why do you say that?" Justine asked.

"Because that's what women like her do. They lie."

Clem mumbled something Rhonda couldn't make out, then she heard Aggie softly sobbing.

"I'll go put on some coffee," Justine said, and Rhonda darted back to her room.

"WILL DANIEL REALLY come back?" Rhonda asked. She and her father were side by side in his old car in the woods.

"Of course, sweetie. Of course he will. Don't you worry."

But Rhonda *was* worried. If Daniel was out of the picture, what was going to stop Clem and Aggie from being together all the time? Surely not Rhonda's mother. Clem would leave Justine and Rhonda and pick up his old life with Aggie. The thought of it made Rhonda's stomach ache. She reached up and touched the wiry stitches above her eye. There were seven of them. Lucky number. *Right.*

Peter got nine stitches. Tock and Lizzy hadn't been hurt at all when the wall came down. But the weird thing was, Lizzy hadn't said a word since that night. Not to Rhonda or Peter, not even to Tock.

"She just needs a little time," Tock said. "Let's all quit bugging her about it."

CLEM TURNED AND looked at their ruined stage once again. "I still don't get it," he said. "Did you all have some kind of fight?"

"Sort of," Rhonda said, unwilling to admit to her father that she really had no idea why they'd torn it down, other than that Peter had told them to.

"It just seems like such a shame," Clem said. Above them, the pirate flag flapped in the breeze, the painted skeleton face the one remnant of their play that hadn't been destroyed.

"I've been thinking," Rhonda said, eager to change the subject. "Nineteen seventy-nine was the year Peter was born."

Clem's jaw tensed. He gripped the cracked steering wheel and stared out at the woods in front of him, imagining some invisible road. "Yes. It was."

"So that means Peter is your son, right? My brother." The words felt thick and bitter in her mouth: *son, brother.*

Clem closed his eyes. Shook his head. "No. He's Daniel's son. You can see that, right? He's the spitting image of his dad."

"But if you and Aggie were married . . ." She opened the glove compartment and found only a tangle of wires and the shredded leaves of an abandoned mouse nest.

Clem sighed. Got that faraway look in his eyes he did just before telling one of his stories.

"I remember standing in front of the nursery window and pointing Peter out to nurses, visitors, any passers-by. My son. My boy. My Yankee doodle, born on the Fourth of July, all-American kid."

Clem played with the gear shift on the steering column, put his foot on the gas pedal, and pushed it to the floor. It let out a rusty squeak of protest, reminding them they weren't going anywhere.

"It was exactly a year before I found out the truth," Clem continued. "Peter's first birthday. We had a little party in the backyard with Daniel. He brought red, white, and blue hats, streamers and sparklers. I went inside to put the baby to bed, but I forgot his blanket. It was his special blanket, he never let go of it. When I came back out into the yard to get it, I saw them: Daniel and Aggie. They were . . ." he cleared his throat. Rhonda nodded, trying hard to imagine the scene—all of them so young, her father married to Aggie, thinking he'd had a baby with her; thinking his life was perfect until that moment.

"When I stepped out the back door into the yard that night, I heard this strange popping sound inside my head, like a little explosion of bright white light cleaning everything out."

Rhonda nodded. It was a little like how she felt tearing down the stage; like everything she knew and understood was somehow over.

"I knew right then that Peter was Daniel's son. I think part of me knew it all along, even in the very beginning. But I pushed that part to the back of my brain. We believe what we want to believe, Ronnie; even when the truth is right there under our noses."

JUNE 18, 2006

SOMETIMES YOU MAKE up a lie and it becomes this safe little house you live inside," Warren said. "But it's not really safe. The foundation is bad, ready to crumble and the people you invite inside with you, they're all in danger, too."

Rhonda bit her lip and took a step back, willing herself not to cry. She stood beside Crowley at one in the morning, listening to Warren's confession against the backdrop of beeping monitors and doctors being paged over the intercom. Warren had pulled the oxygen mask off his face and it lay hissing at his chin, a whispered warning that seemed, to Rhonda, to be saying, *Don't listen. None of it is true.*

Warren had declined the offer to remain silent or to have a lawyer present, eager to hurry up and tell his story at last. The beginning of his story was much like Pat's story: after building a rapport with Ernie with herself in the suit, Pat offered Warren five hundred dollars to come up to Pike's Crossing, put on the suit, and take the girl one last time. She knew Trudy bought lottery tickets and cigarettes every Monday afternoon, after picking Ernie up at school, and that Trudy always left Ernie in the car during this stop. Warren was supposed to take the girl and drop her off in the woods off of Route 6. Pat had picked a spot. The idea was that she'd wander around lost for a few hours, overnight at the worst, but Pat would find her and bring her home. The lost girl would be found. The story would have a happy ending, just like what happened down in Virginia.

"But it didn't work out that way," Warren said, looking away from Rhonda and Crowley. "Pat had showed me right where the drop-off should be, but once I was driving along dressed in a rabbit suit, in a stolen car, I got nervous, you know? So I decided to take the long way around the lake, took that dirt road that snakes through the state forest, it seemed . . . less conspicuous. The map said it would connect with Route 6 just outside of town.

"I was all pumped up, scared as hell, the road was going on forever, all twists and turns. And I couldn't see well through those fucking eyes. I was sweating like a pig. I mean, I've never done anything like this before. And the little girl, she was telling me a story about her day . . ." Warren stopped, swallowed, wiped at his forehead, then continued. "About how in school, it had been Letter F day: they made an F poster, ate fruit, had a contest to see which team could come up with the most words that started with letter F." He mopped at his brow with the back of his hand, and was quiet for a long moment.

"So, we got to this hairpin turn and I didn't see it coming. I was going too fast, I guess. I slammed on the brakes and jerked the wheel to the left, and the little girl, she wasn't belted in . . ." He chewed his lip. Tears welled in his eyes. "It happened so fast. She was knocked against the door and I guess it wasn't closed all the way or something, because all of a sudden, the door was open and she was gone. Just like that."

"You're saying she fell out?" Crowley asked. "The door just happened to open all by itself?"

"The latch—it was broken," Rhonda whispered. Like she'd told Warren days ago: *Shit luck and random chaos.*

"What?" Warren asked.

"Peter was supposed to fix it. It was written in the schedule at the garage. Laura Lee said the door wouldn't stay closed unless it was locked."

Crowley scribbled in his notebook.

Warren started to cry, and Rhonda's first instinct was to go to him, offer comfort to him. But she couldn't. Not knowing that it had been he who looked across the parking lot at her through painted mesh eyes. He who took Ernie on her last trip to Rabbit Island.

She didn't want to believe that it was possible. It seemed like some sick cosmic joke. The only person she'd trusted through all of this, the man she'd started to fall in love with, had been the rabbit she'd been chasing all along.

Maybe you'll catch up to him one of these days, Warren had told her just this morning.

Now here he was. She closed her eyes tight, trying to make it all go away. But there was still the oxygen hiss, the beeping.

Warren had stopped the car and run back to where Ernie had fallen out. She had tumbled down a steep embankment, and lay awkwardly, horribly still, on a pile of rocks. He scrambled down to her and saw at once that she was dead. Crowley pressed for details—how could Warren be so sure she was dead, not just knocked out? Warren described her battered little head, the impossible angle of her neck, the staring eyes, the long, desperate minutes of checking for a pulse, for breath—no, she was dead, and it was his fault. Stupid with panic, he carried Ernie back to the car.

"I knew I couldn't bring her back. But I couldn't just leave her there. So . . . I decided to bury her."

Rhonda shook her head. *Why?* she wanted to scream. And she realized what it came down to: Warren had simply made a series of bad choices. Horrible choices. Choices born of the need for quick cash, the chance to make an edgy documentary, the search for a shortcut, and, finally, sheer mind-numbing panic. Everything seemed like a good idea, or maybe the only option, at the time. Rhonda really saw him for what he was: a scared nineteen-year-old kid.

"I went back closer to the lake and found an old path through the woods. I carried her in my arms. She was so light." He paused again.

"And where was this exactly, Warren?" Crowley asked.

"Hm? Oh, on the north side of the lake somewhere, I think. I got sort of turned around. But there was a clearing in a grove of pines. I found a hole there. Like the remnant of an old well or something. I laid her down at the bottom and piled rocks and dirt on top."

"And Miss Clark's vehicle?"

"I put the rabbit suit in my gym bag and returned the car, just like we planned. I handed the suit over to Pat and told her that everything had gone according to the plan: that I dropped Ernie off at the edge of the state forest, close to Route 6, right where she'd told me."

Crowley looked skeptical. "And you expected that she would not find out the truth?"

Warren considered.

"I don't know what I expected. It just seemed impossible to tell the truth. I could barely believe the truth, you know—like, how did this happen? How *could* it happen? And I told her the lie so many times over the next few days—she got worried fast, couldn't figure out what went wrong with her grand plan—that I started to believe it. To convince myself. I actually started to think that the little girl was going to come walking out of the woods at any minute. I could see it so clearly. Her little face all lit up as she told everyone all about her adventures on Rabbit Island. It seemed so . . . possible."

Rhonda nodded, looked away from him, focusing her eyes on the monitors that kept track of his pulse and blood pressure.

"Rhonda, I don't . . . I'm sorry. Sorry for being dishonest. For leading you in the wrong direction. You know Peter's keys? I got them from Pat myself and dropped them in the cemetery when we were there, so you'd find them. I did everything I could think of to get you off the trail."

"So it was all an act then?" Rhonda asked, biting her lip again. *I will not cry. I will not let them see me break down. There are enough victims in this story already.* "What happened between us. Another trick to distract me?"

"No!" His eyes were moist and sincere. "God, no! Rhonda, what happened between us . . . it was . . . the only honest thing I've done since I've been in Pike's Crossing."

Rhonda nodded, unsure of what to believe. She knew she'd started to fall in love with Warren. And her being with him had helped her to let go of Peter—to move on in some intangible way.

"I think that all along, part of me wanted you to discover the truth. Part of me needed all this to be over. I tried to tell you myself. I tried last night, then again this morning. But I couldn't."

"So what did you do after you left my place, after your failed attempts to tell me the truth?"

"I drove around for a little, thinking it through. I stopped off at the house to change clothes. Then I went to the Mini Mart. I told Pat what really happened that afternoon, said I was going to

Crowley myself. She lost it. She went after me with a crowbar and then I guess she stuffed me in the suit and put me in the car . . . God, she must have been crazy with rage, to do all that. But I don't blame her. She loved that little girl. She kept saying how all this was going to save little Ernie, that she'd be the nation's darling. Have offers for movies and books. Have her face on the front cover of *People*. Her and Pat together. That's the way it was supposed to be."

A nurse came in, lifting the oxygen mask. "You've got to keep this on," she scolded.

Warren pushed it away again.

"Please tell Trudy how sorry I am. Tell her—oh fuck it." He was crying again. "What can anyone say? Tell her that on Ernie's last day at school, during that F contest, the word she came up with was *fable*. Tell her that, would you?"

Rhonda nodded dumbly down at Warren as the nurse attached the mask again, adjusted the flow.

Was that what all this had been? Rhonda wondered. A fable in which the rabbit plays a terrible trick, but at the end they all learn a lesson? But what could possibly be the moral here?

SEPTEMBER 3, 1993

PETER SHOWED UP at Rhonda's door, breathless.

"I need Clem," he panted, shoving his way past Rhonda. Clem came out into the living room.

"What is it, Peter?"

"You've gotta come quick. It's Mom. She's in the bathtub. She used a razor. There's blood all over!"

Clem ran out of the house with Peter. Rhonda started to join them, but her father stopped her. "Stay here!" he ordered.

Rhonda's heart thudded in her ears. She went to find her mother to tell her what had happened.

"There's nothing we can do to help right now," Justine said. "Let's do our best to keep busy."

So Rhonda sliced vegetables for stew, listening to sirens draw near.

Forty-five minutes later, Clem returned with Peter and Lizzy.

Lizzy had a suitcase. Peter carried a knapsack, a sleeping bag, and his old army pup tent, which he went to work setting up in the yard.

"You'll freeze in there," Justine warned, handing over a pile of thick blankets from the linen closet.

"Can't you make him come inside?" Rhonda whined to her parents, who just shook their heads and told her to leave Peter alone for now.

Lizzy went straight to Rhonda's room, set up her suitcase in the corner, and began doing homework at Rhonda's desk.

"Want to talk?" Rhonda asked her. Lizzy didn't even look up.

"Oh that's right, you don't talk anymore. I forgot."

Rhonda stomped out of her room and down the hall, where she caught sight of her parents in the kitchen. Clem was just hanging up from his call to the hospital. Rhonda ducked into the shadowy bathroom to eavesdrop.

"She's going to pull through," Clem reported.

"Thank God," Justine said. "Did they say how long she'll be there?"

Rhonda heard Clem light a match, take a drag of his cigarette, then exhale. "No idea."

"I'd think they'd keep her awhile after something like this. And when she does get out, I wonder what shape she'll be in. Looking after the kids might be too much for her," Justine said.

"Fucking Daniel," Clem hissed. "I can't believe he's done this. Where the hell is he?"

"Like you said, he's probably off on a bender. Hiding out from people he owes money to," Justine said.

"These aren't the kinds of guys you mess around with," Rhonda heard her father say to her mother.

"I just wish we could get in touch with him," Justine said.

"Maybe it's time to call the police. File a missing person's report or something. With Aggie in the hospital, someone's gotta drag his ass out of hiding," Clem said.

RHONDA HAD A good view of Peter's tent through her bedroom window and spent most of the afternoon and evening staring at the green canvas door, hoping Peter would emerge, like a caterpillar from a cocoon, beautiful and changed. When he refused to come in for dinner, Justine brought him a plate.

"Let me take it to him," Rhonda begged.

"Not tonight, sweetie," Justine said.

At nine o'clock that night, Rhonda was watching through her window when she saw Tock arrive, wearing her red hat and carrying her BB gun. Peter held back the front flap of his tent to invite her in. When Tock left the tent an hour later, the gun was not with her.

"She gave him her gun," Rhonda said to Lizzy, who was lying in bed with her eyes closed, pretending to sleep. Rhonda could tell she was faking.

"Can you believe it? She gave him her gun!"

Lizzy just moaned and rolled over.

RHONDA WOKE UP in the night to find the mattress and bottom sheet soaked. She shook Lizzy awake.

"Did you piss in the bed?" Rhonda asked, dumbfounded. But there was no other explanation for the warm, stinking urine that soaked them both.

Lizzy said nothing. She didn't look ashamed or embarrassed. She wore a vacant look, like a sleepwalker.

"I can't believe this," Rhonda muttered, flipping on the light. "Well, let's get it cleaned up."

Lizzy stood frozen in a corner and watched Rhonda strip the bed.

"Take off your nightgown," she instructed. Lizzy didn't move.

"What is wrong with you?" Rhonda yelled. "Take off the nightgown!" She threw a clean one of her own at Lizzy, who stood, frozen.

"Don't just stand there!" Rhonda yelled. "Do something! Say something! Just open your mouth and talk!"

There was a knock on the bedroom door and Justine stuck her head in. "What's going on?"

"Lizzy pissed the bed and won't change!"

Justine surveyed the mattress and wet sheets on the floor, then went to Lizzy and put an arm around her.

"Come on, dear. Let's get you into a hot bath." She led Lizzy down the hall and into the bathroom. Rhonda heard the water running and the soft murmur of her mother's voice.

Justine returned, carrying Lizzy's wet nightgown, and grabbed the sheets and Rhonda's pajamas from the floor.

"What's the matter with Lizzy?" Rhonda asked.

"You need to be a little gentler with her, Ronnie."

"It's one thing to not talk, but to just stand there like a freaking statue . . ."

"Rhonda, Lizzy was the one who found Aggie today."

"Oh." The word felt small and round coming from Rhonda's lips.

"She's been through a lot," Justine said. "A lot more than anyone knows, I think."

Rhonda bit her lip. "Is she ever going to talk again?"

Justine nodded. "I'm sure she will. When she's ready. Pestering her, making a fuss, that never helps anything. We just need to be patient."

RHONDA, IT'S PETER." She hadn't spoken to him since the night she sent the police to his door searching for Ernie. She didn't know how to begin to apologize. And she still had so many questions—like who was he with at the Inn and Out Motel and why had he lied about it?

"I've been meaning to call," she said. "I'm so sorry for everything, and I . . ."

"Ronnie," he interrupted, "last night the police found a body."

Rhonda closed her eyes. At last, it was over. The police had been searching the woods around Nickel Lake for Ernie's body since Warren and Pat were taken into custody. Rhonda had studiously avoided the news stories about the botched kidnapping. She didn't want to hear the pile of charges being heaped against Pat and Warren. The one piece of news she'd heard had haunted her. When the police searched Pat's office, they found a little girl's sneaker soaked in blood, decades old. Pat had kept Birdie's shoe with her all these years, a gruesome reminder of her loss.

Rhonda heard Peter breathing into the phone.

"Where?" she asked. "Where did they find it?"

Rhonda hated herself the minute she said the words, turning Ernie from a *her* into an *it*.

"In our woods, Ronnie. Under the old stage."

There was a long pause. Rhonda drew in a breath. She heard a strange crackle on the phone line. She felt a pain in her head and reached up instinctively and ran her finger over the scar. Rhonda had this crazy idea then. She thought maybe they'd just dug up that old bogeyman. He'd decomposed to the point where they looked at him and thought he'd once been a person. Maybe that was the body they'd found—their childhood fears given form, weighted down by stones, as if such a weight could hold them down forever.

"That can't be," Rhonda found herself saying, more of a gasp than a sentence.

"I want you to get in your car right now and come straight over here, Ronnie. Get here as soon as you can. We have to talk before you see anyone else, especially the police, okay?"

"The police?"

"Yeah, they're going to want to talk to you."

"But I don't understand," Rhonda said, her voice sounding squeaky and strange; it was her eleven-year-old voice.

"I know you don't. That's why you need to come see me. Promise me you're on your way."

"I promise," she said, the words tumbling easily out of Rhonda's tight, dry mouth.

RHONDA HUNG UP with Peter and met Crowley coming up the steps to her apartment as soon as she opened the front door.

"Has something happened to Warren?" she asked. The last time she'd seen Crowley was at Warren's bedside a week ago.

"Warren? No. He's fine. He's out of the hospital and a guest of the department of corrections. Pat too. They kept her in the hospital awhile because she hasn't said a word since you hit her. The docs say there's nothing wrong physically—just won't talk."

Rhonda nodded. *Elective mutism*, she thought. Jingled the keys in her hands.

"Got a minute, Miss Farr?" he asked.

"I was just on my way out."

"This won't take long. Can we go inside?"

She offered him a cup of coffee from the pot she'd just turned off and they sat together at her table, stirring milk and sugar into lukewarm coffee.

"Tell me about the summer of 1993. The August Daniel Shale disappeared. You did a play then—*Peter Pan*, right?"

Rhonda was taken aback by the question.

"Uh, right. I was Wendy."

Crowley sat across from Rhonda, taking notes as they spoke, referring to his black book as he questioned her. But the questions he asked made no sense.

"I'm not sure what this has to do with . . ."

"Just answer the questions, Miss Farr," Crowley cut her off. "Now, if you would please, take me back to that summer. Tell me about the play. About the last time you saw Daniel Shale."

"Daniel? Um, the last time I remember seeing him was the evening of the play."

"Right," he said, thumbing through his book, "the play ended, to the best of everyone's recollection, around seven thirty, then you had a cookout. Now can you remember anything unusual about that evening? About him?"

Rhonda strained to remember. She thought of the photographs

in Clem's album, which showed all of them after the play. Lizzy up on Daniel's shoulders. Daniel sword fighting with Peter.

"He was clean shaven. He'd always had this thick walrus kind of mustache but sometime that summer he shaved. There are pictures in my father's album of him that night."

"I've seen the photographs. Your parents said you have a video of the play?"

"Yeah, I borrowed it a couple weeks ago."

"Would you mind if I took it for a few days?" he asked.

"Not at all," Rhonda said. She got up and walked into the living room, where she found it on the shelf below the television—where she left it the morning she and Warren watched it together, cuddling on the couch. She shrugged the memory off, grabbed the tape, and headed back to Crowley. When she returned to the kitchen, Crowley was up, snooping through papers on the counter—old grocery lists and receipts.

"Can you remember anything else unusual about that night?"

"Not really. We had kind of a party after the play. Families from the cottages down on the lake came because their kids were in the show. We were all in our yard eating hot dogs and burgers. Aggie, Peter and Lizzy's mom, got a little tipsy and accidentally set the picnic table on fire. I guess that's the most unusual thing that happened."

"And things broke up shortly after dark. People went home. What did you do, Miss Farr?"

"I . . . um, went into the woods with some of the kids from the play."

Crowley flipped through his book.

"Hospital records show you and Peter Shale being seen in the emergency room for stitches around ten o'clock that same evening. Everyone I've talked to says that at some point during or shortly after the party in the yard, you, Peter Shale, Lizzy Shale, and Greta Clark went into the woods and tore down the stage. Was there something particular that prompted this?"

Rhonda's head spun. She went over what few memories she had of tearing down the stage, but they were just a blur in her mind. It didn't feel like a true memory anymore. It was just a story she had told and retold so many times that it had long ago left any feel of reality behind. When she told the story, it was like recalling a dream. The dream where she and Peter ended up with matching scars.

"I'm not sure," she admitted. "We all somehow knew it was our last play. Everything changed that summer. Peter and Tock got together. Lizzy was drifting away from us. I guess tearing apart the stage was kind of a symbolic thing."

"Were Daniel and your father fighting that night? About money? Because Daniel had asked your father for another loan?"

Rhonda remembered a time before, on Peter's birthday, when Daniel asked Clem for a loan. He said it was to buy tools, but Clem hadn't believed him—had made some mention of gambling. She and Peter had heard the whole thing from inside their closed coffins.

"That's pretty much the story Clem, Aggie, and Justine tell," Crowley continued after listening to her recollections from earlier that summer.

"You've talked to Aggie?" Rhonda asked.

Crowley nodded. "A detective in Maryland met with her last night." Crowley ran a hand through his short hair, glanced down at his notebook, then continued. "Daniel was in trouble with some gambling debts and your father felt he'd bailed him out enough. It sounds like your father did an awful lot for Daniel. Is that the way you remember it?"

"I'm not sure. I guess so. I mean, Daniel had bad luck. He was always coming up with these schemes, but none of them ever panned out. And it seemed like he always owed money to some-one. That's the impression I got anyway, but I was just a kid."

She thought again of the wings Daniel made, of Peter standing on the shed roof, determined to prove they would work.

"Who took you to the emergency room?" Crowley asked.

"My father and Aggie."

"Your mother didn't go?"

"I don't remember her going. I think she stayed home with Lizzy."

"And Daniel, where was he when you had your stitches?"

"I have no idea. He wasn't at the hospital, I don't think. He must have stayed back with my mother and Lizzy."

Rhonda reached up and touched her scar. She thought of Peter's matching scar. Of the way the blood poured down her face, how frightened she was. There was so much blood on both of them. On Lizzy too, because she was there, trying to help them. She took off her pirate jacket and wrapped it around Rhonda's head. They were all crying so hard. Rhonda didn't even remember how they got back to her house, or the ride to the hospital. She just re-membered being in the same room with Peter and how the doctor pulled the curtain to do the stitches.

"Thank you, Miss Farr, you've been helpful." Crowley was closing his notebook, getting up to go. "One more thing, if you don't mind," he added, fumbling in the pocket of his jacket for a small bag that he withdrew and held out for her inspection. "What can you tell me about this?"

The pink plastic was cracked and grimy, but she recognized it immediately. It had once clung to the roof of her mouth.

"My retainer!" she said at last.

Crowley nodded. "We found it down in the hole with the body."

Rhonda was quiet a moment while she considered this, re-membering the day she and Peter had sat in the hole together and he asked her to take it out. She shivered as she imagined it there beside little Ernie Florucci.

"I used to change costumes down there," Rhonda explained. "I probably left it in the hole the night of the play. I wouldn't have worn it on stage. I probably left it down there for safekeeping. God, I thought it was gone forever."

"Thank you for your time." He snapped the book closed. "You've been quite helpful."

"But I don't understand," Rhonda said. "What does any of this have to do with Ernie Florucci?"

"Ernie?"

"Yeah, with the body you found in the woods?" Crowley looked perplexed, and Rhonda went on, a bit irritated. "It was Ernie, right? You found her."

"We didn't find Ernestine's body in the woods. Not yet anyway, we're still looking. There's a lot of woods around the lake to cover and, unfortunately, Warren hasn't given us many details to go on."

"So, what's this about?"

Rhonda thought again of that old bogeyman, stuffed full of rags and pillows. Of their fears scribbled on slips of paper, folded again and again and dropped into the hole like ruined paper cranes. What had she written on her paper? What did Lizzy and Peter write?

"The body we found has been identified as Daniel Shale. Initial findings are consistent with his being killed around the time he disappeared. Possibly the night of the play. The remnants of his clothes match those shown in the photographs from that day."

Rhonda felt a peculiar rushing sensation around her head, as though all the air had been suddenly sucked off the porch.

"Killed? How?"

"Yes," Crowley said. "The preliminary reports say blunt trauma to the head."

SEPTEMBER 4, 1993

PETER HAD TOCK'S gun out and was practicing his aim, shooting cans off the stone wall at the edge of the yard. Clem gave him pointers, set up the targets, and even let Peter fire his Civil War replica musket a few times.

Rhonda didn't know how to talk to Peter about what had happened to his parents. It didn't seem right to bring it up, nor did it seem right not to. She carried her homework out to the picnic table and glanced up often to see Peter shooting cans, Clem patting him on the back, saying, *Good shot, son.*

Rhonda thought of things to say, how to comfort him, to tell him that everything would be all right—Aggie would get well, Daniel would come home. But every time she opened her mouth to speak, to say the words she practiced in her head, the weight of their inadequacy, their sheer stupidity, kept them in the back of her throat. Her words got stuck there like some vile frog, thick and useless, and when she finally gathered the courage to walk up to him and say something, the only thing that came out was, "Want a Coke?"—to which he just shook his head.

That night, Lizzy didn't wet the bed, but she didn't stay silent either. She moaned, howled, spoke in gibberish. She called out for something or someone—the word a blur that sounded, to Rhonda, an awful lot like *Peter*.

Rhonda shook Lizzy awake.

"He's outside," Rhonda told her, trying to comfort Lizzy, whose eyes were wide with panic. Lizzy grabbed hold of Rhonda, dug her nails into Rhonda's arm. "Peter's just outside in the tent," Rhonda told her. Lizzy put her head back down on the pillow and drifted off to sleep.

Rhonda got up and looked out her window to see Peter standing with Tock's gun. She watched him walk the perimeter of the yard, then return to his tent. From her bedroom window, she studied him, positioned in front of his tent like he was standing guard—holding the gun tight in his hands, gazing off into the distance, looking not brave but somehow resigned, as he stood waiting for some imagined enemy.

JUNE 25, 2006

WHEN RHONDA PULLED into Peter and Tock's driveway, the first thing she noticed was the two girls playing in the yard. There was Suzy, her heavy silver EPILEPTIC bracelet glinting in the sun, her hair nearly white blond. She had a red toy shovel and bucket in her hand. The other girl was smaller, all knees and elbows, with dark hair held back in pigtails. As Rhonda watched, the dark-haired girl dropped something into a hole. Suzy shoveled sand over it, covering it up. The other little girl leaned down and whispered something in Suzy's ear.

Ernie?

"Hey, Suz," Rhonda said, jumping out of her car. "What're ya up to?" Rhonda studied the dark-haired girl: freckles, brown eyes. She looked an awful lot like the girl in the MISSING poster; the girl Warren said had fallen out of Laura Lee's car.

"Nothing," Suzy said.

Rhonda nodded. "Your dad inside?"

"Yep," she said.

Rhonda went up the steps and knocked. Tock answered. Rhonda instinctively took a step back, remembering the other woman's rage when they'd last met.

"Rhonda," she said, stone-faced. "We were starting to think you weren't coming." Rhonda couldn't tell from Tock's expression if she was grateful or disappointed.

"I got held up," Rhonda said. She heard voices in the living room. Peter and a woman.

"The girl playing in the yard with Suzy," Rhonda said, "who is she?"

"Come in," Tock invited, placing a hand gently on Rhonda's back. Rhonda flinched. No, not a knife. Just a hand. Tock was guiding her toward the living room, pushing her almost. Rhonda half-expected the room to be full of people who would jump out and yell *Surprise!* People who would tell her that the past weeks had all just been a trick, a game. Warren would be there in the rabbit suit and say something like, *See, Rhonda, things are never what they seem.* Even Crowley would be there, peeking out from behind the drapes to give her a we-sure-fooled-you-didn't-we? wink.

Rhonda looked in and felt all the air drain from her, like an abruptly punctured balloon. There was no party. Just Peter talking with a woman she recognized at once.

"Ronnie," the woman said. "My God, Ronnie."

"Lizzy?" Rhonda managed to whisper. The name came out like a question, but there was no doubt. Rhonda stood and walked over to her.

Lizzy wore her hair long still, but had it back in a braid. She had dark eyeliner on and was dressed in faded jeans, black cowboy boots, a white T-shirt.

Rhonda took Lizzy in her arms and clung to her. "I don't understand," she whispered.

"I have so much to tell you, Ronnie," Lizzy said.

"You're talking," Rhonda pulled back and studied the face of her long lost friend.

"Not just talking," Peter said. "She's a singer. Tell her, Lizzy."

Lizzy nodded. "I have a band in Seattle. Amazing Grace and the Disciples. We've put out a couple albums."

"Seattle?"

"That's where I finally landed."

There was so much to say, so much to ask. Little by little, they sketched out their lives for one another in broad strokes. Tock brought out fruit, bread, and cheese. Peter opened some wine.

"When did you start singing?" Rhonda asked.

"Now *there's* a story," Lizzy said. "See after I left home, I hitchhiked. Ended up in Boston for a while. Lived on the streets and in a couple of shelters."

"Wait," Rhonda interrupted. "Shelters? But I thought you were with Daniel."

Lizzy shook her head, looked away.

"But that's what you said in your postcards," Rhonda explained.

"That's what I wanted everyone to believe. Maybe, on some level, I wanted to believe it too," Lizzy said. "The truth is, I was on my own. No one knew who I was or where I'd come from. I still wasn't talking. I didn't talk until I was sixteen. Five years of silence. I was in San Francisco then, pregnant with Kimberly, living in this home for pregnant girls. This gal Trish, she asked me if I wanted to be in her band. They needed a guitarist. So one day, I just sat down with them, picked up the guitar, and the next thing I knew, I was singing. I don't know if it was music or Kimberly that gave me my voice back, but the way I look at it, it must have been the combination, 'cause that's been what's kept my life afloat ever since. Kimmy and the music. The centers of my little universe."

"That's Kimberly in the yard with Suzy?"

Lizzy smiled and nodded.

AFTER A WHILE, Peter patted the cigarettes in his shirt pocket. "Ronnie, come have a smoke with me," he said.

"Don't tell me you smoke," Lizzy said.

"Once in a while," Rhonda admitted.

"Once in a while won't hurt," Peter said. "Me, I wish I could give the damn things up."

"You've always got a choice," said Rhonda, thinking back to how she used to obsess over the choices others had made. The choice to leave, which she thought Daniel and Lizzy had made. Now it turned out Daniel hadn't left after all. He'd been buried in the woods the whole time—right next to the bogeyman.

"Peter, I'm so sorry," Rhonda said once they were alone on the front steps, where a tangled hedge of rugosa roses was encroaching on the left side, scratching Rhonda's leg on the way down. Once settled on the step, Rhonda looked up—at the peak of the A-frame was a huge paper wasp nest, a startlingly large layer of gray combs buzzing with activity.

"For what?"

"For thinking you could have had anything to do with what happened to Ernie."

Rhonda looked out into the yard, where, at the edge, Suzy and Kimberly were digging little holes, burying things.

"You were just following the evidence, Ronnie. And it's not like I was very forthcoming with you."

"It was Lizzy and Kimberly you were with that day at the motel, wasn't it?"

Peter nodded. "I actually tracked her down just after Suzy was born. We talked a few times, then she moved again and we lost touch. She called me last year, totally out of the blue.

I begged her to come home, meet Suzy, let me meet Kimberly. She finally broke down at the end of May, said she had some shows to play in New York and Boston, and that she and Kimmy would stop by after. She was really skittish about it and made me swear not to tell. She got in late Sunday night and left the next day before supper to catch her plane. We only went out once to get sandwiches and she made me drive clear down to Wells River for them. I never even got a chance to introduce her to Suzy."

"But why didn't she want anyone else to know she was back?"

Peter shrugged. "I guess she needed to do things at her own pace—take baby steps. It had been such a long time—so much had happened. Coming home was overwhelming."

"God, I was such an idiot!" Rhonda exclaimed. "I thought you two had kidnapped Ernie. And later, when I saw you with that rope . . ."

"It was for moving furniture," Peter explained.

"And the little red shoes?"

"Suzy's. She'd been hanging out there with me most afternoons while I fixed the place up. She brought toys, clothes. Left her stuff all over. Ronnie, I'm sorry, too. Sorry I wasn't honest. And sorry that things turned out the way they did. I don't know what was going on with you and Warren, but finding out he was involved, and everything that happened there in the garage that night . . . it must have been tough."

Rhonda nodded. "I trusted him, Peter. I thought he was the only honest person in my life these last weeks. I really cared about him. I haven't felt that way about anyone since . . ." Rhonda hesitated. "Since you."

Peter took a drag of his cigarette. Exhaled smoke. "Are you gonna go visit him?"

"I just can't. It's not even so much what he did. I admit, it was horrible, but I don't see him as this evil criminal. Just a guy who made some lousy choices. It's that he lied. He lied for so long. And he seemed so genuine. That's what hurts the most. And how can I ever trust someone like that again?" Rhonda looked at Peter. It felt good to be talking to him, saying something honest. To be able to go to him with her problems, as she had when they were growing up.

"Sometimes," Peter said, "it doesn't seem like there's any choice but to lie."

Rhonda shook her head. "He should have come forward, told everyone what happened. That it was an accident."

"He kidnapped the girl, Ronnie. He wasn't going to get off scot-free. Even if it was all Pat's plan."

"Pat! I still can't believe that I never even suspected Pat," Rhonda said. "It all makes perfect sense now, in some twisted way. It's all just so—sad. So very sad."

Peter nodded.

"Crowley came by as I was on my way out," Rhonda said.

"So you know what they found in the woods?"

"When you told me about the body under the stage, I thought you meant Ernie."

"Yeah, they wouldn't have stumbled across him if they hadn't been looking for her. I'm sure her body will be next. And I'm sorry Rhonda. Sorry I didn't tell you on the phone. I wanted you to hear it from me not some asshole cop."

Rhonda nodded. "All those years, we just assumed he was out there somewhere, living another life."

Peter eyed her cautiously, then nodded. "So what else did Crowley ask?"

"He wanted to know what I remembered from that summer. I told him what I could. I'm afraid I wasn't much help."

Peter looked at her for a few seconds, then turned away to gaze down the walk and driveway to the road.

"So what do you think happened?" Rhonda asked. Peter

glanced back at her and raised his eyebrows. "I mean to Daniel. Crowley said he owed a lot of money to people."

"Ronnie, I . . ." He cut his eyes away from her and then back again, searching her face for something he didn't seem to find.

"I don't know," he said finally, crushing his cigarette butt out on the step, putting the spent butt in the pocket of his shirt. And these words, the way he said them, reminded Rhonda of his usual mantra, *I don't remember*—the words he used to defend himself, to keep himself distant whenever Rhonda asked him some question about the past, like about how Daniel had once dressed as the Easter Bunny.

"Tell me about the night we tore down the stage," Rhonda said, a touch of Joe Crowley in her voice.

"You know the story," Peter replied.

"I used to think I did. Now I wonder if I'm missing something."

"Tell me what you remember," Peter said.

"I came out into the clearing and found you, Lizzy, and Tock. Lizzy was crying. You'd all had some kind of fight. And you said I was just in time to help tear down the stage."

Peter nodded.

"We were angry and sad and going too fast. Lizzy was holding a hammer, smashing boards apart. Tock had a crowbar. You were sawing apart the back wall." Rhonda was talking quickly now, almost a recitation. "And then, we pulled the back wall down, and you and I, we were under it. The next thing I remember is you dragging me out from under there, pulling off boards, untangling me. There was sheet on top of me—the backdrop from the play, the shoreline from Neverland, and I was twisted up in it. I was crying then, definitely crying. And blood was dripping down my face, down into my eyes, and they burned and I thought maybe I was going blind. And you were bleeding too, cut on the forehead by some rusty nail. We had to get tetanus shots, remember? And I thought they were like rabies shots. I thought we had to get a whole bunch in the stomach and I cried again in the emergency room when the nurse told us about the shots. I didn't cry about the stitches. They didn't hurt at all. And you, I'm sure you didn't cry. They had us in the same room, but they pulled the curtain to do our stitches, remember? They didn't want us to see. And we had to stay in bed after, to rest for a few days, and our parents were supposed to wake us up every few hours, just to make sure we were okay, that we hadn't slipped into a coma or something."

Peter was silent, staring at Rhonda as he lit his second cigarette. Rhonda leaned over and let herself brush the hair back from his forehead, revealing the thin white line as if she would find her answers there spelled out in a childish cursive: *This is what happened.*

"Am I interrupting?" Lizzy stood in the open doorway, peering down at them on the steps.

"Rhonda was just telling me about the night we tore down the stage."

Lizzy looked down at Rhonda, smiled, then held out her hand to pull Rhonda up.

"Take a walk with me, Ronnie." Rhonda stood up and walked with Lizzy down the steps and out across the gravel driveway, past the two girls playing in the overgrown yard, burying an army man in the dirt; they were so like herself and Lizzy that she shivered.

"I have a story to tell you." Lizzy's voice was calm and sure of itself. It was a smooth and mellow voice. The voice of lullabies.

Lizzy was leading Rhonda toward the woods, as the rabbit had led her in her dreams. She was still holding Rhonda's hand, and she turned now and looked at her, to gauge Rhonda's response.

"I'm going to tell a story and you are not allowed to interrupt.

You have to listen carefully to everything I say. You don't have to believe it. Right now, I'm just asking you to listen."

Rhonda nodded, her throat tightening a little.

Lizzy clasped Rhonda's hand tightly and let out a breath. "Are you ready?" she asked.

Rhonda nodded. Together, they stepped into the forest.

SEPTEMBER 4, 1993

RHONDA STOOD WATCHING until Peter crawled into his tent with the gun. A few minutes later, she saw Tock cross the yard, open the canvas flap, and join him.

Rhonda left the window and got into bed beside Lizzy. Lizzy's back was to her. Rhonda put her arm around Lizzy's stomach, curled her knees up into Lizzy's, their bodies making one giant question mark under the sheet.

"Remember the story our moms used to tell all the time?" Rhonda asked, not sure if Lizzy was asleep. "How we once had our own language? We were the only ones who understood each other."

Rhonda felt Lizzy's body stiffen then relax. Then she felt the quiet motion of Lizzy starting to cry.

"I wish," said Rhonda, "that I could remember some of those words now."

But she couldn't. So she just held Lizzy as tight as she could, rocking her gently, until they were both fast asleep.

JUNE 25, 2006

O NCE UPON A time," Lizzy began, "there were two little
girls who told everyone they were sisters. And they were,
for all intents and purposes. They looked alike, talked alike and
had this weird way of finishing each other's thoughts and sentences. They loved each other very much."

So far, this story, their story, sounded like the beginning of a
fairy tale. Hansel and Gretel. Two innocent children who were
somehow doomed from the start.

The trail beside Tock and Peter's house took them through
the woods that had been logged several years before Peter and
Tock bought the land. All around them was evidence of the forest reclaiming itself: paper birch, pin cherry, and poplars mixed
in with some old sugar maples that had been left alone during
the logging. The path took them down to the stream that fronted
the property. It felt like a good ten degrees cooler by the water.

The banks were covered in ferns. Around them grew birch and sassafras with the funny lobed leaves that reminded Rhonda of mittens. When they were kids, they'd broken off sassafras twigs and chewed them, pretended they were root beer–flavored cigarettes.

Lizzy lay down in the bed of ferns on her stomach and Rhonda joined her, gazing down at the quietly burbling stream, which was clear as a magnifying glass. Water striders skated at the edge. A green frog hopped from a nearby rock and Rhonda watched it glide underwater. She thought of frogs she'd dissected. The drawing in her living room. Then, she thought of metamorphosis. Change. What did the frog remember, Rhonda wondered, from its life as a tadpole?

"The thing is," Lizzy continued, "one of the sisters had a terrible secret. Something she was afraid to tell the other. Are you paying attention, Ronnie? 'Cause here's where things get tricky."

Rhonda nodded, studying Lizzy's face, noticing the tiny lines around her eyes and lips.

Does the frog trust its own memories? Does it think nothing of them? And what, Rhonda wondered, of the frogs who are kissed and turn into princes? What do they remember? What do they know?

Rhonda suddenly felt seized with panic. She didn't want Lizzy to tell this story, whatever it was. She'd been searching for the truth for weeks, but now that she was on the cusp of finally understanding everything, she wanted to go back. But it was too late.

When Lizzy spoke again, she was direct, no more fairy tale musings.

"When I was ten years old, my father began coming to my room at night. He'd say he'd come to tuck me in. Maybe it actually began before then. When I look back, I remember him visiting me in the bathroom for years. Washing me all over in the tub, asking to wipe me after I'd gone to the bathroom. It was only when I was ten that he came to me in my room. It was only then that he not only touched me, but had me touch him."

Rhonda bit her lip. *Not Daniel*, she wanted to gasp, but that was against the rules. And besides, she knew it was the truth, didn't she? She felt it deep in her bones, in the tingle of the scar on her forehead. It had been there all along like a sleeping tiger, the dark secret in the back of her brain.

"He called me his special girl," Lizzy continued. "His star. He said we had a secret bond between us, something no one else could touch. He made me promise never to tell because if I did, it would be ruined and he would be very angry. He told me no one would believe me anyway. No one would believe that I was such a lucky girl. They'd think I was making it up."

Rhonda gazed down into the water. The sand at the bottom of the stream sparkled where the sunlight hit it. She remembered once how she, Peter, and Lizzy had panned for gold with an old aluminum pie plate at one of the creeks that led into the lake. Lizzy thought the mica they found was real silver. She saved it all in a little box and said that when she got big, she was going to have it turned into a mirror.

"It got bad, Rhonda. Real bad. When he was drinking, when the coffin thing wasn't taking off and he was home all the time, he was always after me. He'd take me into his shop and make me do things. Tell me stories about things his father had done to him, how fathers carried this special kind of love inside them. He gave me these coins, these silver dollars. They were my prize for staying silent. But you know what I kept thinking? About the ferryman. You know, the guy who takes people across the River Styx to the underworld in his boat? I'd read about it in some book of Peter's. He was paid by the coins stuck in the eyes of the corpses. I felt like my father was paying the ferryman. But I was the one who kept making the trip."

Rhonda thought of the bag of coins, how it grew all summer. Lizzy's pirate treasure.

"I was so scared, Rhonda. And it was more than fear. I felt alone, and crazy, and just sick. I couldn't protect myself. I tried turning into Captain Hook, thinking that would do it. I thought if I didn't wash, if I was filthy and said horrible things, he would stop. But it didn't matter."

As Lizzy went on, Rhonda felt as if she were falling; falling down deep into the rabbit hole of her dreams. The place where memories dwell. Where the truth lay buried and guarded.

"It took me a long time to gather up the courage to say anything," Lizzy explained, "but I knew I had to—I couldn't go on carrying the weight alone. You were my best friend, my secret gypsy twin, and I longed to tell you. I tried. The only time I came close was the night of Peter's birthday when you slept over—do you remember?"

Rhonda nodded. *I have a secret.*

What if Rhonda hadn't turned away then? What if she'd done what a better friend might have, and actually listened?

"Finally, I decided to go to Peter," Lizzy told her. "If I expected help from any of you, it would have to start with my brother. He was older—I thought he'd get it, know what I was talking about.

"But he was furious. He said it was a lie, and that I was fucked up—it was the first time I heard him say *fuck*, I think—making up a crazy story just to get attention. That I was jealous of Tock, jealous of you, and just a sick little girl making up lies. I told him *everything*. And it was hard, Rhonda, hard to talk about what Daddy was doing to me. What I had done. I mean, I was eleven, for Christ's sake. But I did it. Every fucking sordid detail and still he didn't believe. 'Not Dad,' he said. 'Dad would *never* do that.'

"I was crying, begging him to believe me. Peter said he needed proof. And then, he came up with a plan. He wanted me to bring

Daddy out to the stage that night after the play. He wanted to see it with his own eyes.

"So the night of the play, just like Peter planned, I showed him. I made him believe."

Lizzy paused for a moment. She pursed her lips, gazed out across the stream into the dense and tangled woods. Rhonda looked too. Through squinted eyes, she saw Daniel dressed as the white rabbit, leading the children deep into the woods between their houses, separating them. Lizzy was the last to come back. Rhonda had been so worried. Had she known then? Suspected?

"My father went with me gladly," Lizzy continued, taking Rhonda back to the evening of the play, speaking in a dull monotone, no expression on her face. "He'd had a fight with Clem and was eager to leave the party. He was more than a little drunk. I led him down the path through the woods to the stage and he sat down on the edge, pulling me in front of him. He started touching me, unzipped his jeans and put his hands on my head, knocking the pirate hat off, guiding me down to him. I was used to it by then in a way. I could just make myself tune it out, you know. I could go places, think about other things. Sometimes I would go over all my lines from the play. It was dark in the woods by then, but the moon was out and Peter—he was hiding behind a tree—could see what was happening.

"Peter was crazy when he got to the stage. He came at Daddy, hitting his back as hard as he could with that stupid toy sword of his—broke it right in half. He was just screaming, no words, just a sound like some kind of battle cry. He jumped up onto Daddy's back, wrapping his arms around his throat, still just howling. Dad lost his balance, fell, and they started rolling around on the ground, grunting and thrashing, knocking over folding chairs. Dad got Peter pinned down under him and was like, 'You like to spy? Huh, boy?' just livid, spitting, red in the face.

"I thought, that's it, he's going to kill Peter, then there's this pop-pop-pop sound and Daddy's slapping at his back, cursing and screeching and I see Tock at the foot of the stage aiming her BB gun like a fucking sniper."

Lizzy's tone changed as she described how Peter and Tock came to her rescue. Her voice was more animated, almost excited as she told this part of the story.

"When she ran out of ammo, she charged and threw herself on him, and just the sheer momentum knocked him off of Peter. Peter snatched up one of the chairs and started hitting Daddy with it.

"My father was pissed off then, but I don't think he was scared. He finally grabbed the chair away from Peter and struggled to his feet. He knocked Peter flat on his back and held him there, his arm across Peter's throat.

"Tock was standing at the edge of things now, just screaming this incredible string of profanity, 'You motherfucker cocksucking sonofawhore dipshitfucker get the fuck off him or I'll fucking kill you!' kind of thing. I thought everyone in your yard would hear her and come running. But they didn't. I guess the music was up too loud. And Mom had gotten bombed and set the table on fire."

Lizzy stopped to take a breath, and when she continued, her voice was the flat, familiar monotone once again.

"Daddy had Peter pinned by the throat and Peter was gasping, choking, struggling to get a breath. I knew it was up to me to end it. If I could just hit my father hard enough, he'd black out. I think I had an idea from cartoons that he'd get amnesia, too—and it would be like it never happened, you know? So I went back behind the stage to where we kept the toolbox and grabbed a hammer, then crept up behind my father and Peter. Tock was still screaming. Peter and Daddy were sweating, shaking, glaring at each other. I raised my arm high, swung, and hit the back of my father's head as hard as I could. He went down, just like that. But

I hit him again, anyway. Then again. Then it was like I couldn't stop. Everything he'd ever done to hurt me came back in a flash and I put all those months of lies and pain into each swing of the hammer. It was like that day I killed the bogeyman. I just kept going.

"Peter finally took the hammer away. Tock led me away, up onto the stage, wrapped her arms around me, holding me as tight as she could, rocking me."

Lizzy looked over at Rhonda for the first time since she began her story. Lizzy's forehead was glistening with beads of sweat. Her eyes, which had seemed to lose their focus as she spoke, now gazed at Rhonda with pinpoint clarity.

"Peter and Tock dragged Dad's body up on the stage and rolled him into the hole, closing the trap door on top of him. Then Tock came back to hold me again."

"And that's what I walked in on," Rhonda said. She'd been silent long enough. It was as much her story as theirs from that point on.

"None of us ever knew how much of it you'd seen," Lizzy told her. "I always wondered how long you'd been watching, maybe too scared to make a move, if you knew what I'd done, hated me. Peter said you hadn't seen anything, that you would have done something. Try to stop it, run back for help, something. But I was never sure. And after a while, I guess Peter and Tock wondered too."

Rhonda shook her head.

"No, Peter was right. I had no idea. I thought you all had had a fight. I thought maybe something was going on with you and Tock and Peter was pissed. I couldn't tell."

Lizzy nodded. Blinked hard and continued.

"Well, you were there for the rest of it. Peter decided to tear down the stage; turn it into a pile of rubble and busted lumber that no one would ever think to look under. So we dug out the rest of the tools in the box and tore apart the stage in a crazed frenzy. We were all kicking and smashing the boards apart. You and Peter got hurt when the back wall came down and it was good because later it explained the blood on our clothes."

The mosquitoes had found them now, there in their place in the ferns. Lizzy swatted at her bare arms.

"You wrapped your jacket around my head," Rhonda remembered. She shivered to think that that jacket had already been splattered with Daniel's blood.

"I got rid of my clothes that night—or actually, I guess your mom must have gotten rid of them. While I was in the bath Justine took them away. I never saw them again."

"And you stopped speaking," Rhonda said.

"Peter said we couldn't tell. We could never speak of what had happened in the woods that night. Of course, Tock and I listened to him—he was the leader, right? Always. He went over it again and again—if we said nothing, it was like it had never happened. Nobody would ever know. I was afraid. Afraid that if I opened my mouth, everything would come pouring out. Words seemed dangerous. Does that make sense?"

Rhonda nodded.

"When Mom started to well and truly lose her shit, it was even harder. She was never too tightly wrapped, but thinking Dad had left her was the last straw. And I knew it was my fault, all my fault, no matter what Tock and Peter said. Eventually, not speaking wasn't safe enough. I had to leave. Get as far as I could from what had been done to me; from what *I'd* done."

"What made you come back?"

Lizzy shook her head. "It's silly, really. Peter had been after me for months to come and I was too scared. But then, remember that whole thing with that little girl in Virginia?"

"Ella Starkee," Rhonda said.

"Yes, Ella Starkee. I saw her on TV. When she talked about her kidnapper being dead and how she thought it was sad. She said, 'Sometimes, what a person needs most is to be forgiven.' That's what brought me back, really—that one sentence. It was a light at the end of a long, dark tunnel. It felt like, after all these years, it was time to forgive my father; time to forgive myself."

*N*ine one thousand, ten one thousand. Ready or not, here I come!"

Pat raises her head and scans the yard. The sun is blinding. Sweat prickles her forehead. Her chest and stomach itch. Heat rash. Maybe later, when Mamma gets home, they can go swimming.

Pat crosses the yard, pokes around in the vegetable garden, peers behind the row of giant sunflowers, the little patch of sweet corn. She checks the rain barrels (dry . . .), and the toolshed. No Birdie. Then, turning away from the house, she scans the cedar hedge that borders the yard. There, in the corner, a flash of red. Birdie's dress. Pat pretends not to see. Goes closer, then walks right by, mumbling, "Where can she be?"

Then, turning quickly, she shouts, "Found you!" and reaches through the hedge to tag her baby sister. "You're it!" Birdie laughs, pulls away, slips out the other side and right into the road.

"YOU'RE IT!" THE soft white paw of the rabbit lands on her shoulder, touching the red dress once more. Birdie looks up, laughs, and takes off through the headstones after Peter, who runs in slow motion, hip-hip-hopping until, at last, the little girl catches up, grabs hold of a leg, and pulls him down to the grass.

She's perfected the trick and doesn't need the suit now. She has become Peter Rabbit.

The rabbit sits in a jail cell, waiting. People come and go. The public defender. Jim. They ask the same questions over and over. They want to talk about motive. About Birdie. About the little shoe they found tucked in a box in the bottom of the closet in Pat's office. A shoe wrapped in white tissue paper, like a present Pat made herself unwrap each day, a blood-soaked reminder of what she'd done. What she'd failed to do.

They say the psychiatrist will come soon. An evaluation.

Peter Rabbit says nothing. Just nods, eyes focused on something no one else seems to see.

And when the rabbit sleeps, the dreams are good.

Peter's on Rabbit Island and both his Birdies are there. He hop-hop-hops, chasing them in games of tag and hide-and-seek that go on for hours. And they laugh. God, how those little girls laugh.

When he catches them, he takes them both in his strong furry arms, and holds tight like he'll never let go.

They're all safe. And they're going to stay there forever. There on Rabbit Island.

DANIEL WAS BURIED next to his father in the St. Anne cemetery. Buried in the coffin he'd built himself: *It's better to burn out than to fade away . . .*

They had all gathered at Clem's after the funeral, and were eating casseroles, drinking cocktails, and telling stories about Daniel. Daniel and the peanut cart. Daniel and his crazy ideas. Daniel the Easter Bunny.

Lizzy went to lie down. Everyone agreed it was a terrible strain on her—back in town to bury her long lost father. Peter sat on the couch, while Tock stood behind him, massaging his shoulders. Justine picked at the remnants on her plate: bits of three-bean salad and cheeseburger casserole. Suzy and Kim were on the porch, playing Go Fish and drinking ginger ale with maraschino cherries.

"I'm gonna get another beer," Clem announced, standing. "Anyone else need anything?" Everyone shook their heads.

Rhonda stood up, stretched, and followed her father into the kitchen.

"How are you doing?" she asked.

He got that far-off look in his eyes. "You know, for a couple of years, I didn't speak to Daniel. Right after I found out about him and Aggie and realized Peter was his son. I met your mother, tried to forget about everything that had happened before. Then, the fall after you were born, I was sitting right out there on the front porch and up he comes like some kind of phantom."

Clem looked longingly out the window, took a long sip from the bottle of beer he was holding.

Out on the porch, the girls giggled.

Clem continued. "Daniel came sauntering up the brick walkway, holding a six-pack of beer out in front of him like an offering. We sat and drank the six-pack, talking about our baby girls, about Peter. We just fell into our old rhythm. Like there'd never been a breach in our friendship."

Rhonda nodded, thought about how good it felt to be talking to Peter again. How familiar and comfortable. Like going home.

"After Daniel disappeared, I kept going out to the porch. I'd sit there for hours some nights over the years, smoking, staring off down the road, waiting for him to show up with another six-pack. Now I know he's not going to. And I suppose there's some comfort in finally knowing, but it still doesn't seem fair."

Rhonda nodded. Her father teared up. Looked out the kitchen window onto the porch, like there was still hope his best friend would show up and say the whole thing was a hoax.

The girls outside giggled. "Go fish!" Suzy squealed.

THE POLICE SEEMED to be going on the assumption that Daniel had been killed by one of two men he owed a great deal of money to: Shane Gokey or Gordon Pelletier, both of whom were now dead. Everyone seemed glad to accept this version of events—an answer, however horrible, was better than simply not knowing. Crowley made it clear that the case was by no means closed, which meant, to Rhonda, that there would always be the possibility of being caught. Rhonda was no idiot. She knew that with modern forensics, some small piece of evidence—a hair or a button—and they would be caught. Even Rhonda, who hadn't known about the murder but had helped to hide the body, and later, when she learned the truth, said nothing. She also knew that the truth had a funny way of surfacing when you least expected it. Ten years down the road there might be a knock on her door, and there would be Crowley to say, "I know what you did."

"THE WORST THING is," Clem said, "we may never know what really happened. And of course there's part of me that'll always kick myself in the ass for not loaning Daniel the money he asked for that summer to pay back those guys. The money that might have saved his life."

The little radio in the corner of the kitchen was playing softly, and Van Morrison came on. Clem walked over and turned it up. "God, Daniel loved this song," he said. He held the radio in his hands, swaying a little as he gazed out the porch window, his eyes focused on an imaginary figure in the distance.

He has no idea, Rhonda thought. No idea what Daniel was doing to Lizzy, about what had really happened that last night. And if Daniel's best friend didn't know, maybe their secret was safe.

Justine came into the kitchen, wearing a sensible black dress—no sweat suit today. Her arms were loaded with dirty plates and bowls. She set them down in the sink with a small crash, stirring Clem from his dreams.

"Need some help?" he asked his wife.

She shook her head, started to fill the sink with water, squirted in the soap, her back to Clem, Rhonda, and the radio.

Rhonda remembered the third degree her mother had given her each time she came back from spending the night at Lizzy's house: *What did you do? How late were you up? Was Aggie there? Peter? Daniel?*

Daniel.

Oh my God, she knew all along. Rhonda nearly said the words out loud. For an instant, she imagined placing her hands on her mother's square shoulders, turning her around so that they were face-to-face, and saying, *You knew what Daniel was doing, didn't you?*

She gripped the back of a kitchen chair instead.

"You sure we can't give you a hand?" Clem asked. "There's a lot of cleanup."

"That's okay, dear. Cleaning up is what I do best," Justine said.

A chill ran through Rhonda, beginning at the scar on her forehead and racing all the way down to her toes. *Cleaning up.* Was it possible that Justine knew not just about the abuse but about what finally ended it? Had throwing away Lizzy's bloody clothes been more than just simple housekeeping?

Rhonda squeezed the chair tighter.

"Can you turn that up?" Justine said, her back still to them. "I want to hear the weather."

Clem turned the radio up and the DJ came on to give the top of the hour news. The lead story was that Ernestine Florucci's body had been found by some campers on the north side of the lake early that morning.

Rhonda let out a squeaky sigh, felt her fingers slip off the chair.

"I'm sorry, Ronnie," Clem said, still holding the radio in his hands. He set it back down on the counter carefully, like it might be a bomb.

Rhonda went out to the porch, where Suzy and Kim were giggling over their cards. "You girls want to take a walk?" she asked.

Suzy nodded, said, "I know where there's a submarine." Rhonda's stomach went cold as she followed the skipping girls across the yard and down the path that led to their old stage.

Rhonda hadn't been into the woods in years. Shortly after the play, they'd all stopped using the path that connected their houses, choosing to walk back and forth the long way, down the road. Now Rhonda understood why.

The woods seemed smaller, to Rhonda, closer somehow. The trees had grown, filling in and making the clearing darker than she had remembered, even on a bright day. She looked up, trying to recall which pine it was that Tock had shot her arrow from. She thought she could pick it out, but couldn't be sure. They all looked nearly the same.

The girls climbed into Clem's old Impala and Rhonda followed, squeezing into the front seat beside them.

"Where are we going?" Rhonda asked. Suzy was at the wheel in her dark funeral dress, her hair held back with a ribbon.

"To see the octopus," Suzy said, matter-of-factly.

Rhonda looked to her right. The disarranged pile of wood that had once been their stage was black and sickly green with decay and moss. The police had pulled boards aside to expose the hole beneath. Rhonda turned away, unable to make herself look down into the hole they had once all taken turns hiding in. The hole where they changed costumes and which they used to make the most dramatic entrances and exits. Rhonda remembered falling in her dreams, how she thought she might never stop. She thought of her old retainer, pulled from that hole, held in an evidence bag now, packed away beside the remnants of Daniel's T-shirt and jeans. She scanned the ground, wondering where they'd buried the bogeyman, struggled to remember what she'd written on her piece of paper. What *had* she been afraid of then? Peter not loving her? That she would grow old and forget things? Had she written something as simple as *spiders*? Or something far more sinister?

Under a few boards off to the side, Rhonda spotted a torn bit of cloth and recognized a piece of the painted scene from the play. Blue waves, a bit of palm tree, now blotchy with mildew. Their Neverland, was, Rhonda realized then, a lot like Ernie's Rabbit Island.

SUZY BROUGHT THE sub gently to rest on the ocean floor. She, Kim, and Rhonda got out and sat in the bed of pine needles, which was actually soft sand. They sipped tea and ate small cakes. Rhonda looked around at the ruined stage, at the trees that enclosed the clearing. She thought, for a moment, that she had seen the flash of Tock's flaming arrow pass in the corner of her eye. A bird squawked, and in its squawk Rhonda heard Peter Pan's crow.

The octopus was a fine host and said many things that sent Suzy and Kim into fits of giggles. "Silly octopus," they said. Then, all at once, Suzy got serious.

"The octopus says you can tell us about Grandpa Daniel now," she said.

Rhonda froze, imaginary cake in her mouth, the invisible cup of tea spilled onto her lap.

"What about him?" she asked, her voice as calm as she could make it.

"Tell us a story about him," the little girl asked.

"I'm sure your father could tell you lots of stories," she said to Suzy. "And your mother, Kimberly, she could tell you what you want to know."

"But we want *your* story," Kim whined. "You knew him too."

Rhonda thought about it. About these little girls, who had just watched a man they never met be buried. A man whose body the police had found bludgeoned to death in the woods. Their grandfather. Of course they were curious.

"Well, let's see," began Rhonda with some hesitation. "Once upon a time, your Grandpa Daniel decided that his son Peter—that's your daddy, Suz—should be able to fly, so he made him a pair of wings . . ."

So Rhonda told the story, leaving out the part about Peter alone on the workshop roof, about Aggie coming at Daniel with a shovel. She found herself stretching the truth a little to say that yes, maybe Peter had flown that day, just a little bit, just enough. And, as Rhonda told the story, she thought: this is how the past gets passed down. This is how memories are made. Half-invented, embellished, given a touch of whimsy. Daniel would be a saint now that he was dead. A beautiful man who made his child wings.

RHONDA AND THE girls got back in the sub and began moving toward the future, somewhere off at the edge of the horizon. They rose up out of the sea that was the past, out of the swell and surge of memory. Suzy was pulling at the gear shift, turning the steering wheel. Rhonda worked imaginary hand cranks and stopped occasionally to hold her two hands in front of her face, making them turn the periscope as she searched the horizon for some sign of the familiar.

"Land!" Rhonda finally shouted.

"Surface," Suzy ordered. "We're home."

Acknowledgments

Thanks to my editor, Jeanette Perez, and to everyone else at HarperCollins who helped make this book a reality.

Thanks to Dan Lazar, my wonder-agent.

Thanks to Dudley and Janet Askew, owners and operators of The Maple Valley Café in Plainfield, Vermont. Much of the early work on this book was done at Table 8, fueled by their perfect omelets and awe-inspiring home fries.

Thanks to all my friends and family who have been so indulgent and supportive while I figure out this whole being-a-novelist thing.

And, of course, thanks to my readers. This book wouldn't exist without you.

BOOKS BY JENNIFER McMAHON

ISLAND OF LOST GIRLS
A Novel

ISBN 978-0-06-144588-0 (paperback)

The suspense builds in this chilling novel when two horrible crimes are connected, no one can be trusted, and people are always more complex than initial impressions reveal.

"McMahon never flinches, but her readers will at every dark secret."

—Keith Donohue, author of *The Stolen Child*

PROMISE NOT TO TELL
A Novel

ISBN 978-0-06-114331-1 (paperback)

A chilling debut novel about a woman whose past and present collide when she returns to her small hometown to care for her aging mother on the same night a young girl is killed—a crime that mirrors the haunting murder of her childhood best friend.

"This taut novel is above all a reflection on the haunting power of memory."

—*Entertainment Weekly*